Acclaim for *Live from Medicine Park*

"A rocky encounter with a rock icon changes a filmmaker's life
in [Constance] Squires' heartfelt novel. . . . Squires gets it right
on both sides, making Lena a convincingly grizzled rock [and]
roll survivor while giving resonance to Ray's journey to personal
redemption. You don't need to be a rock fan to appreciate this rite-
of-passage story, but Squires' fellow rockers will also appreciate
her attention to details."

—*Kirkus Reviews*

"Few people write about the seductive energy of rock music
and the bewitching power of place with the grace and acuity
of Constance Squires. With a quirky Oklahoma spa town as
backdrop, *Live from Medicine Park* is a rollicking tale of bad love,
good music, and unwavering ambition gone wrong—all set to
lyrics so evocative, they're bound to haunt you long after you
close the book."

—**Rilla Askew,** author of *Most American:
Notes from a Wounded Place* and *Harpsong*

"Constance Squires creates a strong sense of place, and time,
with characters who reflect the Native and ranching past of
Oklahoma. *Live from Medicine Park*—about the art of music, film,
and living—is nothing but great medicine."

—**Thomas Fox Averill,** author of *rode*
and *Ordinary Genius*

"Constance Squires's potent and lyrical anthem about love, music, and memory also has a lot to say about the complex transience of fame and fandom—and the price that musicians and listeners alike must pay for them. *Live from Medicine Park* is an aching, honest, unforgettable story of a fading legend, as well as a vivid portrait of one of the most mystical places in this country."

—**Adam Davies,** author of *The Frog King*

"Neither roots rock nor the American Southwest has enjoyed such savvy and inventive celebration as in this novel. While the material touches on those clichés of rock 'n' roll, sex 'n' drugs, et cetera, at every turn its narrative pushes past the cartoon to the bruise, past the headline to the whimper, and way past air guitar to the spellbinding noise of families in crisis and fallen people struggling to rise. Bristling with stubborn hopes and wild detours, *Medicine Park* restores us finally to the redemptive power of howling at the moon."

—**John Domini,** author of *Movieola!*

"*Live from Medicine Park* is an emotionally compelling rock-and-roll novel, full of supercharged prose, like Dana Spiotta's *Stone Arabia*. I was captivated by documentary filmmaker Ray Wheeler and rock musician Lena Wells from the start. Using powerful language, Constance Squires immerses the reader in waves of desire, love, and urgency. She is a brilliant writer."

—**Brandon Hobson,** author of *Desolation of Avenues Untold*

LIVE FROM MEDICINE PARK

LIVE FROM MEDICINE PARK

CONSTANCE SQUIRES

UNIVERSITY OF OKLAHOMA PRESS : NORMAN

Also by Constance Squires
Along the Watchtower (New York, 2011)

Copyright notices for song lyrics used by permission in this book appear on page 209.

Library of Congress Cataloging-in-Publication Data

Name: Squires, Constance, author.
Title: Live from Medicine Park / Constance Squires.
Description: First edition. | Norman : University of Oklahoma Press, 2017.
Identifiers: LCCN 2016058498 | ISBN 978-0-8061-5733-7 (paperback : alk. paper)
Classification: LCC PS3619.Q57 L58 2017 | DDC 813/.6—dc23
LC record available at https://lccn.loc.gov/2016058498

The paper in this book meets the guidelines for permanence and durability of the Committee on Production Guidelines for Book Longevity of the Council on Library Resources, Inc. ∞

1 2 3 4 5 6 7 8 9 10

For Nora

"If you really want to understand me, there's some giving up we got to do."

The Rolling Stones,
"If You Really Want to Be My Friend"

We need to know the history of the historian in order to understand the version that is being put in front of us.

Julian Barnes, *The Sense of an Ending*

CONTENTS

LIVE FROM MEDICINE PARK

THE SILVER SUN HOTEL

Medicine Park, Oklahoma
May 18, 2000

Maybe if Ray Wheeler were the kind of filmmaker to make big-budget sci-fi flicks instead of documentaries on a shoestring, he'd be rolling into Oklahoma to tell some high-concept escape story. Futuristic Oklahoma would be a deceptively idyllic penal farm where they'd send Texans for reconditioning. Screw-up Texans, like himself, would shuffle across a green lawn in hospital gowns and think on their sins. The scenario didn't seem too far off the mark as he pulled out his camera and started shooting. A narrow main street and the sun-dappled creek that ran alongside it came into view. As he imagined the hero of his sci-fi plot making a run for it across the two-lane blacktop, a sun-faded billboard too big for the weed-choked side of road where it stood announced Medicine Park, Oklahoma, as the "Home of Rock Legend Lena Wells!"

Ah, Lena Wells. His real main character. As Ray and his producer, Martin Parker, passed the sign, the subject of their upcoming documentary stared at them from under a curtain of long, black hair, hands in the pockets of her buckskin hip huggers. It was an old picture, as of course it would have to be. She hadn't made an album since the end of the seventies.

"That's overstating it a bit," Ray said, nodding at the sign. "Legend."

"You think a lot of famous people come from here?" Martin replied, steering Ray's Jeep around a narrow turn. "We're proud of her."

Ray kept quiet. He didn't give a damn about Lena Wells, but it didn't matter. Love your subject. That had been one of his mantras in the classroom, and Martin, who had been his student before he became his producer on this project, was quick to remind him of it. Ray let the camera follow a red cobblestone promenade that ran along the water until it found a white metal bridge and a low waterfall with a strip of flat stones across the top where water streamed smooth as glass. Close to the banks, a line of tall, old catalpas stood like upright citizens dipping their bare toes in the healing water. The water must heal, or be rumored to heal, if the names on the map meant anything. Medicine Creek. Medicine Park.

He was ready for some healing. Dunking or chanting, bloodletting or snake handling, he didn't much care. He would gladly suspend disbelief for anything that promised to save his soul, shape him up, and set him back on his feet. Even if it kicked his ass. Even if it hurt a little bit. It was the new millennium after all. A cosmic reset that had not ended the world the way some people feared. Maybe if it wasn't an ending, it was a beginning. Time to start again.

Ray pointed at the name of the town in metal letters on a yellow-brick post office. Medicine Park sounded like a spot for druggies to meet and exchange soggy wads of bills for plastic baggies full of illegal what-have-you, but he knew that wasn't the right picture. "What kind of medicine?"

"The good kind," Martin said. He was from here, Comanche County, Oklahoma, and he knew all about the place.

"Do you think it will work for me?" Ray asked.

"No way." Martin laughed. "You're a hopeless case."

On the edge of the water, its cylindrical roof curving down to the red dirt, sat a large Quonset building that Ray guessed was to be the site of the free Lena Wells concert—she was calling it the Medicine Ball—which they would be filming in five days. The only hint of the upcoming show was the presence of a few tents pitched near the building's front doors and a banner strung between the tents with Lena's name block-lettered in purple magic marker. A thin man loped around the impromptu campsite wearing what appeared to be head-to-toe silver lamé, with headgear like the rings of Saturn bobbing around his ears. The early arrival of fans was a good sign. Maybe people remembered Lena Wells, enough, at least, to generate some interest in the documentary. Maybe by the time the concert started there'd be a line of fans snaking halfway to the highway. It didn't hurt to hope.

She had been pretty big for a little while. "I was thinking about the night she tanked on the *Tonight Show*," Ray said. "I saw that."

"Dude! No wonder you don't like her."

"Oh, I don't know. I felt sorry for her. She was so wasted. I was watching with my mom and dad expecting, you know, Phyllis Diller or Richard Pryor. Some antic banter." Ray slid his camera back into its case as they pulled into a gravel parking lot where a couple of cars and two white catering vans sat partially obscured by a stand of cottonwoods. The Silver Sun Hotel, home of Lena Wells, emerged from behind waving tree limbs.

"Looks just like it did on the cover of *Keep Your Powder Dry*," Martin said. The white frame building was three stories high, girdled by a covered veranda as wide as a highway lane, its columns peculiarly made from stacks of round, red stones shaped like cannonballs. Lavender and orange stained glass panels in a starburst pattern filled the center of heavy doors at the top of the veranda stairs. "It used to be a resort hotel," Martin continued. "Bootleggers hung out here in the thirties. Bonnie and Clyde, too. Lena bought and refurbished it in like 1980. Maybe '79."

Nobody answered the door when they rang the bell. They stood around and pressed the buzzer again and again. Gusts of hot wind came along every few seconds and dried their sweat.

"They know we're coming, right?" Ray walked to a window and tried to peer in. Wood blinds on the inside blocked the view.

Finally the door was opened by a small man with slicked-back blond hair dressed in a white catering smock. "The party begins at 7:00," he said.

"We're the film guys," Ray said.

"I don't know a thing about that," the man said. "I'm setting up for the party."

"Couldn't you let us in?"

"I don't think so. What if you're bad guys?"

"Bad guys?"

"Like thieves or something. Robbers."

Ray turned to Martin. "Are you a bad guy?"

Martin tipped his hat back and scratched his hairline. "Isn't anybody else here?"

"We did say 3:00, right?" Ray looked around. Lena's son, Gram Wells, and his wife lived on the premises, at least Gram had said so. Where were they? Ray was taking out his cell phone to call Gram when they heard the loud rumble of a motorcycle engine and gravel churning. They turned around to see a big man ride into the parking lot on an old blue BMW motorcycle with a sidecar. He pulled right up to the stairs and swung off the bike, dropping the kickstand and hanging his helmet over a handle bar.

Obviously relieved, the caterer waved at the guy with the motorcycle and disappeared into the house, leaving the front door open.

"Hi there." The motorcyclist climbed the stairs and offered his hand to Ray. He was every bit of six foot five, with oily braids and a long beard streaked with gray. "I'm Cy."

Ray couldn't visualize the spelling of his name. He only heard him say "sigh" and thought how poorly the wistfulness and resignation, the oh-mercy-me quality of the word fit the man. *Sigh.* "Hey there, Sigh. I'm Ray Wheeler, this is Martin Parker."

Cy pushed his sunglasses to the top of his head to reveal white-blue eyes like a husky's in a sun-darkened face. "I figured."

Cy swung open the stained-glass doors and waved the two visitors into an open room. The Great Room, Cy called it. Gleaming pinewood planks reached sixty or seventy feet to the back windows, where sunlight poured in. Fireplaces big enough to park motorcycles inside, made of those same red cannonball-like rocks and ringed by leather furniture, faced one another from the side walls. From the back wall protruded a short stage covered with overlapping Persian rugs and rigged out with amps, microphones, a black Steinway piano with a red fiberglass tambourine discarded on its top, and a grouping of guitars.

"Looks like rehearsals are underway," Ray said.

"Yeah. Wonder who plays that Höfner." Martin nodded at a green electric bass leaning against the back wall.

When Cy shut the front door behind them, Ray's eyes focused on white, twinkling strings of Christmas lights hung in long, horizontal rows across the ceiling. The main light in the room, though, came from an enormous chandelier made of elk antlers hanging from the middle of the low, wood-beamed ceiling, and a row of track lights trained on the stage. Several gold records, framed and hung along the back wall, grabbed the light and threw it back into the room. A drafting table lamp beamed over a mixing board set up at the old marble-topped reception desk to their right, where decades ago guests would have picked up their room keys. Good light was satisfying, like when a car starts right up on a cold day. He could film here with little-to-no additional lighting.

Who was this big guy? Lena's husband? Boyfriend? Brother? Manager? He felt right at home, that was sure. Whoever he was, the man felt no need to explain. He gave Ray and Martin a broad smile, his white-blue eyes relaxed and merry. "Let me show you to your rooms."

They picked up their suitcases and followed him. On the back of Cy's leather riding vest a patch said *Red Dirt Sober Bikers,* and stitched across the bottom half of his jacket with purple thread were the words:

> *Heavy heavy blues*
> *As my feathers are light*
> *Midnight of the morning*
> *Of American night*

Ray remarked, "I know those words."

"Of course you do," Martin said, sounding embarrassed.

"'Trip the Wind,'" Cy said, without turning around.

Lena Wells only had four or five hit songs, and this was one of them. Once Cy said the title, Ray conjured Lena's throaty alto laying down the words against a sidewinding guitar riff that invoked the smell of roasting meat at a barbecue joint in El Paso where he had worked his first summer job. The owner had played "Trip the Wind" and Gerry Rafferty's "Baker Street" twenty times a day on the jukebox while Ray stoked an old black smoker in an unair-conditioned kitchen. He couldn't remember whether he had ever liked the songs. Maybe he had, but now they were too tied up with sense memories of raw flesh and flies for him to feel anything but distaste when he heard them. "One of her best," he said.

As they crossed the wide room, several people dressed in cooking whites came out of what he guessed was the kitchen, heading for the back door, carrying stainless-steel steam pans. "What's with the caterers?" Ray asked.

"For the party," Cy said.

"I hope we haven't come at a bad time."

Cy looked over his shoulder at him. "Didn't anybody tell you? Lena's throwing you a party tonight."

Behind him, Ray heard Martin clear his throat. "Sorry, Ray, I forgot to mention it."

"Hey, that's real nice," Ray said. He hated parties.

"You'll be staying on the third floor," Cy said. As he led the way, Ray and Martin followed him up the worn oak stairs, slick in the middle from use.

"What's on the second floor?" Ray asked as they passed the landing.

"Lena," Cy threw back, not turning around. Ray looked left and saw only closed doorways down a hallway dimly lit with amber sconces. They took the next flight, and on the third floor, Cy drew two old-fashioned keys from a keychain on his belt and unlocked a door. "This is yours," he said, nodding at Ray. "You're across the hall," he told Martin. "It's not the Hilton, but you know, it's quaint and all, and we're putting you right here on the premises like you asked." He pointed down the hall at a brass-lined dumbwaiter. "Ring the bell and use the pulley, and Edith will help you out if she's in the kitchen—she's the housekeeper and she's here till two or three. Send down a note. I wouldn't ask her for a five-course meal or nothing, but if you need a Coke from the fridge, she'll do it."

Ray stepped into his room. A double bed covered in a peach-colored chenille bedspread took up most of the space. Mission-style furniture crowded the room: a nightstand, a marble-topped bureau, and, over by the window, a table, with two straight-back chairs tucked under it, with a black-and-orange Navajo rug underneath. In the corner, a TV with a DVD player sat on a small stand. The room smelled green and damp in a bacterial way that the sharp chill from the humming window unit suppressed but didn't hide.

"See you at the party," Martin called from across the hall as the door to his room slammed shut.

Ray stretched out across the bed and kicked off his boots, staring at the deep trowel marks in the stucco ceiling and walls. An enlarged sepia photograph of a leathery-faced American Indian leaning on his rifle, hair hacked off at his chin, hung next to the bathroom. Geronimo. Lena had always claimed to be a descendant of the old warrior, but Ray assumed it was a tall tale. The photograph on the wall was one he had seen dozens of times; it seemed like every gas station west of New Orleans had a rack of vintage Wild West postcards, and this particular shot of Geronimo was usually among them. He got up and unpacked a stack of rock documentary DVDs he hoped would enthuse him about this new project.

He was uninspired so far—embarrassed to find himself on the rockumentary bandwagon, which was lumbering forward like a glittery parade float now that the year 2000 had arrived. Psychically, the start of the new millennium had left him in a crater the size of his life when it hit, but everything still looked the same, same grubby, uneven world, and as far as he could see, the millennium mark was nothing more than an occasion to rehash the past, rockumentaries being only one symptom of this tendency. For an art form dedicated to the new and the now, rock and roll leaned hard toward nostalgia. It worked on canonization as it went. And now he would be part of the narrative-forming machine, arguing for Lena Wells's place in the big rock story. Why she was important, why we must not forget the vital contribution of Lena Wells. Rockumentaries. What a downer. If he were going to choose a rock musician from the seventies to profile, it would be somebody underground, not Lena Wells, an artist whose big-stadium shows and fringe-wearing, baroque style were exactly the sort of thing that had sent him and so many other people screaming into the arms of punk rock.

There was a knock at his door. He opened it to find a blond woman with long, wavy hair like she had just taken out braids. She wore cargo shorts and a green-and-white striped T-shirt, and was keyed up, her tan knees rocking back and forth like a kid who needs a bathroom. "Hi!" She flashed a smile. "Are you lactose intolerant?"

"Well—"

She walked into the room, scratching her elbow. "I'm Jettie Waycross. Gram's girlfriend."

Ray stood back and let her pass. "I thought he was married?"

"Well, wife then. That just sounds so—I don't know. *Wife.*"

Ray laughed. "I take it the marriage is new?"

"Just a few months. I'm mostly used to women, so the whole thing's a trip. But fun!"

Full of energy and powerfully built, she had Tina Turner power thighs, a dark tan, liquid brown eyes. The sun damage made it hard to guess her age—she had crow's feet and smile lines but might have still been in her twenties. Had she just said she generally preferred women? He thought so.

She continued, "So you're not a vegetarian are you?"

Ray remembered a brief meatless stint in his thirties that had quickly devolved into a diet of potato chips and cheese pizza. It hadn't lasted. "No."

"Any food allergies, anything we should know about?"

"I can eat anything. You might ask Martin, across the hall." Ray wondered what she would have done if he had said yes to any of her questions. He could smell the food for the party from there on the third floor. It smelled ready to serve.

"They should have asked you before now, they're just so"—her hands flew open like she was tossing confetti—"laid back around here. This party? Oh my god, so far out of their comfort zone. Never mind the concert."

"You're in the Black Sheep, right? Martin, the guy across the hall, saw you play in Austin. You rocked his face off. You particularly."

"I play bass and sing." She beamed. She had the kind of fair eyelashes that were only visible when they caught the light, and her left eyebrow had a blank space like it had been bisected by the world's tiniest lawnmower. "I write the songs, too. I—"

His cell phone rang in his pocket. "Excuse me," he said, glancing at the caller ID on his phone. It was his ex-girlfriend. Now his attorney. He sat on the edge of the bed and answered. "Lauren. How are things in Austin?"

"Are you there yet?"

"Just got here."

"What's she like?"

He glanced up at Jettie, who stood next to the open door bouncing one knee, the back of her flip-flop snapping against the wood floor. "Lena Wells? Haven't met her yet."

"I just love her."

"That's why we broke up."

Lauren laughed. "Keep telling yourself that." In fact they had broken up when Lauren got involved with another attorney, whom she called a "grown-up" after trying for a few good years to make Ray quit making high-minded films that made no money. She had needed a more practical man, a materialist like herself. What could he do about a thing like that?

"I assume you have news," Ray said. The room was freezing and he could see goose bumps raised on Jettie's toned arms. He wished she'd leave, but she flashed him another wide-open grin when he locked eyes with her, so he stepped into the tiny bathroom for privacy, sitting down on the sliding lid of the toilet seat.

"Chester Lord has offered you a settlement."

"Aha! He's come to his senses!" Ray pushed the bathroom door so that it was nearly shut. "What's his offer?"

"He'll drop his lawsuit if you'll pay for his rehabilitation—"

"Sure!" Ray said. "The man needs his arm. I get it."

"Well, his arm is useless. Rehabilitation won't change much about that." Ray imagined Lauren pacing behind her glass-topped desk, pulling at a gold hoop earring while she stared out the window at the old Spanish-style church across the parking lot from her office. Our lady of something or other. She explained, "I spoke with his physician who continues to insist that the bullet tore the muscles of his bicep too severely for him to work as a security guard again."

"Maybe he could learn to shoot with his left hand?"

"Jesus, Ray."

It sounded callous, and Ray didn't feel callous, but he did feel angry. And innocent. "I'm just saying—"

"You didn't let me finish. The other part of the settlement would require you to pay for his daughter's college education. All of it, all four years."

"What?" Ray grabbed the hair at the top of his head. "That's insane!"

"Apparently she's a smart kid. She's gotten into Rice, but they can't afford it."

Ray laughed. "I can't pay for that."

"I think you should give it some serious thought, Ray."

"Do you really? You're supposed to be on my side." He spun the roll of toilet paper and watched it unspool into a pile on the floor. "No way. Tell him no way. Four years at Rice University? My god. I'll never understand why he didn't go after Johnny Reyes. He's the one who shot him."

"Johnny Reyes has no money. He's a little thug. The shooting happened while you were filming. You're a filmmaker."

"A broke one."

"Don't I know it. But Chester Lord doesn't seem to appreciate the difference between documentary and feature filmmakers."

"Any news on Johnny?"

"Stop worrying about him, Ray. He's sitting in La Tuna serving his time, same as yesterday and a lot of days to come. Think about yourself. You like the moral high ground. Pay for this kid's college and I think you can start crawling back up to that rarefied air you like so well."

"What do you mean—I like the moral high ground?"

There was silence on the other end of the line. She wasn't going to answer. Finally, he said, "Forget it. It's a terrible offer, Lauren."

"That's right, Ray. Keep doing things your way. Some day it just might work."

He stared at the phone. A new lawyer, maybe? But Lauren gave him a good deal, the ex-sweetheart's discount.

When he came out of the bathroom, Jettie asked, "What's why you broke up?"

"So you weren't listening at the door?"

"I mean, I didn't have my ear to the door. I might've gotten pretty close, though." She shrugged. "Couldn't hear much."

He laughed. "She's my ex."

"I could feel that. Who's Johnny Reyes?"

Her eyes concentrating on Ray, Jettie idly began swinging on the front door handle, drifting in and out of the room like an oscillating fan while he told her how he was being sued in civil court by Chester Lord, a security guard at a pharmacy in Rio Marron, Texas. Lord was shot by Johnny Reyes while Ray was filming a documentary called *What's in the Water?* And Lord now had a withered right arm too weak to fire a weapon. Lord's career, such as it was, was over, and he was looking to Ray for a payday. Upon hearing of the lawsuit, the university where Ray had taught classes for ten years without tenure "failed to renew" his contract.

"We were following him—Martin and I—with the camera running. Johnny's this charismatic little tweaker. I'd decided he was the face of Rio Marron's type of drug crazy."

"Your film was about drugs?" She swung into the room. "I got to say, old son, that sounds kind of done-to-death."

He chuckled, surprised. "Not those kinds of drugs. Rio Marron is a town in West Texas where the city fathers decided back in 1962 to start putting lithium in the water supply."

"Can they do that?"

"They were doing it."

"But now the shooting—it wasn't you who pulled the trigger, right?"

"Right." He almost laid it all out for her, but he was afraid he might lose her apparent sympathy if they stayed on the subject too long. "I guess innocent is a relative term," he said.

She reached up and patted him on the shoulder, giving him a warm smile. "Sorry, old son, I didn't mean to get you upset."

"I'm not upset."

"You are, but anyway, I'm glad you're here. Sounds like you shook up that little town. Maybe you'll shake things up for us, too."

"You say that like it would be a good thing."

"I always like a little shake, rattle, and roll. See you downstairs after a while." She stepped out into the hallway. Just as he was closing the door, she said, "Was that a no to the lactose intolerance?"

"Yes. I mean, that was a no."

After she left, Ray tried to turn the air conditioner unit down but found the knob stuck in the high position. While he jiggled it, he sent something like a prayer out into the universe. To his surprise, the plea came in the form of lines from one of Lena Wells's songs, one he had developed a grudging fondness for while listening to her CDs on the drive up from Austin, somewhere between Wichita Falls and Burkburnett. It was called "Need":

> *I'm a lone low gambler*
> *Need a three-card miracle*
> *I'd take a daybreak spiritual*
> *I'd do a voodoo ritual*
> *Done took the measure of you*
> *I'll take whatever you got.*

2

HOT BURRITO #1

Two tall, leather-skinned men stood on the Great Room stage like strips of beef jerky with guitars playing a familiar folk song whose title Ray couldn't come up with. Near the stage stood a small group of people nodding to the music, including a skinny black guy with a side-parted afro, two rockabilly girls in flared skirts, and Martin in his porkpie hat, his fleshy face and prominent waistline reminding Ray of Alfred Hitchcock in one of his sly cameos. As Ray strolled the crowded wood floors, he overheard bits of conversation.

"—thought it'd be fancier."

"Where is she?" The question came from a heavily tattooed woman holding a paper plate piled high with blue corn tortilla chips.

"Pretty boys. Out-of-towners, usually. What do you call a harem when it's all guys?"

A fat man wearing a big white Stetson was saying, "—eight of her damn buffalo out there in the middle of the road. Took two days to get somebody out to fix the fence."

"Have you seen her yet?"

"I mean, it's not that big, Graceland isn't. Not like you expect. Same as this place." A man with a shaved head and close-set eyes peered around like a disappointed sightseer. "I don't know, I guess I expected solid gold floors or something."

"You know, I hear she picked his bride for him. That little gal's her biggest fan. Pretty good, huh? I wish my daughter-in-law was my biggest fan."

"—she goes to the Monday night meeting in Lawton, the one at the strip mall with the discount liquor store. Why are those meetings always next to liquor stores?"

"I bet she don't even show up."

"Excuse me, are you the film guy?"

Ray had nearly reached the sliding glass door at the back of the Great Room. He looked down to see a woman with a shiny chin holding out a beer to him. She smelled like hair spray.

"Thanks." He took a long swallow.

"I heard Julia Roberts was going to play her."

"No, it's not—"

"That gal's teeth are too big."

"It's not that kind of film. It's a documentary."

"Oh." The woman pulled a face. "I heard it was going to be a real movie." She looked like she wanted to take back the beer.

"Sorry," he muttered, as she moved off. He was getting the picture that, while Lena Wells might have been shelved firmly in the where-are-they-now file for the rest of the world, here in Comanche County, Oklahoma, they knew exactly where she was, and they had definite ideas about how best to show her to the world. Ray downed his beer and grabbed a whiskey from a passing tray, knocked it back, and then grabbed another. She was somewhere close. Eyes out for Lena, he checked the kitchen, cruising past gleaming stainless-steel counters with black-and-white nature prints arranged along the white-tiled walls above them, then took a turn around the Great Room, passing through conversations like a plane through weather patterns.

As long as nobody knew him and nobody wanted anything from him, he felt fine. It was when the small talk started that he had troubles. Small talk killed him. It had a rhythm and a set of rules he had never learned, and he could become claustrophobic in the middle of a chat like a feral squirrel trapped in a house. In fact he might not have been fired from the university if his small talk weren't so deficient. He had attended a party at his department chair's house the previous fall and had slighted her pinhead husband somehow. He wasn't even sure how, but a month later, when Chester Lord's lawsuit hit, his chair had been so eager to let him know that the university couldn't risk being sued that Ray knew she still had it in for him because of the insult to her husband. "You're such an artist," she'd said, as she peeled his name off his office mail cubby, "I'm sure you'll land on your feet."

Tonight, though, so far so good. He slid open the back door and found himself on a wide deck strung with lights and crowded with people. The sky flushed hot pink as the sun sank behind the serrated peaks of the Wichita Mountains west of Medicine Park. The air in the backyard smelled like charcoal smoke and barbecue, cigarettes and wine, and, occasionally, the green thread of pot smoke. A group of men holding beer bottles congregated near the barbecue grill, standing off to one side near a long, narrow stable where Cy was overseeing a serious outlay of meat, his face squinting from the heat of the fire.

Closer to drunk than he usually got, Ray walked over a wide stretch of lawn toward a white-trellised gazebo lit with orange Chinese lanterns and crowded with young guys all smoking pot, judging by the odor. Men and women wandered down sidewalks that radiated from the gazebo like spokes. He circumnavigated a group of wide, middle-aged people, one and all in Wrangler's jeans and cowboy boots, the women with ratty perms and big bangs. The men stood with their legs apart, arms crossed as if bracing for a blow.

Ray regarded them. "What's the story there?" He asked the question more to himself than anything, but a woman who had been cruising the edge of the group like a small moon responded.

"Cattle." She wore a white sleeveless tunic with silver bracelets on both wrists.

"Oh, I'm sure they have some individuality," Ray said. "Maybe."

There was a pause, and then the woman laughed. "I didn't mean they *are* cattle. I meant they're *in* cattle. The cattle business."

"Oh. I thought you were being Nietzschean—herd morality kind of thing."

The woman's bracelets jangled. "You could be right," she said. "I don't really know them."

Two tall men in straw cowboy hats approached the woman, American Indians wearing bolo ties with turquoise-and-silver settings that looked like a year of Ray's adjunct teaching pay, and stiff, pressed jeans, their hair pouring over their shoulders slick and dark as oil. As the two men began to talk, their backs to him and hiding the woman, he heard one of them say, "Lena, you're hard to find."

Lena. He had been talking to Lena. Christ almighty. Ray tried to peer around the men's slim backs to take a good look at her, but he could only see her bare feet on the grass and hear her silver bracelets jingling. Herd morality. What a jackass.

He wanted to wait on the two men to leave but it was weird, his standing so close to them on such a wide, empty stretch of lawn, so he paced a few yards toward the gazebo. He was crunching ice with his teeth, relishing the way it drowned out the stale sounds of the cover band, when he felt a tap on his shoulder.

"Howdy."

Ray turned and this time really looked at the woman in the long, white tunic smiling up at him. They were in the darkest part of the yard, but the yellow glow from a string of lights twenty feet away showed the high cheekbones and smooth forehead of a very familiar face. This woman now looked a lot like Lena Wells. "Hi!" he blurted. "I'm so sorry. Fuck, I didn't realize—I'm sorry I said fuck—"

She covered her mouth and watched him, her eyes full of mirth.

"I didn't look at you; I'm sorry, I—"

"Relax, Ray. Or Mr. Wheeler. Maybe it's Professor Wheeler? Is it okay if I call you Ray?"

"You can call me anything—shithead—whatever. You can call me—"

She made a gentle clucking sound like she was approaching a skittish horse. "I'll call you Ray. Since that's your name."

"Sure." Ray took a deep breath and rolled his neck across his shoulders. He hadn't fallen apart like that in front of a girl since junior high when he had asked a girl if her eyes were real.

After a moment she said, "And you can call me Lena."

"Yes! I will. Lena. Lena Wells. She of the cosmic riffs and the hoot owl screech."

"You're not even drunk, are you?"

He was, actually, somewhat drunk. "Nope. Just a natural fool."

She watched him steadily, pulling at the tips of her long hair. She didn't look appreciably different than she had twenty years ago. Same delicate bone structure, same dark eyes, same long, dark hair. Although she had been world-famous while he was just a college kid in Texas suburbia, they weren't far apart in age, just a few years that now spanned the back of their forties. She said, "I should have introduced myself. I was about to say something to you, but those guys wanted to talk to me. They're good people. I'd like you to interview them for the film."

"They're—were they in your band?"

"Just friends. Good people."

Ray felt a small wave of irritation. So he was going to be conducting interviews because Lena Wells thought the subjects were good people? No. He wouldn't. "I've got the interview list established, but we can certainly talk about anybody you'd like to add."

Lena crossed her arms under her breasts, throwing her collarbones into high relief. He wanted to bury his mouth in the shadowy hollow below her neck, a fleeting and subterranean urge. She said, "How do you know who you should interview?"

"I've read up on the subject—on you—I've got a sense of what's important."

"Oh, you do?" She nodded. "It's good that you can tell me what's important about my life. I have some thoughts on that subject, too, oddly enough."

"Of course," he replied, the glimmer of eroticism snuffed. They were heading into the worst kind of small talk—small talk that wasn't really small. There was some sort of preliminary negotiating going on here, and his impulse was to step right over the line and start talking business, straight up. But he knew that wasn't the way to go about it. Instead, he would have to figure out how to spar and parry and be charming without giving away whatever power he possessed over the film.

He hadn't expected to find her attractive and didn't want to, but there it was, chemical, electrical, or something. Lena put off a strange energy, slow but not easy. She wasn't trying to make a presentation of herself the way people do when they meet someone new—it was more like she had known him for a while. Or maybe she assumed he already knew everything about her that she cared to share. And he did. Once the fact of the upcoming Lena Wells project was a fait accompli, Ray had done the due diligence. He had hunted on the Internet and at the library for anything there was to hear, see, or read about Wells, from homemade fan sites that were more like shrines to the unevenly digitized serious articles in magazines like *Creem* and *Rolling Stone*, some of which were available in full text online, some of which he had to find in microfiche. He hadn't owned any of her music, so he bought her CDs and listened to them all, learning the lyrics. Although he hadn't yet read the media kit, which had arrived from Lena's manager, Katerina Davies, the day before he left Austin, he felt like he knew the dimensions of Lena's life, the topography.

Her vibe wasn't what he'd expected, though. She was magnetic in a still, modest way that was taut with energy, like a hawk on a fence post. Given her drug and alcohol problems in the past, he'd thought she might be blousy, loud, still a party girl, but there was none of that. Her voice was low and her Okie accent had thickened since her most recent interviews, her vowels stretched flat as asphalt. She was also more petite than he expected, almost childlike, her hips so narrow it was hard for him to imagine her giving birth to a child. And then there was the fact that she was distinctly—

"Short. Wow, you really are very short, aren't you?"

She nodded in a slow, exaggerated way. "You said that out loud, do you realize?"

Ray downed his drink. Was it his third or fourth? He was buzzed, that was for sure. Way buzzed. It was some verbalized observation like this about the chair's husband that had cost him his teaching job. He said in a strangled voice, "Sorry, you just look taller in your pictures."

"That's okay," she replied. "Those platform heels did their job. That's why I wore them."

"Being short's not a crime."

"No, it isn't."

"So, you're going to make a comeback, huh?"

She blinked. "I have new music. You think that's what they'll call it? A comeback?" She raised her fingers to her lips.

"A comeback, yeah. Because you were gone, and now you're coming back." He hadn't meant to sound sarcastic, but he did, he definitely did, and now he watched her startle and pull back. He tried to explain. "There are a lot of them right now—something about the new millennium. Comebacks, reunion tours. A lot of seventies folks make these where-are-they-now docs to help with the promo, too, so you'll be right in there. Our film should really help."

"Where-are-they-now? That's a category?" Her black eyes fixed on him, appalled. She pushed her hair behind her ears. "I never thought of myself as 'seventies folk.' I didn't know."

"Hey, I'm sorry," he said. Was she kidding? He felt a rush of warmth and wanted to put an arm around her. "Our film is going to be a cut above, don't you worry."

She gave him a hopeful smile so he pressed on, trying to be supportive. "And maybe there will still be an audience for you. I mean, that whole bell-bottomed cowgirl thing is way over, of course, but I'm sure your agent will get you hooked up with a stylist or something. You haven't lost your looks, and that's going to help a lot."

"Wow." She stared at him. "Bell-bottomed cowgirl thing? You don't think much of me, do you? Would you have said any of that if I were a guy? It's almost like you don't want this job."

"No, I just meant, you know, a new look for a new century kind of thing," Ray said. "And I meant you're beautiful, that's all. I do want this job, I really do!"

"I've been working on the music like that was all that mattered. But the business bullshit—it's all coming back to me now. Boy, is it ever." She had been looking off, but suddenly she pulled her attention back to his face. "I'm not feeling too good about this. About you. I'll tell you what, Ray Wheeler." She rocked back on her heels and leveled a finger at him, her eyes snapping with energy. "I'm giving you a week."

"I beg your pardon?"

"I said a week."

"A week?"

"Call it a probationary period."

"You're putting me on probation?"

"I'm going to need you to impress me, Ray. You're going to need to rock my little hillbilly world. Because right now, I don't have much faith in the likes of you." She got up close to his face and said, "Do you think I can't tell?"

"Tell what?"

"You're drunk."

Ray put his hands out in front of him. "Hey, hey, listen. I'm not usually like this."

"You know, darling, I've probably spilled more booze than you'll ever drink. So I don't judge. Drink all you want on your own time. It's just that you're on my time now. This here's work. You knew we'd meet tonight. I've been sober too long to spend the next however-many-days it takes to make this film splashing around the shallow end with some smart-ass drunk. I don't live there anymore." She turned without smiling and strolled across the grass, her white tunic drifting over the lawn like a stingray rippling across a sea bottom.

He caught up with her and grabbed her by the arm. "Please," he said. She looked at his hand on her arm and he took it off. "I'm nervous, okay? It's making me act like a dick. I'm sorry."

She nodded, but her expression remained wary. "One week." She turned and walked off across the lawn, heading straight to Cy, who still stood over the grill. She rested an elbow on his shoulder and said something to him. Ray watched as they laughed at something. Him, they had to be laughing at him. He had blown it. Fucking Lena Wells. She *was* short!

Lena smiled at the group of people standing around. A guy in a yellow golf shirt was playing air guitar to illustrate a point as he grinned and talked to Cy. His sycophantic posture pulled Ray up short. Cy gave the guy a weary, tolerant nod, and Lena backed off to let Cy slap down raw meat on the grill. She pushed off from him like she was on roller skates. It was the same fluid motion Ray had seen before in concert footage, where she would separate from her lead guitarist, Cyril Dodge, to let him take a solo.

Cyril Dodge. Cy. Not Sigh. He had had short, curly brown hair back then, and a surfer's tan. His riffs had taken the band's music from something rootsy to something less predictable, something that gave off sparks like metal dragging concrete. He had always seemed content to let Lena take the limelight, but watching him shake salt over the meat on the grill, Ray remembered the one time he had ever seen Cyril Dodge pushed to the front—that night in 1981 when Lena effectively ended her career by spacing out on the *Tonight Show.*

Ray had been in El Paso with his parents, a hungry college kid who had come home from the dorms for a late-night snack and for help typing a paper due the next morning. He had paused behind the couch on his way to the kitchen to see who the musical guest was and recognized Lena Wells and the Lighthorsemen. That summer he was deep into new punk music coming out of L.A. by bands like X and Agent Orange and couldn't have cared less about anybody vanilla enough to be on the *Tonight Show,* but he idled behind the couch and watched anyway. Lena Wells was always worth watching, smoking hot in a dirty hippie kind of way. She was about a minute into "Black Ice," sweating under the lights in a purple tube top, her skin greasy like she hadn't bathed that day. She grabbed the mic, a curtain of black hair falling across her face and concealing the crisis for a moment even as her voice faltered and stopped. Stopped.

The momentum of the song surged into an abrupt hush like a wave hitting a seawall. Ray had grabbed the back of the couch. Ed McMahon's big laugh boomed into the broadcasting silence, then sounded again, the second time like a downbeat of dread.

The Lighthorsemen tried to loop back and play the chorus again so Lena could jump in. The camera cut to Johnny Carson, but he looked nervous, so it cut away. Silence spread like a stain.

Even Ray had known the words. He would never have copped to liking such a mainstream jam, but the song was everywhere that summer. Ray and his mother and his father spoke out loud the lyrics that should have come next, giving one another embarrassed glances as their voices rang out simultaneously. All across America, people shouted the words at their television:

> *Next time you play you'd better deal me in*
> *I'll bet the farm and then I'll let you win.*

Everybody remembered the words but Lena. Later, global transient amnesia became the official diagnosis, but in the moment everybody knew it was the booze and drugs. From the couch, Ray's mother said, "That girl is lost," and took a long drag on her cigarette. As the silence held, Ray squirmed. Too real, too raw, the moment was intolerable. He wanted to snatch the afghan spread over his mother's legs and throw it over the television screen to cover the shame they were witnessing. Where was the cut to commercial?

Then, hope. A new sound erupted, and the camera found Cy's blue-sky eyes. There he was on lead guitar, improvising a solo that gave Lena smelling salts and took her on a walk around the block. What ensued was musical triage. The drummer and bass player joined in, a top-shelf laugh boomed from Ed McMahon, and a cut to Johnny Carson showed him pulling a face that said, "All righty, then!" Whatever Lena was doing stayed out of view of the television audience, but Cy was staring pleadingly at her as he sang. There was not another shot of her until the second verse. Then she was there again, her voice roaring in like a dead plane engine surging back to life just before the plane crashes into a mountainside. The band brought the song to a big close, and the cameras showed the studio audience on their feet. Still, nothing could make it look like a deliberate performance. There was just no denying that silence, a rend in the fabric of *Tonight Show* time, a bullet hole blown in the chest of Tuesday night. Lena had lost it and everybody saw. When the song was over, Carson went straight to Cy, shaking his hand with what had looked to Ray like honest-to-god gratitude.

Now Cy grabbed a rack of ribs with heavy tongs and laid it on a plate held by a waiting caterer.

Ray had planned to run down all her old bandmates for interviews, and Cy's presence right there in Medicine Park would make his job a little easier, but only if he had a job. He was feeling worse by the minute, convinced he had blown it again. It was becoming hard not to notice that his problems were basically of his own making. What was he doing wrong, though? He was a good filmmaker. He was. He wasn't a whore or a hack, he made films he believed in, and he made them well. Nor was he a drunk—he had told Lena the truth about that. He thought about her collarbones and how if she fired him he would never see them again, and he felt a fresh injection of the regret that had lately become his new normal.

A man with big, freckled arms stumbled into him and left a smear of barbecue sauce across Ray's shirt. He watched one member of the catering crew, a Hispanic girl in a white smock, push the sliding glass door shut with her hip as she carried a cheese tray. He wondered if she was legal. Ever since his second film, *Barking Mad*, which he'd finished in 1994, Ray had felt a special bond with the illegal workers he ran into. They didn't feel the bond, but he did.

Barking Mad was about a coyote—a man that brought illegal immigrants across the U.S.–Mexican border—who was a serial rapist preying on his powerless clientele. Ray had been dating Lauren, and it was her housekeeper who'd given him the idea for the film by telling him the story. She had helped him contact other illegal immigrants, who all told horrific tales about what was obviously the same man. Ray had pieced together a picture of a spindly-legged guy in a ball cap that said PORT ARTHUR PAWN. The man kept a wad of tobacco in his jaw and drove a white van in which he played the music of Ted Nugent, a detail Ray had put together after hearing three of the man's ex-clients, two female victims and one teenage boy, describe a song "about cats who bring illness," "*loco gato.*" He finally played "Cat Scratch Fever" for one of the women and she nodded, "*Si, si.* That's it."

The film had been a feat of editing. Ray spliced the interviews so the similarities in the eyewitness accounts accreted, and he let the natural predator/prey analogy that emerged with "coyote" and "Cat Scratch" do its work. A year later, when police caught the guy in Port Arthur, Texas, they credited Ray's film with building the profile they needed. The film had made a difference. Ray felt validated after that, and he'd been confident that his next film, *What's in the Water?* was going to solidify his reputation for truth. Instead here he was about to get fired from a where-are-they-now thing that might or might not run on VH-1. So much for plans.

At the barbecue pit, Cy had stepped away from the heat to drink a Coke. Ray combed the clusters of people, looking for Lena's long, black hair and white tunic, but he didn't see her. The pot smoke emanating from the gazebo was becoming a mushroom cloud. It was a party given in his honor, but Ray decided to split before he did any more damage.

Heading in the direction of the house, he was confronted by an enormous white dog. It sat in the middle of the sidewalk, gazing at him mildly. He stopped and looked at it, unsure whether to pet it or try to walk around it. Ahead, familiar voices rose in anger. He tentatively stroked the top of the dog's head.

"It's not fair!" This was Jettie's voice. Ray wasn't sure what to do. The voices sounded like they were in front of him, and if he kept to his trajectory he'd interrupt them. But he wasn't sure what the dog would do if he tried to walk away.

Then the other voice said, "Say hello to Cimarron, Ray."

"Hello, Cimarron." He petted the dog again and took a few steps until he could make out the dim outlines of two figures sitting on a bench a few feet away. "Hello, Gram."

Jettie opened a space between herself and Gram and patted the seat. She said, "You want to come to our show tomorrow night at the Signal Flare?"

"Good to see you," Ray said, sliding in between them. There was a haze of energy in the air between them, the incomplete circuit of the fight that he had interrupted. Jettie had fired off the last shot, and Ray had stumbled on them before Gram could fire back. It was funny how you could feel things like that.

Ray and Martin had met Lena's twenty-two-year-old son a couple of weeks earlier back home in Austin at a club called Bandolero, where Gram had been about to perform with his and Jettie's band, the Black Sheep. In response to Martin's proposal about a Lena Wells documentary, Gram had invited the two of them to drop by the club the afternoon before the show. Ray had gone along with Martin for moral support. Or so he thought. They had sat on a back patio strung with chili pepper lights, drunk seaweed-colored margaritas, and chatted for half an hour. Gram had surprised Ray by knowing his films. "Mom and I loved *Barking Mad*, and that other one, *Paper Trail*, that was good, too."

He had spoken to Ray as if there were some prior knowledge between them. As if Ray had agreed to direct.

Up to that moment, Ray hadn't been aware that Martin's fan-boy documentary had any real chance of getting made. But right then and there, Martin had revealed that he had applied for and received a $30,000 grant sponsored by some rich Oklahoma oil family to make a film about "an Oklahoman of cultural significance." Martin and Gram had high-fived and ordered tequila shots. Taking in Gram's self-conscious stoop, spiky black hair, and meaty earlobes weighted down with earrings, Ray had been noncommittal, silently furious about what was becoming clearer and clearer as the conversation continued. He rounded on Martin as soon as they were back on the sidewalk. "You told them we're a team? That I want to do this film?"

"Look, I knew you'd be mad," Martin conceded, "but they wouldn't talk to me otherwise. They'd think I was just a fan."

"You are just a fan."

"But you're not. You've got chops. You got a rep. Don't bust my balls, Ray, I just want to do something—" Martin's long fingers flitted across the frayed edge of his hat brim. "You've helped me a lot. Letting me work on *What's in the Water?*—that was most excellent experience. I just want to return the favor."

"You want to do something—for me?" Martin felt sorry for him; that was the deal. He was throwing him a life rope by asking him to direct his pet project. "Martin, you've been corresponding with Lena Wells and her people, saying I want to direct this thing?"

"Come on, man, you're going to thank me."

Ray doubted it. And now Martin would have nothing to thank him for either, when Lena sent them packing in the morning. He had never even liked her music. Ordinarily he would have turned the project down flat. But ordinary was over. He was in no position to say no to a job. Oh, why didn't reality have a rewind button? Then he could fix his first encounter with Lena the way he fixed things in the editing room. Rewind, Delete. Record new footage. But reality didn't work that way. He turned to Gram and asked, "You live here on the grounds, right?"

Gram gestured toward a white carriage house with black shutters at the back of the property. "That's our place. Gives us a little privacy. Did she put you on the third floor?"

Ray allowed that he was staying on the third floor, letting a note of irritation creep into his voice as he explained that no one had been on hand to greet them when they arrived until Cy had shown up and shown them to their rooms.

"Yeah, it was the butler's day off," Gram said. He leaned back and rested his elbows against the back of the bench. "I hope you found everything to your liking. Do let us know if there's anything you require. I'll leave a chocolate on your pillow my own self if I have to, man, that's how much we aim to please."

"No problem, no problem," Ray said. He was getting the dross of Gram's anger at Jettie, and he tried not to take it personally. "I'm without a valet, myself, unless you count Martin, which I don't."

Jettie laughed.

"I thought Martin was the producer," Gram said, uncrossing his legs.

"That's him."

"So doesn't that make him your boss?"

"You bet," Ray said flatly. "Maybe the valet is me, huh?"

Jettie leaned forward. "Come to our show, Ray. Come check us out tomorrow night. You might think there's all kinds of nightlife around here to choose from." She waved a hand at the big sky darkening above them. "But you'd be wrong."

"Right," he said. "What's this about a Signal Flare?"

"It's a club in Lawton, right outside Fort Sill." Gram jerked a thumb to the east. "You could film us."

"Well—" Ray palmed his knees and leaned forward. Did footage of Gram and Jettie's band belong in a Lena Wells documentary? Maybe it did. When they weren't playing their own music in the Black Sheep, they were basically Lena's core musicians, never mind that they were also her family. But it wouldn't have mattered if they had invited him to film them grooming their big dog—he'd have said yes. The conversation needed a yes. "I'll be there."

A good note on which to leave. Ray stood up. "I love this idea. Let's talk about it in the morning."

"Sleep well," Gram said. "If there's a pea under your mattress, why, you just give me a call, princess. I live to serve."

Ray forced out a good-natured laugh and waved. As he crossed the yard, he grabbed a drink off a waiter's passing tray and slammed it. Gin. Ugh. How much worse could the evening get? He saw Martin standing in a group on the lawn and went the other way to avoid talking to him. Back in the house, he passed through the orbit of a few couples in the Great Room slow-dancing under the strings of white lights to a pleading rendition of "Hot Burrito #1." He took the stairs two at a time in propulsive gusts of frustration and self-disgust. He had pissed off the entire Wells family tonight. Ah, he could screw things up. Before mounting the final flight to his room, he stopped on the second floor landing and peered down the hall. Lena's private quarters. Gleaming wood floors reflected warm light from chevron-shaped amber sconces mounted along the walls. The third door on the right stood open. He tiptoed down the hall and ducked in.

The sodium glow of a streetlight outside the windows poured into the dark room and showed a long parlor lined with floor-to-ceiling barrister bookshelves crowded with books and CDs. A dozen blown-glass globes tied to jewel-toned ribbons dangled in the window, reflecting the streetlight in prismatic patterns across the floor and turning the surface of his khaki pants into something trippy and liquid, red and pink and orange. Thousands of records stood in crates along the floor of the south wall, where windows faced the screened-in porch at the front of the building. He smelled incense. Not the stoner kind, more the ecclesiastical variety. Frankincense or myrrh. A buffalo-skin rug was spread in front of a fireplace in the corner of the room made of Medicine Park's signature red cobblestones. Surrounding the fireplace were plants, kilim pillows, and lacquered boxes, a suite of dark leather couches arranged around it. Framed photographs stood on the shelves. They were hard to see in the lowlight, but he could make out Gram as a boy. Gram and Lena. Publicity shots from the albums—sexy, staring, in-your-face shots Ray had seen before.

He picked up a group picture of Lena with the cast and crew of *The Ballad of Belle Starr*, a Western she had made in 1978, her lone foray into acting. A second photo showed her in buckskin outlaw costume, fingering a coiled horsewhip while looking over a script with Keith Carradine, who played her husband.

Ray set down the picture and toured the room, hands joined behind his back, peering at the books and CDs. Exotic knickknacks sat about. An old disc gramophone stood in the corner, its blackened brass horn arcing from the base like the entrance to a black hole. A stuffed cougar was poised to leap from behind the reaching fronds of a Sego palm. He stood in the low kaleidoscopic light looking around until the silence in the room began to indict him.

Still, he couldn't leave. He let his eyes run over the room. On Lena's leather couch, hidden halfway under a cushion, was some sort of fabric. It lifted easily from its hiding place, and he was holding a black-and-blue plaid button-up shirt, woman's size small. He pinched the shoulders and held it out so that it hung before him, the shell that proves the cicada, the shed skin that proves the snake. So small—Lena was small. He imagined her buttoning the shirt on a cold day, fast fingers pulling at wooden buttons. There was a light smell of deodorant at the armpits, he discovered, as he brought the soft flannel to his nose. Breathing deeply, he closed his eyes and took in, for the first time, Lena's smell. It brought her to him in another dimension, made her animal. He drew another deep breath. How exciting. How strangely exciting. When he opened his eyes, he saw a shadow in his peripheral vision.

Someone was there. He glanced up, the shirt still to his face, and saw a barefoot woman in the hall, just outside the doorway, her arms wrapped tightly around her ribs inside an airy white tunic. She quivered like a rabbit. Time slowed, and it seemed he had watched her for hours and become long accustomed to her big-eyed curious presence. But it must have been only a second.

He dropped the shirt and stood up. "Lena—there you are—I wanted to apologize—" But she didn't hear him out. She vanished down the hall and he heard a door shut.

He stood in the empty room and listened to his own battering heart. The swirling light reflected from the blown-glass orbs in the window seemed to pulse like blood. The back of his throat caught. He grew dizzy. He fingered the soft fabric of the shirt. Stepping as softly as he could back into the amber-lit hallway, he made for the second-floor landing, again taking the stairs two at a time. When he was safely inside his room, he looked at the small plaid shirt he was still holding like it was on fire. He dropped it into his suitcase and sat on the edge of the bed, cursing and cursing into the cold room.

3

FORTUNE COOKIES

In the morning Ray enjoyed a sliver of peace before memories of the previous night overwhelmed him. He raised himself onto his elbows to peer into his suitcase, which lay open on the floor. There was the black-and-blue plaid of Lena's shirt. He groaned and dropped back to the pillow, flooded by the memory of Lena standing in the doorway watching him sniff her shirt. Had he really done that? He opened his eyes and studied the swishes and swipes of the trowel marks in the stucco ceiling. They resembled clouds, their patterns presenting him with outlines of objects that seemed to shift. As he hugged his knees to his chest, he saw in the troweled paint the shape of a fortune cookie with the wispy slip of a fortune sticking out. What would that fortune say if he could open it? *Probation is over, go straight to jail.* Or, *A beautiful woman thinks you are a fool.* Or, *Steal from others, lose peace of mind.* Something like that, if the fortune cookie knew anything at all.

He stretched out under the covers. Outside the window, birds chirped, and he could see from a crack in the blinds that the sun was shining. What a nice day to start a new project. Now that he had truly blown it, he realized he had been telling Lena the truth when he said he wanted the job. He did. It wasn't just the grant money Martin had procured. It wasn't that, thanks to Johnny Reyes and Chester Lord, he had no other film or teaching prospects on the horizon. It was that he needed to do something right, to show himself that he still could. He needed a win. And the grant money wouldn't hurt; his own meager reserve of funds would run out by the end of summer. He saw himself washing beer mugs and stocking liquor, bartending again, his career as a filmmaker over. He saw himself talking about his films to bar customers who wouldn't believe him.

Who was he if he wasn't a filmmaker? He had lost love and money and time to be what he wanted to be, but filmmaking was becoming less like a career and more like a fantasy that would never pan out. Yet if he had learned anything from making documentaries, it was that people believed in their fantasies more than they believed in reality. Reality wasn't of much interest to most people, and he was no exception. He was intent on finding the inevitable gap between the real world and what people could take in, that cushion—of stories, of personal myth—that people created in the space between themselves and the world outside to make life tolerable. That was where people really lived, and that was what he was after. To find it. To show it. Here in Medicine Park he could already see that zone opening between world and mind, between story and reality. This hotel sat in that space, a collective fantasy starring Lena Wells, who had written a bunch of new music without a thought as to how or if the world would receive her. That was a story he wanted to hear and to tell. That his desire to do so was a feature of his own fantasy, he knew. He just didn't know how to proceed otherwise. Anyway, when those personal myths succeeded, they came alive in the real world, too. A real comeback album. A real film.

His reverie was interrupted by rustling in the hallway and the appearance of a piece of folded white paper under his door. He swung out of bed and plucked the note from the floor.

Just so we're clear: this is a rockumentary. It's about Mom's music, that's it. If you ask about who my dad is, I'll kick your ass, straight up. That does NOT go in your movie! If it's none of my business, it's damned sure none of yours. You think you can find out what even I don't know? If anyone should know, it should be me, her son, hers and someone else's. Whoever he is, he must not want to know me. He's probably a dick. If she chooses to keep him a secret, she must have her reasons. Nobody's business. If you can't follow that rule, then go the fuck home.

Ray carried the note to the rickety round table by the window, where he sat down and reread it. The note was handwritten in the neat, small handwriting of someone who was used to writing track lists for mixtapes. The kid didn't know who his dad was. Ray knew this; he simply hadn't thought much about it until now. But of course it was a big deal. For Gram, anyway. Poor guy. What was Lena thinking, not telling the kid who his dad was?

Just then he saw another sheet of paper glide under the door. He jumped up and flung the door open, finding himself looking down at a crouching Gram. "Please come in," he said.

Gram frowned and stood up. "I've got to go."

"Well, what's in the new note?"

He handed Ray the note. "You can read it."

Ray unfolded it. An apology for the first note. He glanced up at Gram and smiled. "That's okay, man. No problem at all." He had expected it to contain the line "By the way, my mom says forget about the probation, you're fired" and felt a rush of kindness toward Gram for not delivering that news to him.

Gram yanked one of his earrings, a small skull, spinning it with his thumb. "Jettie wants out of here, bad."

The comment seemed to come out of left field, the kind of nervous non sequitur a person throws up when he feels the power dynamic in a conversation shifting away from him. Ray registered the shift, too, and it felt good. "Sure she does," he agreed smoothly. "This is no place to launch a career."

"I can't leave now. Mom wants us to tour with her. I can't leave her in the lurch. I mean, she gave up music for me."

"Come on, she did not." Lena's musical moment had passed, that was all. Disco, new wave, punk rock all played a part. Besides, she had that substance abuse problem to kick. Ray leaned against the doorjamb, gleeful to be giving advice. "You shouldn't blame yourself. She had her reasons, like I'm sure she has her reasons for not telling you who your dad is. Just between you and me, I can't imagine what that reason could be, but whatever. That subject's off limits—I hear you, man."

Downstairs, on his way to the kitchen, Ray found Jettie onstage in the great room. "Amateurs!" She looked around, toeing a pile of power cords, hands on her broad hips. The equipment moved offstage for the party last night had been moved back but not been set up or plugged in.

Ray stopped in front of the stage and eyed her. "What's wrong?"

"You'd expect some professionalism, wouldn't you? With the success she's had?"

"Sure."

"Look at this shit, Ray." She motioned at the instruments on stage. "We have a live show, her first live show in almost twenty years, in four days. But what are we doing right now? Are we practicing, maybe?"

"No?"

"Correct!" She pointed at him. "We are not practicing. We are having breakfast, we are sleeping in, we are doing whatever the hell else, but we are not practicing. Because, hey, when you're a genius, you don't need to practice."

"Genius? You mean Lena?" Ray stepped up onstage. "Does she play that card?"

She grimaced and looked down. "Oh, not really. Ignore me. I'm just a little bit of a perfectionist."

"I get it. I'm that way, too. If you're going to do it, do it right, am I right?"

"Indeed." She high-fived him.

"You know," Ray offered, "Aristotle thought making metaphor was a form of genius? And almost anybody can make a metaphor. He wasn't thinking of a genius as some rare freak with exceptional talents. More like the spirit of the mind."

She cocked her head. "You don't think Lena's a genius?"

"Hell, I don't know. I do think that word gets thrown around too easily, especially when it comes to musicians. Everybody's a genius in rock."

"Let me show you what I'm talking about." Jettie sat down at the piano. "What don't you see here?" She nodded at the front of the piano.

Ray looked at where she was pointing. "Sheet music?"

She swung around, straddling the bench to face him. "You know why there's no sheet music? Because she doesn't use it."

"A lot of musicians don't read music. Even the so-called geniuses—Paul McCartney, I've heard."

"It's not that she doesn't read it. She does, just not fast enough to keep up with what she's doing. She plays so goddamned fluently that reading the music slows her down. So she memorizes it all. Memorizes it."

"So you do think she's a genius. Whatever that means."

She positioned herself in front of the piano keys and spread her fingers gingerly across them without hitting any notes. Her eyes on her hands, she said, "I've had to work so hard, that's all."

"Can I tell you something?" Ray ventured, cautiously. "You sound jealous."

She grinned. "Do I? Shit. Sorry to vent. It's just that I want to jam and there's nobody else ready."

"I bet you were that kid that wanted to actually study in study groups, weren't you? The one who did the group project by yourself before anybody else got the chance?"

"Of course."

"I guess I'm more surprised to learn she plays piano than that she memorizes everything. She's never played it on stage, has she? Or on an album?"

"She composes on it, but she's shy about anybody hearing her play it. I don't know why."

The door to the kitchen swung open and Gram appeared with a jar of apple butter in one hand. "Hey, Baby—oh, morning, Ray. Breakfast, y'all."

"You can't expect people to practice before breakfast," Ray said, jumping down from the stage.

Jettie threw up her hands. "Let's eat, then."

In the kitchen, Martin sat at the table across from Gram with Cimarron standing next to him, eye level with a plate of eggs that she looked like she might make off with any minute. A woman with short gray hair and skin-tight jeans stood at the sink rinsing a frying pan. Jettie said, "Edith, this is Ray. Edith keeps this place in order."

Edith wiped a red, raw hand on a towel and shook Ray's, nodding soberly. She had small, heavily made-up eyes, and ruddy, vein-mapped skin. "Help yourself to anything you find," she said.

Jettie poured Ray a cup of coffee. "What do you take?"

"Just black."

"Ray," Martin said, his voice tight, "Gram tells me we're shooting the Black Sheep show tonight?"

Ray sipped his coffee and leaned against the counter. He kept forgetting that Martin was in charge. He gave his new boss what he hoped was a deferential look. "That okay?"

Cy walked in through the back door and grabbed a piece of bacon off Gram's plate. "That'd be fine."

"I mean," Martin said, "the documentary's not about them, but I like it. Great idea, I—"

Ray studied the guitar player's expression, looking for signs that Lena had found him last night and told him she wouldn't work with Ray. But Cy's expression showed nothing but pleasure in eating bacon.

Ray turned to the group. "What's the lineup?"

"Gram on lead, Jettie on bass, me on rhythm and second lead," Cy said.

"You're in the Black Sheep," Ray said. "That's a lot of guitar."

"That's a lot of good," Jettie corrected him.

At the table, Martin looked like he wanted to jump into the back and forth, opening his mouth a time or two, but nobody noticed, and to his credit, he soon gave up trying to insert himself. Ray saw him relax and start to go with the flow. It was a damn good trait he wished he possessed.

"Who's playing drums?" Ray asked.

"Rinaldo West," Cy said. "He ain't been coming around lately, but you'll see him tonight. He gets born again every so often and when he does, he don't hang out with us. It's one of them times."

"Whatever happened to Lena's drummer?" Martin asked. "Ellis Wolfe?"

"He's living in the Philippines," Cy said. "Lena and I visited once, but it was some funky shit. I hardly got out of there without Lena taking a bunch of his kids home with her."

"A bunch?"

"Whole mess of them running around."

"What about Desmond Jones?" Jones had played bass with the Lighthorsemen on every album. He was older and more experienced than the rest of the band, had already had a career as a session guy for Phil Spector before he joined them. Critics often cited him as the band's secret strength, the heavy underpinning that kept their sound galloping forward. Jettie had his job now. "He's not around?" Ray asked.

With a look of distaste, Gram said, "That old coot. Who knows?"

They were all up onstage plugging in amps and instruments and tuning. Coffee mugs steamed atop the piano. Ray sat on a couch a few feet away getting his camera ready. He didn't know what else to do but proceed as if nothing had happened the night before. Martin dropped down in a leather chair in the Great Room and said, "So, you kind of blew it with Lena last night."

Ray sat forward and felt like he was draping his neck over a guillotine. He hadn't expected Martin to be his executioner, but Martin was the producer, after all. Lena wouldn't fire Ray in person. It made sense. "Who told you?"

"Lena did. Listen to that sentence, would you? Lena did, because we were talking after you went to bed—Lena Wells and I were talking!" His eyes glowed with the pure joy of a kid who still believes in Santa getting to sit on his knee at the mall. "And she was so nice. I still can't get over it."

"I'm glad you got to meet her. That's really what this project was about anyway, you and your fan-boy needs. So, am I fired or what?"

"Ah! No!" Martin stroked his soul patch with comic exaggeration. "And why is that? Because I, Martin Parker, saved your grumpy ass with my savoir faire."

Ray leaned back. "Didn't know you had any of that."

"When we started talking, I didn't know you'd even met her yet. I was just being my usual charming self."

"Lena Wells's number one fan."

"That's right. I told her how when I was growing up, I lived just down the way in Lawton and how me and my parents used to always drive by the Silver Sun on our way out to the wildlife refuge, how I always wanted to get a glimpse of her. Oh, and I told her you were a huge fan, too. She said she doubted it, which is how I knew you stuck your foot in it, but I told her you were just shy."

"Shy?"

"Well, I have to say, Ray, I have noticed that you're not nearly as articulate when you're not in front of a class. Regular Ray is maybe a little shy."

"Martin, she put me on probation."

"She told me. But she can't really do that, I'm your boss."

"But if she won't work with me—"

"That's true."

"What did you say to her?"

"I said you were the greatest documentary filmmaker I know and I couldn't imagine who we could replace you with that would have half your talent."

Ray scratched his ear. Much as he loved the flattery, Martin's hero worship stressed him out. He had a bad feeling he'd let him down one day. "I don't know why you overestimate me the way you do, Martin, but I thank you."

"She said she still wants the week's probation, but I wouldn't worry about it, bro. Just do your job. It will all be A-okay."

But Martin didn't know about the shirt sniffing. His estimation of Lena's good will came from a moment in the last night's timeline before she caught Ray trespassing in one of her private rooms sniffing her clothes. Ray shut his eyes. Oh, God.

"What's A-okay?"

He opened his eyes. It was Lena who had spoken. She was coming down the stairs barefoot wearing a pair of jeans and a Chess Records T-shirt.

"Everything," Martin said, beaming at her like he wanted to raise a lighter in the air and yell her name as she walked toward them.

She seemed amused. "Everything including that film y'all made last year. I just finished watching it—good stuff! You have a release date?"

"I thought you'd like it!" Martin said. "It'll be out one of these days."

"That Johnny Reyes is one sexy beast. I could watch a whole film of him blinking."

Ray scrutinized her face but found no trace of anger. He was confused. And how had she seen *What's in the Water?* All he had was a rough cut; he'd had to take the money he planned to use on postproduction to pay Lauren when the lawsuit hit. Even with the footage of Reyes breaking into the pharmacy and shooting Lord cut out, he still didn't know if the film would ever see the light of day.

He turned an accusing gaze at Martin, who gave him a thumb's-up and said, "I think it's Ray's finest work." Ray couldn't stop staring at his former student. Right before his eyes, Martin was turning into a real producer. Did he have any idea how much damage he had just controlled?

Behind them, the opening vamp for "Rank Outsider" came tinny and uncommitted, a finger exercise on an electric guitar not yet turned on. Ray assumed it was Cy.

"I'd rather think our little project here will be his best," Lena said. She widened her eyes at Ray, smiling, and for a moment the full knowledge of everything that had already passed between them showed on her face. Pressure inside him released with a hiss. Until that moment, Ray had thought it just possible she hadn't realized he was sniffing her shirt, that it was too dark in her study, that she hadn't checked the couch after he'd left and hadn't found her plaid shirt gone. But the way she looked at him now showed full knowledge. She knew what he had done, and somehow it was okay.

He smiled back. He wasn't fired. Not yet, anyway. He clapped his hands. "You can count on me," he said. The prospect of work lifted him in its satisfying grasp. He needed plans for the day, he needed to make a schedule, needed to hire extra camera crew for the live show, only four days away. He raked his palms down the front of his pants and looked around. "Okay. Okay. Who's available today?" he asked. "Who wants to talk to me first?"

Lena raised her hand. Ray glanced back at the stage to see if Jettie had overheard Lena exempt herself from practice, but she was bent over her green Höfner, her back to them.

That afternoon Lena and Gram took Ray and Martin out to see Lena's buffalo herd. Heading out of town, Ray began filming, appreciating for the first time the oddness of the place. A jumble of scenes streamed by, challenging Ray's ability to prioritize and choose what to frame, what to shoot. Hills rose steeply away from the creek bed, pocked with hard-to-see houses adorned with houseplants, wind chimes, and old cars. The architecture was truly weird. Homes and public buildings alike were built out of red granite balls, same as the porch pillars and fireplaces at the Silver Sun. Cottage after cottage lined the street, built entirely of the rough granite balls. Lena called them "Oklahoma creek rock," explaining they were harvested from the creek beds. The walls looked like cobblestone streets standing upright with windows cut in. Some of the windows were made of wagon wheels set into the walls with cement, some were made of the empty frames of old televisions.

The bison fed in the tall grasses on land that Lena owned northwest of the Wichita Mountain range. "They weigh about a thousand pounds each," she said, standing in front of a cattle gate that marked the entrance to the property. Only a few of the animals were visible, grazing on a yellow hill far in the distance. The sky was china blue with no clouds, obstructed only by the noisy passage of a Chinook helicopter that Lena explained would be landing at Fort Sill to the east. "The size of the herd goes up and down, but right now I own just under a thousand."

"A thousand," Ray said. "And I thought you were living off your greatest hits."

"Where are the rest?" Martin asked.

Lena turned and waved her hand to encompass the horizon. "Out there somewhere."

Ray was behind the camera adjusting the light settings to get rid of the shadow on Lena's face cast by the straw cowboy hat she wore. "What do you do with them?" he asked.

"Bison meat is good for you," she explained. "Lean. And I don't use any growth hormones on them. All organic."

"I thought they were endangered," Ray said.

"Used to be—they were nearly hunted to death in the nineteenth century. When they wanted to save them they had to get breeding stock from the Bronx Zoo, that's how close to extinct they were. There were a few other herds—an old boy up in Kansas had some—but my herd descends from that shipment from New York. They're thriving now. We only sell a percentage for food. A few we sell to Native tribes to use for their rituals."

Next to him, Martin struggled to keep the boom pole out of the shot.

Gram seemed bored. "You should show them the car dealership," he suggested. "We could go to the city."

"The car dealership?" Ray asked.

"I own a Toyota dealership in Oklahoma City," Lena said.

"I saw something about that online—I thought it must be a different Lena Wells."

"Lena Wells Toyota." She grinned. "The manager's always trying to get me in the commercials. I hate that part, but it's a very successful business."

"Are you in the ads?"

"God, no," she said.

Ray laughed. "Why not?"

She shrugged. "I can't sell out quite that far."

"So there are cars on the road that say Lena Wells Toyota on them?"

"Lots of them," she said. "Just keep an eye out—they're everywhere."

Ray was amazed. He had come to Medicine Park with the idea that Lena was a sort of hermit, a faded character trying to revive herself with a new album, but that wasn't the whole story. She was busy and prosperous, a private citizen with irons in all sorts of fires. She was savvy, too. He was still reeling from her change of disposition that morning and doubted whether the rough footage from *What's in the Water?* had really been so masterful that it had erased the bad impressions of the night before. More likely, she wanted this documentary more than she admitted. She wanted it to go off without a hitch, without delay, without conflict. She really wanted it.

"Do you have any other businesses?" he asked.

"Just rock and roll," she said. "But that's not business. More like a religion."

"The storage units," Gram reminded her. "She owns a few of those storage unit rental places. Temperature controlled."

That evening, Ray waited on the wide front porch of the Silver Sun for Lena to drive with him to the Signal Flare in Lawton, where the Black Sheep would perform. He thought about her reaction to selling cars. *I can't sell out quite that far.* The big, bloated seventies and their stadium shows, their monster albums, their stars trailing entourages of gurus and groupies and drug dealers were what selling out looked like to Ray. Lena had been part of that, had even embodied it for a short time. Her scruples about the car ads surprised him.

The last of the daylight was sinking behind the Wichita Mountains. Martin had left for the Signal Flare with the band a couple of hours earlier, all of the group piling into a white minivan parked at the front of the old hotel. Ray was sitting in an Adirondack chair and listening to the music coming from a boom box down the street where the group waiting for Lena's concert was settling in for an evening of revelry. From that distance he could make out the man in the silver suit with the Saturn rings pouring bags of fresh ice into the coolers. What were they listening to? It took Ray a minute. Roky Erickson! Good taste, spaceman. He almost went down to join them.

"You ready?" Lena leaned her head out of the screen door.

"All set," he replied.

"Sorry to keep you waiting."

"No, no." He stood up. "No hurry."

She stepped out onto the porch clutching a little black purse. Her lips were shiny and she was wearing tall boots with her jeans. She came up to Ray's shoulders tonight.

"I've never seen them play live," she said.

"Never?"

"Nope. I stay out of their business."

"Except tonight," he said.

She turned away from him, locking the front door. With her back turned, she said, "I mean I hear them play my stuff. I know how good they are. I've just never heard any of their original music. Jettie's music."

"She's never played you her songs? How about Gram and Cy—do they do any of the writing?"

"Gram should try, but he won't. He's like Cy that way. He likes to play, that's it."

Ray swung the shoulder strap of his camera over his arm. She looked at it. "I was hoping we could talk in the car," he said.

She agreed to the taping, and they rode into town in her car, a black late-model Toyota Avalon with a gold "Lena Wells Toyota" logo on the back. Now that they were alone he wondered again if he should apologize for the events of the night before, but he let it go; they were comfortable together now, and there was no cool way to broach the subjects, either his probation or the pervy shirt-sniffing incident.

As she drove, he stuck a boom mic on the camera and turned it on, leaning against the passenger side door and framing her profile. He began, "So talk to me about selling out."

"What about it?"

"You won't do it for the car ads, but what about for the higher-stakes game?"

She pulled her eyes from the road and shot him a wary glance. "What do you mean?"

"Did you ever sell out for rock and roll?"

She tilted her chin back. "What's your music, Ray? What CDs do you have in that Jeep of yours right now? Because I get the definite feeling that my music is not your thing."

"Film, that's my thing. I can tell you all about it," he said. He couldn't tell her the story of one of his college girlfriends, an intense creature with pale-pink nipples who was always saying how *symbolic* everything was, who had made a mixtape for the first time they had sex and had crammed it full of Lena Wells songs. So he said, "Music's okay. I don't live and die by it like Martin. I'm already turning into one of those middle-aged people who doesn't know anything about current music. I tend to like bands that not everybody knows about, bands that play in little clubs, unpretentious stuff."

"Are you saying my music is pretentious?"

"It's earnest. You know what I mean? Dead serious and set on casting a spell up there onstage, totally committed to the belief that music can cause people to transcend their circumstances. Like today when you said it was a religion."

"If you don't think music is transcendent—"

"Yes and no. Let's face it, transcendence is a lofty claim. Everybody's been suspicious of all that since the sixties and seventies. I mean, all that shamanism went hand in hand with a great big business. It got a little sickening, all the righteous posturing coming from these drug-addled millionaires, you know?"

She nodded, seeming to concede the point. "So you'd never sell out, huh?"

"I've never had the opportunity, but I'd like to think I'd stay clean. So far, so good."

"How do you stay clean, Ray?"

"I only do a project if I love my subject."

"Who's earnest now?"

He laughed. "Fair point."

"So you love me? Your subject?"

No, he was doing this film for the money. Not just the money, he wanted to help out Martin, too, but Lena Wells was Martin's passion, not his.

"You know what I think?" she continued. "I think you want to sell out. You'd like to, you're just trying to make a virtue out of the fact that nobody wants what you're selling. You punk rockers have always reminded me of the Puritans and all their hell fire and brimstone against sex. But for you it's the filthy lucre you're against—that's the Sex Pistols, right? You pretend like you don't want it. You turn on bands that you used to love when they get successful. And it's all because you're not honest with yourselves about your true desires. I think you want it, Ray." She turned and wrinkled her nose at him. "You want it." She slapped the steering wheel, laughing.

"Want what?"

She shrugged.

The conversation had taken on shadows he couldn't see into. More big small talk. How he hated it. "But I'm not a punk rocker," he said helplessly.

His light was fading. The sun was setting behind them and storm clouds were rolling in. He didn't need footage of himself being interrogated anyway, so he turned off the camera. He regarded Lena, who sat forward in the seat with her chin raised, back straight, and gripping the steering wheel like a little bird. His high school girlfriend had driven like that.

"What are you then?" she asked.

"I'm Captain Kirk," he said, stretching his legs.

"Oh, brother."

"When I make a documentary my code is to influence the events on screen as little as possible. Like Kirk's prime directive. You don't interfere with the civilization you're interacting with."

"Interacting with *is* interfering with. That prefix. Inter. I don't know Latin, but I'm damned sure 'inter' means getting tangled up with people."

"That's not how I do it. I want to catch things on camera the way they were before I walked in with my camera."

"You can't. We change a room the moment we walk into it."

"Maybe *you* do."

"Anybody does, never mind a guy with a big-ass camera on his shoulder." She turned to him, her black eyes searching. "I want to do the opposite. I want to tear out people's hearts, take them to the soul of the world, leave them changed. Art is supposed to draw blood, Ray. It's supposed to. Otherwise it's just entertainment."

Ray thought of Chester Lord bleeding all over the floor of the pharmacy. Was that art? Should he have stopped Johnny Reyes from breaking into the pharmacy? Philosophically, his answer was still no. But often in the mornings the streets of Rio Marron evaporated like a picture drawn in a fogged mirror as he awoke. He felt guilty all the time. And he knew he should tell Lena the whole sordid story. He should.

"Anyway," she said, "I thought you said you loved your subjects. Can you love without interfering?"

"I have to explain this a lot," he said.

"Because you've put yourself smack in the bull's-eye of a contradiction, darling. It doesn't make a lick of sense."

"I guess you're not a *Star Trek* fan. Kirk cared a lot, but in the end he never violated—"

"The prime directive," she laughed. "I like that, Ray, I do. You and Captain Kirk, huh?"

"Love and distance—they're like yin and yang—"

"Uh huh. Save it," she said, peering up at the sky through the front windshield. "I need to pay attention. Sky looks bad."

Ray was used to a certain amount of incomprehension from people, and that was all right. Lightning flashed, revealing moss green clouds hanging over the highway, and the Avalon was rocked by gusts of winds that hit like punches. Lena flipped on the radio. A loud, mechanical siren sounded over every station, then a disembodied voice that sounded like it was coming from a safe house a thousand feet underground explained the speed, wind velocity, and severity of the storm they were in. Mucho severity. The voice told them to take cover and listen to the radio. Three tornadoes had dropped just outside Apache.

"Where's Apache?" Ray asked.

She pointed to the north.

"Should we maybe go back to your place? You have a basement, right?"

"Relax. It's not like earthquakes in L.A. *Those* scared me to death. They hit everybody. Tornadoes usually let down in the middle of nowhere. Of course, if it's a mile across and stays on the ground for miles—but that's not likely," she said, switching the radio off.

He had been in tornado watches in Texas, but never a tornado warning. A warning meant that one had descended from the clouds and was coming soon to a patch of land near you. "Have you ever seen one?"

She turned and flashed a smile at him. "Stay loose, Ray. I'll take care of you." The rain started then, coming down in sweeping sheets.

Lena switched the wipers on high and leaned into the steering wheel. "I can't see a thing," she said.

"Over the steering wheel, you mean? You being so short and all—"

She reached across and punched him in the leg.

4

HIGH LONESOME

Lawton was bigger than Ray had anticipated. He and Lena drove east through town for several miles down a main drag of unremitting fast food and chain restaurants before they turned onto Fort Sill Boulevard, where the Signal Flare stood, a squat cinder-block building with neon beer signs filling the small windows. The place was packed with people as unfazed as Lena by the weather reports, and decorated in a way that no amount of fancy camera work could make interesting. Free posters provided by beer and liquor distributors were arrayed on wood-paneled walls, and that was it for ornamentation. At either end of the bar, life-sized cardboard cutouts of bikini models and NASCAR heroes holding beer bottles tottered stiffly beneath the breeze of the ceiling fans. Black tabletops, adorned with tented Jose Cuervo advertisements and black plastic ashtrays, dotted the long, rectangular room. Some of the people in the crowd were GIs from Fort Sill, as their buzz cuts attested, and the rest were locals of all shapes and sizes, guys in cowboy hats and Metallica T-shirts, in khakis and button-down plaid, and women wearing everything from tight, black club clothes to cutoffs and tie-dye.

The Black Sheep were onstage at the far end of the bar playing loud. When Jettie and Gram saw Lena come through the door, they lit up. Cy, the consummate professional, gave Ray and Lena a swift nod and held it together, along with Rinaldo, the drummer, a skinny kid who hadn't noticed anything. Lena and Ray threaded their way through the crush of tables and bodies toward a relatively private booth across the dance floor from the stage. After a minute Ray detected Martin crouched on one knee, videotaping from the left side of the stage. Two pickle buckets stood a few feet from each other on the dance floor, catching rain from the storm.

Lena pushed ahead of Ray, her head down and eyes focused on her feet. She slid into the high-backed red vinyl booth on the side that kept her back to the audience, and he took the other side, which gave him good views of the stage, the crowd, and Lena, who leaned her wet umbrella against the wall, set her little black purse on the bench beside her, and regarded him with a smile. "I hate bars," she said, leaning forward and speaking loudly to make herself heard.

A tattooed waitress with dark hair pulled into a tight ponytail came over to take their drink orders. She leaned down so they could hear her. "I'm Annette, y'all. What'll it be?"

"Whatever's on tap," Ray said. Annette's tattoos were tribal, her black T-shirt so tight Ray could see her abdominal muscles, firm and individualized, through the fabric. She wore a black bar apron across her hips that said Signal Flare in red and yellow block letters.

Without looking up, Lena ordered soda water.

When the drinks arrived, they were carried by a thick-bodied man with acne-scarred cheeks and shiny hair slicked back from his forehead. "Wanted to bring these over myself," he said. "I'm Torres. This is my joint. It's an honor."

Ray shook his hand. "Thanks, Torres. I'm Ray. Did the fellow with the camera have you sign something?"

"Yeah, we're cool. It's an honor to be part of the movie," he said, addressing the top of Lena's head. "Gram's so much like family, it seems like we ought to know each other better." Lena glanced up at him. "Any chance you'll sing for us tonight, ma'am?"

"Not my show," she replied. "I don't want to cramp their style."

"Well, it sure would be a thrill for everybody to get to hear you."

"Come to the Medicine Ball," Ray said. "You can hear her then."

They turned their attention to the stage, where the Black Sheep were stomping into a slow opening, heavy on Jettie's bass. Cy was laying down a rhythm on his guitar that began building as Jettie sang, softly at first, a lover's complaint escalating to a warning. They had a big sound—if you closed your eyes you'd think the band must be huge. Gram's guitar took off then into a furious solo that was like driving fast down a narrow, hilly road with no shoulders. Ray leaned forward, watching to see if Gram could finish without slowing down or straightening out. A skinny track with hairpin turns, it seemed nearly impossible, but Gram pulled it off, bringing the ride to a clean stop before going off a cliff into the unpaved air of Jettie's vocals. Her voice lacked the timbre and bottom of Lena's voice; her range was narrower, but within that range, she had a perfect voice for rock, a rough alto with a delivery that said *FUUUUCK YOOOUUU* in thunder.

"Jettie can wail," Ray said. The Black Sheep's music was much closer to his own alternative sensibilities than Lena's music. This was his kind of show.

Lena nodded. She was staring at the band with a look Ray couldn't read.

Martin, still crouched on the empty dance floor, had his camera trained on Jettie. He moved to the front of the stage, flying Ray a grin and a thumbs-up as he scuttled around. Jettie swayed against her bass, its woodwork glowing green under the lights. She wore a short sheath dress, ice blue with a mandarin collar, fishnets, and Mary Janes with thick heels. Her lipstick was the impossible red of car paint.

During Gram's solo, Lena closed her eyes, her fingers tracing loops across the tabletop. While Jettie sang the chorus, Lena leaned back in the booth and nodded her head. "What do you think of their look?" she yelled. "I've never seen Gram dressed like that. Or Jettie."

Gram was wearing the same Levi's he had been wearing every time Ray had seen him, but instead of his usual black T-shirt, he had donned a western-style shirt that looked like an original Nudie Cohn design, mint green with red silk yolks, mother-of-pearl buttons, horses, suns, naked women, and marijuana leaves embroidered over the shirt. He wore black cowboy boots instead of his usual white Converses. Even Cy had put on a brown-and-yellow western-style shirt, although it was hard to see beneath his long beard. Rinaldo, the born-again Christian, was hairless and shirtless in black gym shorts, entirely unadorned except for heavy black eyeliner reminiscent of Lena's.

"You don't think it's awfully gimmicky?" Lena asked, her eyes on the stage.

"Gimmicky?" Ray shot her a skeptical glance. Images of Lena in her signature baroque get-ups flashed through his memory like playing cards. She'd blended her cowboy-and-Indian persona into every detail: feathers and leather, chaps and glitter, European lace and Indian beadwork, bandana halter tops and fringe skirts, matching platform heels custom made for every dress. "Not a bit."

The song ended and Ray found himself shouting into the sudden silence. The electricity flickered, cutting out the power onstage for half a second before surging back.

"Jettie was living in Austin before she came to see us," Lena explained. "Playing some small shows, happy hour gigs, mostly. It wasn't working out too well."

"Is that right?" Ray imagined Jettie on the loose in Austin, her guitar and her girlfriends and her willful work ethic chipping away at the indifference of crowd after crowd. "Hard to make a splash in Austin. It's crowded."

"She just hopped on I-35 and drove up one day. Knocked on the door and asked me to teach her everything I knew."

"And did you?"

"I don't think she understands this, but she's got what she's got. She doesn't need what I know."

"She thinks you're a genius."

Lena shook her head. "I'm a fool is what I am."

They sat for a few minutes as the music washed over them, a patterned intricacy unusual in music with such raw force. Then Jettie called out, "Here's a new song for my new friend Ray," and gave Ray a grinning salute as the band launched into a galloping road song. It was sad under its velocity, a lonely song that could have been played with just an acoustic guitar. The Black Sheep played it big and loud, but the ache of the chorus still came across in Jettie's voice as she sang:

Ice storm on a Greyhound
I read Dog of the South
Write cuss words in the window steam
That I make with my mouth.

There was some musical note that instantly conveyed loss, but Ray didn't know enough about music to know what it was. You could hear it in "Shenandoah," or "The Night They Drove Old Dixie Down," in "Angie" or "Wild Horses." That note, whatever it was, was there in Jettie's song, and it carried everyone in the room with it as she built a causeway in the air with her syllables, between herself and her character, where she could speak in the voice of a liar, a brave and hard-to-reach liar, one who insists she isn't lonely while every sign shows the opposite.

Lena leaned across the table and grabbed Ray's hand. When he looked at her, she nodded in the direction of the stage and said something.

"What?" Ray yelled.

"High lonesome."

"Hi yourself."

There was a lull between songs and Lena lowered her voice. "That tone, that thing. We call it 'high lonesome.' Not many people have it."

The term was new to Ray, but he knew what she meant. There was a wretched ache, and a pinnacle in the music, a perilous place high up in the song from which a fall would be fatal.

Her black eyes roved over him, worry crossing her face. "You got that, too, don't you?"

"Got what?"

"High lonesome. It's in your face. The way you listen. The way you look around."

Ray suddenly felt self-conscious. "I thought it was a tone."

"High lonesome's a thing. I don't know. A mood."

"If you say so," he said. "You're the musician."

"Women love you, don't they?"

Ray laughed. "Oh, I don't know. Some of them. Sometimes. For a little while."

"And you don't quite know why."

"Well, I am pretty cute."

A slow smile spread across her face. "That curly brown hair, those green eyes. Sure you are. That's not it, though. It's that thing. High lonesome."

"Is it working on you?"

She looked down at her hands. "I'm going to fight it."

They both turned their attention back to the stage then, relieved for a distraction as a hard-driving song kicked off. Part of him, the well-oiled machinery that started turning when a woman expressed an interest, clicked and hummed right along, but another part was freaking out a little. He was remembering the argument he had had with his freshman dorm roommate, who had wanted a poster of Lena Wells, this very woman, on the back of their door while Ray had argued for a Joy Division poster. Ray had lost the argument and spent a lot of time that year in a room trying to ignore Lena Wells's intense little face. That part of him was having trouble, like he had climbed into the cheap plastic frame of the poster and found a world of sweat and need on the other side. Like that poster had been staring back at him all along.

A big guy stumbled up to their table, wiry-haired in a billowing Eskimo Joe's T-shirt. He planted a fat, red hand on the table. "Hey, girl," he said, looking at Lena like they were old friends. "Girl! Listen to Big Jim talking shit! You ain't no girl, right? You're Lena fucking Wells. You're probably thinking, Who is this dickweed calling me a girl?" He pressed his palms into the small of his back and stretched like he was having back pain. "Hey, I just wanted to tell you, I saw you one time in Encino with Boz Scaggs. That show kicked some ass!"

"Encino," Lena said. "That was a hot night."

"Was it? I was real fucked up, but man, I sure remember you." He asked her to sign a coaster, his hairy bicep, and his fanny pack, and she obliged by autographing all three. As the band started back up, he lurched away, rejoining his friends and receiving high-fives all around the table.

She leaned across the table. "God love that guy—"

"Big Jim."

"Big Jim, right—but I feel like I need a bath now."

A few minutes later Lena nudged Ray and pointed at Gram, imitating his fretwork with a disparaging shake of the head. Ray couldn't tell what she was referring to, but Gram was playing in a way that she didn't like. What was she talking about? The boy was everything onstage that he wasn't off. He was good, and the chemistry between him and Jettie was there, as Ray had known it would have to be. What he had observed of their relationship so far was inauspicious—they didn't seem to fit together—but here was where they made it up. Jettie glanced constantly over her shoulder, grinning at Gram, and he played with his dark eyes fixed on her most of the time.

When the song was over, Lena excused herself to go to the restroom. As Ray watched her go, he thought again how difficult it would be to be Gram Wells. Having your rock style critiqued by your mom—that was rough.

Ray took out his camera and joined Martin on the empty dance floor. Martin gestured to the stage. "Jettie, man." He pounded a fist over his heart. "My goodness gracious."

She flipped them off and winked. "Yeah," Ray agreed, "she's pretty great."

Martin had already set up a couple of light stands, and now he attached a Rode mic to his boom pole as Ray turned on his camera, a nearly new Canon XL1. In a minute they were ready to go and got out in front of the band.

Watching them, Jettie said from the stage, "These guys are going to film us, y'all. Just act natural. This one's called 'Calamity.'"

She glanced back at Rinaldo, who tapped his sticks three times and struck a stuttering walk into the song like a nonswimmer creeping into a lake. Then the guitars kicked in and the nonswimmer disappeared under a violent wave.

Ray first shot Cy and Rinaldo, but then he went back to where the action was, closing in on Jettie's face. She held the mic in both hands and bared her teeth at some specter in the middle distance, shouting the chorus:

All that I wanted was your eyes on me
But if you won't look
Then you're sure gonna see
There's fragments, like ice chips
All over your car
Where my soul went broken
Too bad to get far
So it slipped in the dash
Like a brand new CD
And now your car, Daddy,
Don't play nothing but me.

Some recessed part of Ray flung open, and he wished for better things, for clear connections on all personal transmissions, for honor all around, and for the personal ability to make things right for all the women whose hearts were broken in cars. He glanced over at Martin. He was feeling it, too. At a few of the tables surrounding the dance floor sat couples that were obviously looking for opportunities to dance. They'd give each other questioning glances and nod at the dance floor, listen for a few seconds, and then shake their heads. You couldn't dance to this music. Not unless you knew how to stand on the dance floor and vibrate like an eel. But nobody was bored; the whole crowd was with the band, their collective support pushing toward the stage.

After a while, Ray felt a finger jab his shoulder. Lena was standing next to him, her long, black hair looking purple under the lights. He grinned and held the camera in place. She leaned up and said into his ear, "Cut that out."

"What?"

She looked at him, the low spots in her face hollowed out by the stage lights.

He continued to hold up the camera. "Lena," he said. "We're just getting a little bit."

"Come here." She pulled him through the bar with surprising force, out the front door where they stood on the sidewalk. Rain fell like bullets from the gutters. Ray drew close to the wall to stay out of the rain, shielding his camera with his body. He looked down at her face as the lights from a car pulling into the parking lot raked across it. She said, "I didn't like that."

"Like what?"

"You filming them."

"But you knew that's what we were going to do."

"I know."

"But?"

She pushed her hair behind her ears and stared at him. "Please just stop."

She was scared; he could see it in her face. They hadn't talked about the documentary yet. She had no sense of what he wanted to do, and the first thing she'd seen, aside from his making fun of her party guests, calling her short, sniffing her shirt, and all but accusing her of being a sell-out, was his filming the Black Sheep. So she was on the offensive. He should have picked up on it sooner.

Gently, Ray said, "I'm imagining a scene of you here, watching them play."

"Sitting in the audience in this shitty bar."

"It would be real and warm. People will want to know why you dropped out. They'll see you watching Gram, and they'll get it. He's your legacy."

"Legacy? As if my own career were over," she said. "It's not my fault I hit it big when I was still a kid, Ray. I needed a break."

"But, you know, the last twenty-some years—" He was trying to tread lightly, but it was hard to hold back on making the point, and having to shout over the rain and the noise from inside the club made him sound more emphatic than he intended. "I mean," he continued, "most people assumed you were gone for good."

She shook her head. "Here's the thing. Gram thinks whatever comes his way is due to being my son. Sometimes he even thinks Jettie's in love with me, not him. He's insecure, you have no idea."

"So—" Ray paused to assimilate what she had said. "You think if the Black Sheep show up in this doc the world's going to come knocking? And he won't be able to enjoy his success because he'll think he owes it to you. Is that it?" He rubbed his chin. "I love your optimism, Lena."

"They're not even signed," she said, pointing at the front door, which was swinging open as another customer entered, letting the sound of Jettie's voice rush out into the wet night. "The film would give them exposure, even if it's modest, and he'll think it was all because of me."

"All right," Ray said. "But I'm looking for some kind of truth to anchor this film. Without your son—well, that's a pretty big hole."

"I didn't say leave him out of the whole thing, did I? I didn't say that."

"Kind of sounded like it."

She flipped over both of her hands and studied her palms as if reading her own fortune. Then she reached out and caught the door before it shut. "All right, then. You want to film tonight? Come on."

He followed her inside and watched her stride right up onstage. The Black Sheep were in the middle of a song, and Jettie's face struggled against confusion as she watched Lena come toward her. Ray laughed out loud when he saw what Lena was doing. She was Alexander the Great solving the problem of the impossible-to-untie Gordian knot by taking his sword and slicing it in half. There—problem solved. Now make me your ruler.

The band stayed on track, but no one was paying attention to their song anymore. Amid clapping and shouting, Lena drew up next to Cy with her head down, waiting for Jettie's song to be over. As Cy played, she stayed quiet and draped a pale arm around his shoulders as she had at the barbecue the night before. He leaned into her. At the center mic, Gram and Jettie drew together, trying to recapture the energy in the room that had slid palpably toward Lena. Rinaldo spun his sticks and crashed through the rest of the song.

When Jettie finished, she gazed out at the crowd. "You know what?" She smiled with her hands clasped in front of her. "We planned a little surprise for y'all tonight—"

The crowd hollered, and she smiled, waiting for them to settle down. Ray laughed to himself. That was the way to do it. Act like it was her idea in the first place.

Jettie continued, "Don't say I never gave you nothing. Ladies and gentlemen? Lena Wells—"

Lena had stepped away from Cy while Jettie spoke and stood next to her to receive the introduction. As Lena stepped to the mic, Jettie yielded it like she was letting a homely girl have a dance with her boyfriend.

That was when the lights went out.

"Transformer!" someone called out from the audience. People laughed, and several took out their lighters and raised them in the air. The red candles on the tables glowed around the room, along with the burning tips of cigarettes. The place grew quiet as everyone waited to see if the power would come back.

Behind the bar, Torres lined up shot glasses from one end to the other and filled them, his wrist rocking like an oil field pump jack. While everyone cheered, he lit each shot glass, so that when he was finished, a line of fire ran down the bar. The waitresses each grabbed a handful and began passing them out. Then, as Torres commenced lighting and handing out votive candles he apparently kept boxes of, they heard the sound of an acoustic guitar. It was Cy onstage playing "Tornado Weather," from side one of *Keep Your Powder Dry.* Lena had meant it as a ballad, but it had become something of an anthem, especially in this part of the world.

"Light it up!" someone yelled.

More and more people recognized the opening chords as Cy continued, and approving utterances shot into the air like flares.

Hushed whistles and soft applause came from the crowd. There onstage Lena grew like a long shadow until somehow the stage was too small for her. Wrapping her arms around herself, she seemed to strive for low key, but there was something so cogent and masterful about the way she raised her chin and looked out at the crowd that it was impossible not to feel he was watching a major event. Ray had heard she was best live, and it was true. Lena sang like she was telling ghost stories around a campfire, her voice ringing through the dark bar despite the lack of electricity to the microphones. She had the focus of someone listening hard for a faint and desperately important transmission that only she could hear, and when she heard the message, it was what she sang. The audience leaned forward to hear it, a secret told at maximum volume.

In the golden glow of all the candles, he started filming again. The studio version of "Tornado Weather" was a lingering evocation of somebody feeling stuck and low, but she had been years younger when she wrote the song. Now her voice threatened a plunge into despair, flirting with a black finality that cauterized the ends of her phrases in a way Ray had never heard before. Yet the song was also more alive for being live, Lena's voice vibrating through the air, the floor, and Ray's body. The song rode up his leg bones, tickled his kidneys, massaged his sinus cavities, a living force no recording could capture. He had never liked the song before, but he liked it now. He held the camera on Cy and Lena as she crooned:

> *No, she could not believe things would ever get better*
> *Like living forever in tornado weather*
> *Tornado weather*
> *The map reconfigured*
> *The bones of the truck stop*
> *All broken and twisted.*

He didn't know if Lena would keep resisting the Black Sheep's presence in the film. To hear her tell it, Gram would resent her for helping him and probably resent her for not helping, too. Damned-if-you-do-damned-if-you-don't. Still, Ray didn't entirely buy the absence of self-interest in her motives for leaving the Black Sheep out of the film, no matter what she said. There was always subtext to the text, the covert to the overt like the belly to the back.

In any case, he doubted she would want to do without the footage he was getting at that moment. Jettie and Gram had joined her and were singing along. On Jettie's face there was only an acolyte's devotion as she watched Lena sing and backed her up. Ray taped as the shadows of the crowd began to pull in around the stage, a sea of candles surrounding the family sing-along.

5

DISTORTION

Back in Medicine Park, Ray took a walk in the garden of the Silver Sun. The storm had blown over, leaving a clean-smelling, green darkness. It was almost three in the morning, but he was too keyed up to sleep, his ears ringing from the loud rock show. Lena had kind of hit on him in the car on the way home, and he was jangling with the energy of the encounter. She hadn't grabbed him or anything. She had used words instead. "You've got that reaching energy, Ray. I've always been so attracted to that kind of energy."

"Reaching?"

"Like a plant turning its leaves toward sunlight. I love that. So elemental."

"What about you?"

"Me?" She thought a minute, her eyes glinting in the darkness as she steered the car out of Lawton and onto Highway 49 to Medicine Park. "Sometimes I'm the light."

"Not always?"

"I wish, Ray. I truly do. But you know what? I could be that light for you. I sure could."

Under the bright moon, Ray followed a sidewalk from the kitchen door of the hotel to the gazebo. Maybe she hadn't meant anything by it. He considered this. The words had been ambiguous enough, but the fine, fizzing feeling in the car was unmistakable. No, no, she had made him an offer.

Ray remembered stories about her love life that had floated around when she was still in the public eye, but he didn't know which, if any, were true. She had been linked to one of the session guys who played for Steely Dan, rumored to have been on hand in Berlin when David Bowie made "Heroes," and tied to Steve McQueen in some vague way. Among the more far-out apocrypha, there was the lesbian witch rumor, the football team rumor, and one propagated by a guy Ray bartended with in Austin who knew a guy who knew a girl who knew a guy who said he installed her stereo system in L.A. and had stayed with her for two days and nights of nonstop sex. But as far as real facts went, all he knew for sure was that she had never been married. She had never said who fathered her child. He still couldn't quite figure out her relationship with Cy, and he didn't know what she had been doing for sex for the last twenty years. Maybe not much.

In the moonlight the weeds and vines seemed sentient, the whole garden alive as though he were walking across the face of a large creature as it breathed and watched him from below. He climbed the steps to the gazebo. The moon poured in over his shoulder and pooled in the gazebo's center, leaving the other side in darkness although he dimly made out the pillars. Wind brought the smell of ashes and burned barbecue sauce as it blew across the cold grill. He rolled his neck across his shoulders and stretched his arms over his chest. As his eyes continued adjusting to the light, Ray realized he wasn't alone. Someone was leaning against one of the pillars, facing him.

"Hello?"

"Ray?"

"Shit, Gram," Ray gasped. "You could give a guy a heart attack."

"Couldn't sleep?"

"I'm pretty wired."

"Here," Gram said. "This will help."

A fat, burning hole appeared in the dark and the smell of pot drifted over to him.

"No thanks," Ray said.

"You sure? It's a peaceful high. Makes the night kind of purple and blue. And soft."

"The night's just like that." Ray was glad Gram was high; it lowered the odds of any big small talk. But as for Ray himself getting high, he generally avoided it, not on any sort of moral grounds, but because the mellow high most people experienced eluded him. Every time he smoked pot, he became hellishly paranoid, which didn't keep him from giving it another try every so often, just to see if anything had changed.

"Peaceful, bro. Come on."

Peaceful. Ray found the word so attractive that he said yes. And shouldn't have; in a minute he felt the old misery closing down around him like storm shutters. He took a deep breath and tried to fight the feeling. "Dammit."

Gram laughed from his dark corner.

Whenever anyone who knew Ray's father heard him laugh, they said Ray sounded just like him. He wondered who Gram sounded like, what mystery seed was responsible for this being breathing in the dark with him. And Gram wondered, too. That much was clear.

"You ever been to El Paso?" Ray asked.

Gram laughed some more, the throaty giggle of an inhalation interrupted. "Never have."

"There's this cemetery there, Concordia Cemetery. My dad likes that place. He's one of those genealogy buffs, you know. But we don't have family buried there. He just likes it. We always leave a bullet for John Wesley Hardin, and sometimes we get drunk and sing 'El Paso.'"

"Out in the West Texas town of El Paso," Gram sang.

Ray joined in. "I fell in love with a Mexican girl."

"Marty Robbins. That man had the most beautiful head of hair." Gram laughed, then paused for a moment. "Mom used to take me to the Apache cemetery on Fort Sill to Geronimo's grave. When I was little I thought that place was a playground. She'll take you there. He's her great-grandpa, but I'm sure you knew that."

"That story's true?"

"Sure it is. I'm his great-great-grandson. That's pretty cool, right?"

Ray realized that a lot of what he had heard coming out of Gram's mouth so far, starting at the club in Austin, had been parroting his mother. Her stories, her desires, her interpretations. "Have you ever been away from your mom, Gram? College?"

"I've always lived here."

"So, do you really know about your mom's reputation?"

"What the fuck do you mean, her reputation?"

"As a musician. Her artistic reputation."

"All those rumors about her are bullshit. I mean, you'd think she fucked every guy she ever stood in the same room with."

"What?" Jesus, the kid was touchy. "No, I didn't mean that, dude, I'm talking about her music."

"Nobody knows her but me," Gram said.

"I hear you."

"There's a bush over there." Gram pointed. He looked like he needed a little more of the peaceful high he was touting. "Back by the fence, some wild berry bush. When I was maybe nine or ten she taught me how to make paint with the berries. We painted all my little plastic soldiers, just sat there doing them up, painting them. That's the kind of thing she's been up to. Being my mom."

"That's very cool, Gram. Did she teach you music?"

"Her and Cy."

"Yeah, he knows his way around a guitar. I expect big things from the Black Sheep."

"Just help me get my mom off on her own thing first." He gave Ray a pleading look. "This comeback of hers could be a problem for us."

"I can see that, especially if she tours. Do you think she will?"

Gram shifted against the column. "It would be a short tour. Half a dozen cities. At least I think so. I hope so, because otherwise she'll have to do without us. The Black Sheep have a chance to tour with Los Lobos next summer."

"Los Lobos?" Ray said. "That's amazing—you guys haven't even made a record yet."

"Tell me about it. Their manager heard us play in Austin. He recognized Cy—I guess they used to know each other. I don't know, man, those two went to Denny's after our show and the offer just materialized."

"I bet your mom's thrilled for you."

"She doesn't know."

Ray cleared his throat, which was dry and scratchy now from the weed. "How do you think she'll take it?"

Gram shrugged. "Doesn't matter. We've gotta do it."

"Sure," Ray said. But Gram sounded like a kid whistling in the dark to fight back fear. He was under Jettie's influence tonight, so the Black Sheep's future was unrolling before him like an inevitability, yet Ray couldn't imagine him really breaking away from Lena. He sensed that for Gram the world out from under his mother's shadow might be a too-too-bright world.

"Tell me, where's Cy in all this? Is he ready to leave the Lighthorse-men and tour with the Black Sheep?"

"He says we have to find a replacement for him," Gram said. "He's sticking with Mom. Besides, he has kids here. They live with their mom, but still, he won't want to leave them. Los Lobos is cool with that. Apparently Jettie's singing was the real clincher for their manager."

"Cy's got kids?"

"Yup."

Ray absorbed that news. He had just about decided that Cy had to be Gram's father but kept hitting up against a wall when he tried to guess why Lena and Cy wouldn't tell him. Maybe to protect his other family. Maybe because it wasn't true. "How old are his kids?" he asked.

"Lizzy's a few years younger than me—she's a senior in high school. And Sonya's fourteen. She's a pistol."

Ray spun a story in his head about Cy trying to keep two families all these years, the kids close in age. Lena would have been the woman who knew the deal and Cy's wife would have been the one who didn't. Until maybe she found out? Something had caused the divorce. But no. He couldn't really imagine Lena putting up with that. She and her son on the B-side? Never.

"You were right about the pot," Ray said, standing. "I'm turning in."

"Hey, see you in the morning," Gram said. "Sweet dreams."

But Ray's dreams were strange. For the sweet part, he was awake, roused by the sound of guitar strumming just before dawn. He had only been asleep a couple of hours and probably wouldn't have heard a thing had he been sleeping more soundly. The music was coming from outside his window, not far away. He shimmied open the window and leaned out. The low light of a dying campfire burned down by the water amid the dark shape of tents full of sleeping fans, and he could hear the steady susurrus of Medicine Creek rushing in the darkness. The guitar music was coming from above. There was a rusty fire escape near the window. Ray grabbed it, found it steady, and swung himself onto it. After a few steps he found himself peering across the black-shingled roof. From a house across the creek, the sound of wind chimes jingled in the air. The pale quarter moon was still out, and the sun was about to break the rosy horizon in the east. High branches of the catalpas that lined the front of the hotel brushed the gently sloping roof, which was littered with generations of the trees' long, brown seedpods, curling and splitting. A few yards in front of him on the steep incline of the roof, Jettie sat cross-legged with her back against a chimney, strumming an acoustic guitar. "Morning," she said. "I must have woken you up. Did I?"

Half asleep and still a little stoned, Ray clambered to a spot next to her and sat down, leaning his back against the chimney. "What the hell are you doing?"

"I like to see the sun rise."

"Well, Jesus, don't fall."

She had been watching him cautiously crouch and settle onto the rough shingles but she looked quickly down and concentrated on the frets of her guitar. "I can see it all, you know."

"I believe you can, Jettie. You're something else."

"No, I mean"—she extended a leg and lifted the pant leg of Ray's boxer shorts with her toes—"I can see it all."

Ray looked down at his underwear—the slit was gaping open. He cupped his hands over his crotch, felt his face burning in the cool air. "Sorry."

She laughed. "It's like something out of an old book."

"An old book? My—" He scooted his back against the chimney and pulled his knees up. "What is?"

"My song. Oh—" She bent over the guitar, laughing. "Not your dick.

Did you think I meant your dick? How could it be like something out of an old book?"

Ray felt old and shy. He answered like he was correcting a student paper. "Your pronoun reference was vague."

She laughed more. "Maybe it *is* like something out of an old book!"

"Depends on the book."

"You want to hear it?"

"Hear what?"

"My song, my song, old son." She began strumming, a quick, whimsical opening.

> *Dark night*
> *Flashlight*
> *Searching through the grass*
> *Looking for your car keys*
> *You find instead the past*
> *Ghost girl, pale shape*
> *Flashing through the sage*
> *Wandered from another time*
> *The wind blew back the page*
> *Run with me*
> *Barefoot high*
> *Above the frozen ground*
> *Come with me*
> *Run with me*
> *'Cause I am glory bound*
> *You may think I'm lost*
> *But I knew to find you here*
> *In this field of early frost*
> *Where the drop ahead is sheer.*

"That's all I got," she said. "I can't figure out how to finish it."

"A ghost story," Ray clapped. "Will you sing that for me later in front of the camera?"

"You're not good at being in the moment, are you?"

"Why do you say that?"

"I was just talking to you about your dick. Most guys would try to prolong that moment."

"There was a song in between." Ray picked up a catalpa seedpod and split it open, pouring the smooth brown seeds into his hand. He had an erection, but he couldn't think of how to tell her that. This wasn't exactly small talk, but he wasn't any good at it either, whatever it was. He continued, "Anyway, you should let me videotape you singing, even if it doesn't show up in the film."

"Which it won't. I'm not against the idea, but tell me why you think I should."

"Well," Ray replied, "because unfilmed time feels like it doesn't count. Who's to say this ever happened? If I film it, there's a kind of proof."

"You're trying to cheat death, is what it comes down to. Songs are like that, too. I'm just trying to throw up a flare."

"Not a lot of people going to see your flare, Jettie Waycross. Way up here. Way out here in Medicine Park."

"I won't be here much longer. We'll help Lena with her comeback, then I'm gone. We're going to tour with Los Lobos! Can you believe it? A year from now I bet we'll have our own album coming out. *The Black Sheep: Calamity.* That's one of my songs. It'll be the title track."

"Sounds like a plan," Ray said, but the instability between the "I" and the "we" when Jettie spoke suggested she wasn't 100 percent sure she could keep Gram on her team.

"That's a secret about Los Lobos, by the way. We haven't gotten up the nerve yet to tell Lena. Or Gram hasn't. I'd have done it by now, but Gram wants to be the one to tell her, and he keeps stalling."

"I won't say a word," Ray said. "What if you have to leave without him?"

The sun was pouring over the horizon. The golden light reflecting off Jettie's pale lashes made her look somehow blind. "Without Gram? Why would I do that?"

"I don't know. What if he likes working for his mom?"

"He's dying to get away."

"Oh. That's good, then. That's good."

6

ABOVE GROUND

I think it's Steve McQueen. I really do, man, and I'm not just saying that because he's so fucking cool. I remember her telling me something about him when I was a little tike—she probably thinks I don't remember. You can put that in the documentary if you want—Steve McQueen is my dad!! I'll stand by you on that. I don't know what Mom will think. Let's try to talk her into it.

Ray studied the note. Steve McQueen. Gram didn't look a thing like him.

He wrote his own note, asking for a cup of coffee, and sent it down the dumbwaiter to Edith. The coffee arrived, steaming, a minute later on a wicker tray, which Ray carried down the hall to his room.

Lena had wanted to practice for the upcoming show that morning. "When we sound better, you can film," she'd said. But for the day, Ray and Martin were explicitly uninvited.

So Martin left to visit his parents in Lawton while Ray devoted the morning to phone calls and reading in his room. His first job was to track down people he wanted to interview. Lena's old drummer, Ellis Wolfe, was indeed gonzo in the Philippines, from all Ray could discover. Most important was Desmond Jones, Lena's bass player from the beginning when she had first shown up in L.A. in the early seventies. Aside from his work with Phil Spector, Ray didn't know much about him, and he had no idea where to start looking for him now. Shane Allison, Lena's manager for all those years, would have been invaluable, but he had died of a heart attack in 1980.

Ray expected to talk to Lena's current agent, Katerina Davies, sooner or later but had learned from Lena that she wasn't even coming out for the Medicine Ball. She clearly didn't have much interest in Lena's comeback, and he didn't think she'd know much; according to Lena, she had hired on right before Lena left the business, had only met her twice, and there had been little for Davies to do in the ensuing years except keep the music in up-to-date formats.

Then there was Lou Wilmot, the producer who had arguably put Lena on the map, and Lars Engstrom, director of the film *The Ballad of Belle Star*. It was an hour of leaving messages, but the administrative assistants who took Ray's calls all sounded excited by the project. "Oh, I remember her! What a good idea!"

From his suitcase Ray retrieved the cardboard box that had showed up in his mailbox in Austin, courtesy of Davies, the day before Ray and Martin left for Medicine Park. The media kit. The box was full of DVDs containing concert footage; archival television, including the all-important *Tonight Show* fiasco; and a brand new reissue of *The Ballad of Belle Starr* with a rich list of DVD extras including film commentary by Lena, Keith Carradine, and Rip Torn. There was a lot of material. To start, Ray set his coffee on the nightstand and settled against the creaky headboard with the print portion of the media kit and began to read:

Press Kit

A brief history of the career highlights of

Lena Wells and the Lighthorsemen

SELECTED MATERIALS: REVIEWS, SONG LYRICS, INTERVIEWS

Compiled by Rank Outsider Productions

All rights reserved

Prepared for Martin Parker and

Raymond Wheeler

Box 1084

Austin, Texas 78610

Reproduction or distribution prohibited

Creem review of *Rank Outsider*, by Lena Wells and the Lighthorsemen, 1977, Raven Records.
If you thought last year's "Don't Fear the Reaper" from Blue Oyster Cult's *Agents of Fortune* cornered the market on ominous, think again. *Rank Outsider*, the debut album by Lena Wells, delivers ten well-turned songs, at least two of which—the title track and "Tornado Weather"—make "Don't Fear the Reaper" sound like "Help Me Rhonda." Wells and her band, the Lighthorsemen, all from Oklahoma, who signed with Raven Records after a summer of brilliant appearances around the L.A. club scene, seem on a mission to remind us of something true and unnerving about the flyover states.

While comparisons to The Band are inevitable due to the essentially rural, sepia-toned sensibility of her music, Wells rocks harder. The Lighthorsemen do not have the chops of The Band—who does?—but they're big and loud and complicated, and Wells herself generates a revved-up feminine longing absent in rock since the death of Janis Joplin. Wells writes lyrics full of wind and rain and dust, of gamblers and ghosts, small towns and the fury therein, but unlike most country music, which shares some of Wells's sensibilities, the songs on Rank Outsider avoid reliance on domestic betrayal. Instead, these songs drive with magisterial hurt over lonesome roads, death-soaked and God-haunted.

The title track tips its hat to "Tumbling Dice": "Hey now baby, I'm a rank outsider / you can be my partner in crime"—and indeed one can read every note on *Rank Outsider* as a response to *Exile on Main Street* and the outsider status the Rolling Stones laid claim to with that album. With this music the claim has claws, issuing from the country's wild center, and Wells has her outsider bona fide, claiming to be the great-granddaughter of Geronimo. The eponymous track is a ballad, with something of the Animals' "House of the Rising Sun" about it, that sets the tone with lines like, "Hair curled like cigarette smoke / Rising from a full ashtray / She didn't heed the warnings / And lived to rue the day."

This note of survivor's guilt carries through to the last and darkest song, "Roadside Attractions," which details a drifter's killing spree along Route 66. It's a ballad in the style of Dylan's "The Ballad of Frankie Lee and Judas Priest." Cyril Dodge, lead guitarist for the Lighthorsemen, embroiders Wells's lyrics with lush streaks of color that the often-flinty lyrics deny. There is a lighter mood in the album, too, as evidenced by the winsome sweetness of "Black Ice," the album's third track: "Next time you play you'd better deal me in / I'll bet the farm and then I'll let you win."

With this mighty debut, Lena Wells and the Lighthorsemen, rank outsiders though they may be, have shown their hand and it's a good one. It is a safe bet that they will change the game.

From *Rank Outsider*, Raven Records, 1977
BLACK ICE
I stood behind you and I saw your cards
Deadman's hand, it left my heart in shards
Fold, I told you, let's get out of here
You did it fast and then you let me steer
 CHORUS:
 Roll like water, better push off slow
 I'll sleep till Tucumcari
 Then be ready to go
 Roll like water, better push off slow
 Black ice is waiting for us under the snow
I'd travel with you till the end of time
Steal all your money and then beg a dime
Drink firewater just to put you out
Sing hallelujah and then start to shout
 CHORUS:
 Roll like water, better push off slow
 I'll sleep till Tucumcari
 Then be ready to go
 Roll like water, better push off slow
 Black ice is waiting for us under the snow

Thank God your saddle's got some room for me
Ain't easy riding but the highway's free
Without you I'd be walking in the weeds
Knee deep in grief and all my other needs
Next time you play you'd better deal me in
I'll bet the farm and then I'll let you win
Drive all night if you'll stay up and talk
Drink truck stop coffee and turn up the rock
    —turn up the rock
    —turn up that rock.

From *Keep Your Powder Dry*, Raven Records, 1978
GRAVEYARD JIMMY
Graveyard Jimmy, you know, he likes to talk
Tells spooky stories when we take a walk
I get so scared and then he says all right
Pulls down the darkness then turns on his light
Oh Graveyard Jimmy makes me love the dead
I've seen them hang on every word he said
When I first saw him standing by a tree
Peeking around and staring right at me
Started to run but then he called me back
He brought a message for me in his sack
I can't tell you what his message means
Graveyard Jimmy, now he's full of schemes
Sometimes I run from him, sometimes I stay
Sure wish that I could see him in the day
We struck a bargain with a rusty knife
I asked a question, though it meant my life
"Are you Old Scratch?" I asked, real close to him
"Some call me that, but you can call me Jim"
    CHORUS:
    Graveyard Jimmy, you know, he likes to talk
    Tells spooky stories when we take a walk
    I get so scared and then he says all right

Pulls down the darkness then turns on his light
Oh Graveyard Jimmy makes me love the dead
We're bound to hang on every word he says.

**"The Decline of the West-ern," *Film-Flam Magazine*,
November issue, 1980.**
Given that Lars Engstrom's last directorial outing featured mud-caked
Vikings cutting a bloody swath through rustic villages full of naked
nymphs, I suppose we should be grateful that, in his new film, *The Ballad of Belle Starr* (American International Pictures), almost everybody
stays dressed and nobody gets beheaded with an ax.

Lest you wonder why a hippie-fixated Swedish auteur has
undertaken a retelling of the post–Civil War reconstruction period
in American history, let me point you to an interview run in this very
magazine last August, when Mr. Engstrom explained his conviction
that rock-and-roll chanteuse Lena Wells, in Lars's own words, "carries
the Wild West in her eyes." I'm not sure why this fact has inspired
him to set Ms. Wells down, for her first movie role, in the Missouri of
the 1870s—a wild but not particularly western locale—but I will say
the singer makes a more convincing bandit queen than Gene Tierney did almost forty years ago in Twentieth Century Fox's *Belle Star:
The Bandit Queen*. While Ms. Tierney, with her contoured shoulders
and girlish inflections, was clearly channeling Vivien Leigh's Scarlett
O'Hara, Ms. Wells is *sui generis*. Nobody else in a Western—or for that
matter, any other film I remember—looks or acts anything like her.

Forget the fact that Ms. Wells, like everything and everybody else
in this movie, is usually covered in a fine sheen of dust. Forget also that
the lines she stiffly speaks seem improvised and have little to do with
the plot, a convoluted affair involving the Starr gang's plan to rob a suf-
ficient number of banks to finance armed resistance to the gall-durned
Yankee carpetbaggers battening down on the region. In fact, forget the
script, credited to Mr. Engstrom, which splices together snippets from
Gone with the Wind, *Bonnie and Clyde*, *Boxcar Bertha*, and *Easy Rider*
in an anachronistic and unidiomatic soup. And forget the fact that just
about everybody else in the cast has apparently stumbled into one of

those deep-Missouri marijuana fields we hear so much about on the daily news. I say forget all these gaffes—but you will forget them. You won't be able to remember them, because ... well, for all his eccentricities and false moves, Lars Engstrom has gotten one thing right. There is something of the Wild West in Lena Wells' eyes.

Ray read slowly, jotting questions that leaped to mind. A picture was starting to form, a pattern emerging the way a constellation whose shape, in the city sky, is anchored only by its brightest stars, becomes densely articulated in a field outside of town somewhere.

He was less than halfway through the press kit when his cell phone rang. He watched the phone vibrate across the nightstand hoping it would fall off and break, but he grabbed it just before it went to message. "Hi, Lauren."

"Me again. Chester Lord's daughter has won a partial scholarship to Rice."

"Good for her! Does this mean he'll quit asking me to pay?"

"He's more determined than ever. They can't make up the difference."

"Did you tell him I declined his settlement offer?"

"She got her scholarship from an essay contest. She wrote about her dad getting shot. You're a featured character."

"Nice, that's really nice."

"Ray, have you thought about this?"

"I'm not sending some kid to a better college than I went to just because her dad, who I've never even met, got shot. This isn't fair."

"Nothing's ever your fault, is it?"

"Lauren, come on."

"You need to settle, Ray. It will go better for you."

When he got off the phone, he sat and stared across the room at the black metallic vents of the air conditioner. Chester Lord, that moaning, cursing, little ginger man Ray had found in the pharmacy crumpled against a shelf of antacids, holding his arm, bleeding heavily, was now the one with the gun, and he was holding it to Ray's head. It seemed incredible that there could be such consequences. He picked up the press kit and dropped it again, unable to concentrate. What was he doing here, a hired hand on his ex-student's fan flick? Lauren didn't even ask him about his personal life anymore.

He slid the DVD with the *Tonight Show* footage and sat on the edge of the bed to watch. So much about it seemed dated—the film quality, the colors on the set, Johnny Carson's plaid leisure suit. As part of his personal memory, that night felt like the past, but not the distant past. He was connected by feeling, by the continuity of his own personality extending from that moment to this one in an unbroken line. But to see the footage cut free of context, a stand-alone artifact, was to see distance. More shocking still was Lena.

There she was, a kid, black circles under her eyes, those sexy collarbones rising out of her thin frame, feather earrings dangling nearly to her shoulders. There was no trace of the competence or control she exhibited now. When she stopped singing, wild panic flitted over her face. Then she looked at the floor like a scolded child, stacks of glittering bangles sliding down her thin wrists as her hands dropped away from the microphone. The camera got up under her hair somehow, went close on her black-rimmed eyes, and it was like they were portals into the Real, some inchoate timeless deep, around which the bright artificiality of the show turned shabby. It was like looking into the eyes of an owl or a deer, something that knows you're there but not what you are or what you can do to it. He felt a sudden urge to go back to their first meeting and treat her differently. Better.

He heard a knock at the door.

"Come in," he called out.

Martin marched in holding a pile of papers. "Have you read this? The media kit?"

"Most of it. Why?"

"Gotten to 'January Ground' yet?"

Ray hadn't.

Martin grabbed a chair and spun it around, sitting down and resting his forearms on top of the chair back. "Read it. It's the last thing in the packet."

Ray flipped pages until he found a yellow sticky note with handwriting on it: *Found this in a box of stuff I inherited from her old agent. It's new old Lena Wells! Never recorded. XO Katerina Davies.* He peeled off the sticky note and found a page of handwritten lyrics. He had never seen Lena's handwriting, but he assumed this scrawl, hard pressed and leaning right like trees in a driving rain, was hers:

JANUARY GROUND

Stan just got his license
We're here in his new car
"And would you like to take a ride?
We won't go very far"
"I shouldn't," said Evangeline
"But I guess just for a minute
This soda sure tastes awful
What on earth did you put in it?"
"Drink some more," the boys said
"Let's all get in the back
Let's pull over at that park now
She's limp as any sack"
"Good thing she's light"
They said, though having trouble with her clothes
"Those jeans are tight enough," they laughed
It's too dark, nothing shows"
The ground was wet
Their knees turned black
They saw she might be dying
So they threw her in the trunk of Stan's
New car and started driving
"She'll ruin the upholstery
Did we get all her clothes?
Where can we take her
So we can split and no one knows?"
Well, Evangeline, she had a friend
Her name was Lena Lee
So they drove to Lena's house
And rang the bell, prepared to flee

But Lena answered wide-eyed
In her nightgown at the door
They looked numb and dumb and mean
When she asked them, "What's the score?"
Evangeline, she's still not home
Her parents called, they're freaking
"Come here," said the boys
"She's in the trunk, she's sleeping"
"In the trunk? She's in the trunk?"
"She's naked and she's sleeping"
They lifted her by arms and feet
Her body was convulsing
Evangeline, she vomited as
They laid her on the lawn
Mort thought to drop her clothes
And said, "I think one shoe is gone."
"You be cool," said Norman
As they sped off Lena knew
Evangeline was fading
On the lawn, her skin was blue
The two girls in the front yard
Had gone through the world together
But they were both alone now
And would stay that way forever
When the ambulance pulled off
And Lena went inside
She called up an ex-boyfriend
And she told him and she cried
"Gang rape, trunk of car, Evangeline convulsing"
"You're just making a big deal of this
As an excuse for calling."
The rape kit was conclusive
And Lena told their names
But Evangeline's parents
Felt sorry for the rapists just the same

"Boys will be boys," they said,
"We can't destroy their future,
She had no business in that car
Let's hope she'll learn some culture."
Evangeline's one blessing?
She did not recall a thing
Lena carried it like bricks
Right until she learned to sing
So the moral of the story
Because every story's got one
Is that to the least there will be done
Everything and then some.

Ray realized his whole body was clenched. He felt like a voyeur witnessing some private crisis, something, like the *Tonight Show* footage he had just watched, not meant for public consumption. "Are we supposed to have this?" he asked, looking up at Martin.

"In the song she uses her own name."

"That's not so unusual. Remember 'We are the Clash?' John Lydon did it to kill off his Johnny Rotten persona. Bo Diddley—one of the best times I ever had at a show was chanting 'Go, Bo Diddley' over and over with Bo Diddley."

"But Lena never self-references. She writes in first person, but it's always kind of a mask, a dramatic monologue in character."

"So what?" Ray was still inside the song, on a muggy, dark lawn with those little girls.

"Maybe it's a true story. It's what the documentary needs—a surprise. Besides—" Martin rocked forward on the chair. He was amped. "It's an unrecorded song. She could debut it on camera."

Ray had the same feeling reading the lyrics—this song was different. It was too long and had no chorus. It would be hard to put to music. All its elements told him its shape was driven by the events it was telling. It used Lena's first name. It felt true. He felt the quickening that happens when a project takes on a life of its own and starts to tell you what it's about. It had happened in *Barking Mad* when two interview subjects mentioned the rapist's Port Arthur Pawn hat, and in *What's in the Water?* when he found the pharmaceutical company that had sold lithium to the city of Rio Marron all those years. Ordinarily this would be the moment when a project came to life as Ray tried to answer new questions raised by his subject. But he couldn't imagine Lena sharing anything she didn't want them to have, and he wasn't sure he wanted his fluff piece documentary going dark. After all, he was on probation.

He said, "Doesn't a new album trump some old draft she must not have thought enough of to record? How can we focus on an old song with the new songs on deck?"

Martin pinched his nose and shut his eyes. "Good point."

"There must have been a reason she didn't record it, Martin. What-ever it is, I doubt she's changed her mind." But he was intrigued. A little bit intrigued.

Up until now, he hadn't cared much about her private story—the sex, the drugs, the usual. And her rags-to-riches rise to fame, it was too Horatio Alger for him, too David fucking Copperfield. He just wondered why she had retired so fast and so early. That was the question he hoped to answer in the documentary. After all, she only made records for four years. In that time she had invented a brand of psychedelic High Plains rock that was still synonymous with her name twenty years later. It was her brand and she could have stayed with it, kept on making music, at least until the tide turned against her, which it did for most of the eighties and nineties, when she had been very uncool, too tied with that seventies wanna-be-Indian vibe, that sex-drugs-and-righteous-indignation camp that was so easy to laugh at in the more ironic later decades. In the mid-eighties, liking Lena Wells and her psychedelic High Plains thing was as verboten as admitting to a continued allegiance to the Bee Gees after disco died.

But now, in 2000, Lena was moving into that just-right category of recherché. Rediscovering her catalog was a mark of distinction among music fans who prided themselves on championing artists the public has pigeonholed. The day after Martin asked Ray to direct the documentary, Ray had seen a skinny hipster dude walking down 6th Street in Austin with Lena's face on his T-shirt. She had become so uncool that she was beginning to be cool again.

7

GERONIMOOO!

Edith made the kind of breakfasts cattle drivers ate on the trail, the kind of fare Ray always imagined Walter Brennan was cooking in *Red River*, hearty and meaty and tasting uniformly of the same cast-iron pan. It was half past eight, and Ray was at the kitchen table with his filming schedule spread out before him, plowing through a plate of biscuits and sausage covered in gravy. "How do you make this gravy?" he asked.

Edith offered a name, "red-eye," as if it answered his question. Her back was to him as she stood at the sink scrubbing the cookie sheets on which she'd baked the biscuits.

"I guess I don't know what that means." He tried not to snap at her, fighting the irritation he always felt when his schedule was off-track. Arrayed before him in wishful color-blocked hours, there wasn't a single section of his schedule that had gone according to plan. He thought he'd need a 5:1 ratio of raw footage to finished film, a good twenty hours at least, but so far he had only seventy-four minutes of footage, and he looked grimly ahead at a day that would probably be whisked out of his hands just as the day before had.

"You never heard of red-eye?" She glanced over her shoulder. "Aren't you from Texas?"

"The suburbs. Sorry."

"It's made out of coffee. Coffee and the leavings in the pan and some flour."

"I got it," Ray said. "Red-eye because it's caffeinated."

The sliding glass door opened and Jettie appeared with Cimarron behind her. She gave Edith a hug and waved at Ray as she went to the refrigerator and grabbed a yogurt.

This morning, unlike yesterday morning, would be productive. He would insist upon it. Yesterday afternoon hadn't turned out badly; after his morning spent reading Lena's press kit, he had spent the second half of the day recording a chat with Jettie and Gram in the gazebo. Lena had disappeared into her bedroom after wrapping up the afternoon rehearsals she had forbidden Ray and Martin to watch, and Ray, frustrated by the total lack of filming that day, had corralled the young couple and asked them questions on camera until they started to repeat themselves. Gram told a couple of childhood anecdotes that would work to help fill in Lena's missing years, and Jettie's self-deprecating account of how Lena took her in when she showed up from Austin made Lena sound fantastic, a cross between an oracle and earth mother. Good stuff, but Ray left the interview feeling sour. Listening to them talk, he had seen how much more Jettie had to say than Gram, and he couldn't help but resent Gram a little bit for having two such talented, beautiful women looking after him. It didn't seem fair.

"That shit'll kill you," Jettie said, nodding at Ray's plate.

"It's keeping me awake, is all."

"Why don't you come outside with me and get some exercise?"

When Jettie finished her yogurt, he followed her and Cimarron into the backyard in socked feet, wishing he'd come downstairs in shoes. Jettie smelled like a fresh shower. She wore drawstring gym shorts and a white T-shirt with fuchsia Nikes, her hair held back in a clip. Cimarron sat down in the grass, dropping her long-haired white tail and haunches to the floor like a snowdrift settling. The dog gave Ray a challenging, intelligent look.

"Does she fetch?" Ray asked.

"Better than that. Watch."

Ray watched as Jettie took off across the lawn in a graceful sprint toward the back fence. Within seconds, Cimarron had come up beside her and was pushing her heavy body against Jettie's legs as they ran. The dog had Jettie's wrist between her teeth, too, but Jettie didn't scream. Instead she laughed as she and Cimarron ran a broad circle with Cimarron on the outside, steering Jettie back to the center of the yard. "Do you see this?" she called. "She's herding me. Amazing, isn't it?"

"She's hurting you?" Ray took off toward her, unsure what he would do when he got there.

Jettie laughed again. "*Herding* me. Great Pyrenees are herding dogs. Sheep, usually. I guess it's in her genes."

Relieved of rescue duty, Ray stopped running. He felt heavy from breakfast, hot and uncomfortable, his socks wet from the morning dew still on the grass.

Jettie glanced down at her wrist, firmly held in Cimarron's huge maw. "I couldn't get away if I wanted to, but she's not hurting me. She doesn't let her teeth break the skin." She came to a stop in front of Ray and dropped to one knee to pet the dog. Intent on rubbing the area behind the dog's ears, she said, "If you can relax like I did just now, you'll do better here."

Ray stared down at the straight part in her honey-colored hair. "I'm not used to being told what to do."

Jettie glanced up at the windows of Lena's rooms on the second floor. "Neither is she."

"Is it that obvious?"

"That you want to get your work done and get out of here? They live at a slow pace around here, old son, and you're moving at a different speed. It's like we've had the turntable set for 33⅓ and you show up and drop a 45 on the spindle."

"From what I've seen, you're more of a 45 yourself," he said. "I'd say we're alike that way. How are the rehearsals going?"

She made a face. "Great, when they go."

"When they go," Ray said. "That's frustrating. How do you do it?"

She stood up. For a moment she gave him a look that flung open rooms behind her eyes he hadn't seen before, and he knew that she had stories to tell and that she wanted to trust him. He wanted her to trust him. But the look was gone in an instant, replaced with a guarded smile. "You know my plan," she said. "Zoom, zoom, zoom! Los Lobos then the moon!"

With the dog at her side, she trotted off in the direction of the carriage house, throwing a wave over her shoulder. Ray thought about calling her back. He thought about taking her wrist in his mouth. As if she could read his mind, Cimarron looked back with a canny expression that abashed him. The dog knew. But what did the dog know? The difference between herding and hurting. It was more than Ray did.

A couple of hours later, Ray and Martin shook hands with the two extra camera people and the sound tech they had hired for the Medicine Ball, a heavily muscled, retired GI named DeAndre Snowden, who ran camera for the Lawton ABC affiliate, and two kids, Molly and Kyle, who were just out of college and who both looked about twelve years old. Ray and Martin sat with the expanded crew around a picnic table on the back porch and blocked out a floor plan of the venue, assigning roles. Martin had hired too many people—syncing all that footage from all those cameras during editing would be a much bigger headache than it needed to be—but Ray rolled with it, not wanting to undermine him in front of the crew.

They were wrapping up when Lena came through the sliding glass door. She shook hands with everyone and then said to Ray, "Come on. I want to show you something. Bring your gear."

"Nice to meet you all," he said, rising from the table. It felt odd to leave the conclusion of the meeting to Martin, odd that any part of the project could happen without his involvement. He had always been a one-man show, directing, producing, and calling all the shots. Now he essentially had two bosses, Martin and Lena, and was having to prove he was up to the job. He took leave of his first boss as his second one stood waiting in jeans and a navy blue T-shirt, her long dark hair pulled over one shoulder. "You got this?" he called to Martin.

"We were supposed to meet with the Gacks."

"Excuse you?"

"The Gacks. The oil family who are funding this film, Ray."

"Can't you do it?" Ray asked. He hated business meetings, especially the kind where people told him how he could and could not spend their money.

"They want to meet you—remember? At the theater at 4:00."

Ray looked at his watch. It was only 10:30. "I'll be back in time."

"Go," Martin said. "Have fun."

Ray grabbed his equipment, exhilarated by the productive turn the day was taking as Lena steered him out the back door to a covered garage on the side of the hotel under a stand of catalpas. She pressed the garage-door opener inside her purse and ducked into the building. Along with her car it was crowded with boxes, old file cabinets, and bicycles. He got into the car beside her, and she backed it out, turning left from the driveway onto the road that had brought him into town. On the river side of the road, fans were sitting outside their tents in lawn chairs. When they saw the black Toyota coming down the driveway, they all stood up, a few running toward the car, some cheering.

"They want to eat you," Ray said.

She gave a long look in the rearview mirror, her lips tight. "You're joking, but that's about right. I'm a consumable product." She grimaced.

"Oh, come on, they dig you, that's all."

"I forgot this feeling." She tapped her short nails on the steering wheel. "It's the reason I quit."

"*The* reason? There's one big reason?"

"One of the reasons," she conceded. "When I was making music, I realized I was stuck in a story. I came out of nowhere and rose fast. Flying too close to the sun, that whole thing. It's a deep, old story, and it's got one shape. The crowd, they were waiting on the ending. Only one way to pay for all that good luck."

"What way?"

"What goes up must come down."

"You mean they wanted you to fail?" he asked.

"They wanted me to die."

"Really die?"

She nodded. "The pressure, man. Last time I was on stage, right after that fucking *Tonight Show* thing, I could feel this gleeful, ghoulish watching from the audience. They loved me, but it was like in a Western, you know"—she reached out and turned up the air conditioning—"when the cowboy's been shot and he's bleeding in the dust and he looks up and sees vultures circling overhead? That's a crazy moment—you realize you're already dead in their eyes. They knew I was on drugs and they were waiting for me to go, sure as shit. I collapsed that night after the show."

Ray twisted in his seat and saw three fans running and waving, trying to trail the car as it kicked up red dust heading east. "They look friendly enough," he said.

"Ray, I don't mean my fans were consciously cruel. It was the *story* I was in. It had a life of its own, an expectation they all recognized. Like when you see a movie and you know what's going to happen."

"I read a *Tattler* article about the 27 Club in your press packet."

"Someone sent you a press packet?"

"Katerina Davies."

"And that's what she put in it? Some idiot piece of trash gossip?" She opened her hands above the steering wheel. "God, I wish Shane was still alive. Now *he* was a manager. What else did she give you?"

Ray told her about "January Ground" and the note Katerina had attached. "Powerful song," he said. "You should sing it."

She set her teeth. "Do you really want to listen to a song like that while you're driving down the road? Washing your car, making something to eat? Nice little song about a gang rape?" A dry laugh escaped her. "Yeah, right. I shelved it for good reason. Katerina's got weird ideas about what's important." She guided the car down Highway 49. "The grave is in the Apache cemetery on Fort Sill," she said. "Not far."

In another minute the blacktop that led onto the military base appeared. They turned right and passed through a checkpoint, continuing south across gently rolling country.

"What if 'January Ground' is the best song you ever wrote?" he asked.

"It's not."

"How can you tell?"

"Can't you tell when you've shot something great? You can, right?"

"Yeah," Ray admitted. "Usually."

"What's the best footage you ever got?"

"I may never release the best I ever got. Tied up in legal bullshit."

He knew she was leading him away from "January Ground," but

he went willingly, deciding to finally come clean about the stink over *What's in the Water?*. "I got my best footage in Rio Marron, Texas."

"Yeah, I'd agree with that. The stuff Martin showed me was really compelling. That Johnny Reyes—"

"There's more to the story than what's in the film. Johnny, I didn't choose him just for his looks. He was such a bad addict. Heartbreaking. The guy was looking to feed, to feel better no matter what. This one night Johnny was strutting down the sidewalk, his shoulders rolling like pistons, and Martin and I were following him, just trying to get some moving shots of Johnny to use for transitions, when all of a sudden, bam, Johnny cranks over to one side and karate-kicks a foot through the pharmacy's front window."

Lena let out a delighted laugh. "He was showing off for you."

"No!"

"Sure he was."

"You sound like the security guard's lawyer. He's suing me."

"What security guard?"

"He was in the pharmacy. He startled Johnny, and Johnny shot him. And people say it's my fault. That I should have stopped Johnny somehow."

"What did you do?"

Ray felt warmth flood his face. "I filmed."

"You kept filming while somebody got shot?"

"I didn't know what was happening. Martin and I were on the sidewalk with the camera trained on this shattered front window, kind of trying to decide what to do, but my impulse was to keep rolling, so we stepped through into the pharmacy, but I couldn't see much of anything. I was about to turn off the camera and leave when we saw this flash and heard the shot."

"You followed him in? Why didn't you call the cops?" Lena pulled her eyes from the road and looked at him.

"I did. The cops—I did. It's all a blur, you know, but apparently I waited like six or seven minutes."

"Six or seven minutes while a guy was bleeding?" Lena looked at him hard. "They're going to get you, huh?"

"No!"

"The security guard, what happened to him?"

"Chester Lord was hurt bad. His shooting arm's useless now, so he can't work his trade."

"That poor man," Lena said. "And Johnny Reyes?"

"La Tuna Federal Prison right outside El Paso."

"So you *do* know something about making art that draws blood."

"Literally," Ray laughed.

"Yeah," she nodded. "I didn't mean it literally. Literally's no good."

The road dipped into a prairie of yellow Coreopsis. Lena sighted along the dash to a sheer cliff face barely visible in the distance rising from the plains to the west. "Medicine Bluff's out there. It's a holy place. Also where the first camp at Fort Sill was," she explained. "General The-Only-Good-Indian-Is-A-Dead-Indian Sheridan came out here to stomp Comanches after the Civil War."

"The one who scorched the Shenandoah Valley?"

"He led six cavalry regiments out here with Buffalo Bill and Wild Bill Hickok as scouts. There was a lot of dying." She fell silent for a minute, and he thought she was thinking about the bloody history of Fort Sill, but when she spoke again, she asked, "So what were you doing for six or seven minutes while the security guard was laying there shot? He must have been yelling, right? Begging for help?"

Ray sighed. Whatever sexual chemistry he thought he had detected earlier seemed like a laughable misinterpretation on his part. Lena was looking at him like she might toss him out of the car.

"Cussing, yelling, yeah, all that, and I was telling him we'd get him help. But I was kind of frozen. I kept thinking how it was an accident, how Johnny didn't mean to hurt the guy. I'd been spending a lot of time with Johnny, and I was really rooting for him, you know? I wanted to see him clean up his act and get out of that little town. I put him in touch with a buddy of mine in Austin who's been sober a long time, and they talked. My buddy, he agreed to be his temporary sponsor and Johnny was cool with that. I even called an admissions counselor at my university in Austin, thinking there might be a way to get him in. The kid had—has—tons of potential, Lena, and I balked at what was going to happen the minute the cops got there. He was going to jail, there was no way around it, but I kept trying to think of a way to save him." He scratched the side of his cheek and stared out the window. "Finally I realized there was nothing I could do."

Lena nodded. "I get it."

"What do you get?"

"You got really involved. Really, really involved." Her voice had softened. She reached over and patted his arm. "That's what you mean by love your subject."

"I guess," Ray said. But when the shooting had happened, Ray had been thinking quite another way. He had been thinking he shouldn't interfere—that was why he kept the camera rolling instead of turning it off and trying to stop Johnny the moment he broke the pharmacy's glass.

The winds were picking up, and they studied the sky, which was greening up like an unkempt swimming pool. The Toyota rolled past rows of Spanish-style stucco buildings with red-tile roofs and immaculate lawns. Only the frequent appearance of old tanks, cannons, and Howitzers enshrined in parks belied Ray's feeling that he was on the campus of some well-endowed private university. In a few minutes they turned and took a narrow gravel road behind a building Lena identified as the Officer's Club, where a long red awning that extended over the sidewalk was filling with air and then emptying, the long column spasming like a snake trying to digest an animal its own size. The tall cottonwoods surrounding the genteel old structure were whipping and bending. A storm was surely coming.

"I read an interview where you said your dad was a GI. That true?"

"According to Edith. Says he was from Iowa and was wild about my mama."

"Your housekeeper?"

"She was a good friend of my mother's. They used to work together at the Silver Sun back before it closed."

"Your mom worked at the Silver Sun?"

"Medicine Park was a pretty busy little resort back then."

"Wait, wait, wait a minute." He started to film. "So Edith knew your mother. And they both worked at the Silver Sun? When was this?"

She glanced at the camera. "Hang on. This is the road to the cemetery." As the Avalon bumped along over the rough dirt road, they passed under the I-44 bridge, and, after a short while, pulled into a gravel parking lot with a historical marker in its center. Where the parking lot ended, a chain-linked gate marked the entrance to the cemetery. "Come on," Lena said, throwing the car into park.

Ray kept his camera rolling as they walked through the gate. A canopy of burr oaks put the graveyard almost entirely into shadows that grew deeper as the cemetery extended east to a creek where the trees were especially dense. Rows and rows of white marble graves stretched down to the water.

A sidewalk led to the middle of the cemetery, where Geronimo's grave stood. It was a largish pyramid, made of the same strange cannonball stones that had been used to build Medicine Park. A cement-covered area stretched in front of the pyramid as if to show right where the body was located. A stone eagle with a black head perched atop the pyramid. Piled at the statue's feet were various items left behind by visitors: a pouch of chewing tobacco; a long, striated feather; a handful of sage; and a cigarette. On the pyramid a concrete sign spelled out the name in large letters: GERONIMO. The headstones of the warrior's wives and children stood beside the grave, the way the family would have stood for a group photograph. Flanking Geronimo's pyramid, old junipers offered shade, their lower branches covered with bandanas, a pair of dog tags, purple-and-green Mardi Gras beads, dreamcatchers, faded plastic flowers, American flags of varying sizes, and a black-and-white Vietnam POW-MIA flag. Lena carefully extracted a cigarette from her purse.

"You smoke?" Ray asked.

"No." She broke the filter off the cigarette and emptied the tobacco on the top of the grave at the eagle's feet, spreading it with her fingers. Then she gave the grave a friendly pat as if it were the old warrior himself and dropped gracefully into a cross-legged position next to it.

"Scoot in," Ray said. "If we use the grave to block the wind this might work." He dropped to one knee in front of her and turned on the camera. "Give a count of five before you answer me. I'll have to edit myself out." She nodded, and he continued, "So, please finish telling me about Edith and your mom. What was her name?"

"Ruby. She and Edith—"

"Her full name."

Lena pursed her lips. "Ruby Wells. I don't know if she had a middle name. She worked at the Medicine Park Inn—the Silver Sun—when I was little. '55, '56. My first memories are there."

"That's so different from what I read. I read that you grew up in an orphanage in Apache."

"You're interrupting a lot."

"I know. It's going to be a bitch to edit. Go on."

"The orphanage was later."

He imagined years lifting from the Silver Sun like layers as Lena painted a picture of the building as a working resort hotel in the 1950s with a couple of young maids and a small girl living on the grounds. His thoughts wandered to the split-level on the east side of the Franklin Mountains where he'd spent his early years in El Paso. His dreams were often set there, and he had a recurring one in which the turquoise-colored gravel that constituted their front yard had washed out into the street after a heavy rain. Rock lawns, brightly colored like the pebbles made for fish tanks, were the norm there, where it was too dry to grow grass. In the dream he tried in vain to scoop up all the bright rocks as they tumbled down the street, but they had mixed with the rocks of the neighbors' yards, rose and canary and lime, and he knew he could never reclaim them all. The last time he visited the city he had been truly angry to find that the new owners of his childhood home had replaced the eco-friendly rock-and-cactus garden with a sodded lawn that looked like it belonged in Massachusetts, not on the mountain in the desert. If Ray could buy the old place he would restore the turquoise rock yard of his youth. In fact, it was becoming a goal, so he understood perfectly Lena's impulse to reclaim her childhood home. "So when you bought the place, it wasn't just a nice piece of real estate. I wondered why you didn't stay in L.A."

"I always thought of the Silver Sun as home. My mother and I were there until I was six. And I didn't understand that, you know, my mom was a maid. She and Edith were maids. But we stayed and all the other people came and went, so I thought they were *our* guests. And that's what we called them, right? The guests. The guest in Room 209 needs extra towels. The guest in Room 112 wants a wake-up call. Meanwhile, I lived on the grounds, knew every inch of every floor, the basement, the attic, every inch of that garden, every outbuilding. I felt it was my home. Then Mama died and I was carried out of there like the trash. They didn't even let me take any of her things."

"I guess you showed them, huh?"

A smile spread across Lena's delicate face. "It was all closed up when I bought it. Full of junk. I paid next to nothing for it." She shrugged. "But it was still home. And she's always there."

"What do you mean?"

"My mom's still reverberating in the old place."

Ray had no idea what she meant, none at all, but he was too pleased with how the interview was going to say anything.

Lena traced the fingers of her right hand through a patch of red dust showing through the grass. "My mother died and I went to the orphanage. Edith tried to get me, but they wouldn't let her."

"So Edith—"

"She contacted me a few years ago. She was running a breakfast joint in Lawton. Told me who she was and that I needed her and she'd come be my full-time housekeeper. I agreed."

"Did you remember her?"

"I sure did. She taught me how to make a cat's cradle and how to peel a banana. I also remember her eyeliner. She used to do this Egyptian thing, you know, every single day, just to clean rooms."

"She inspired your look," Ray said.

"She was my look. When I was little, I'd watch her put on her makeup, make that line wing out past her lids. It was always a secret joke. There I was, on these big stages and in all these magazines, in a hotel maid's makeup."

"She have lots of stories?"

"Well, she's not all that talkative, but if she puts her mind to it she can make Ruby real for me."

"Your mother's death. She must have been pretty young."

"Twenty-six. It was a car wreck."

"I'm sorry."

"She was drunk."

"What you were saying before, about feeling like you were stuck in a story that had to end with you dying—"

"It changed." She beamed, with a look of amazement she was asking the camera eye to share. "I was in concert at Red Rocks in Colorado. I was about nine weeks pregnant, and the news that I was expecting had just come out a few days earlier, so the crowd knew. I was up there braced for the usual greedy-vulture-death vibe from the audience, but it wasn't there. Instead there was all this care coming at me." She took a deep breath. "This concern. I felt they'd have carried me around on a satin pillow across the top of the crowd. Always before I felt they'd have trampled me to death if I got too close."

"They changed because you were pregnant?"

She picked a dandelion whose white fluffy stuff had long since blown away in the wind. Splitting the stem and peeling it, she said, "I didn't think I could manage without the drugs, you know, so I'd never have gotten pregnant on purpose. I had no idea there was any way out of the story. Thought I really would have to die—and I was expecting to myself, banging dope hell for leather. But getting pregnant landed me in another kind of story. Turns out nobody wants to see a pregnant woman die, Ray. Nobody. Turns out the story of new life, rebirth or whatever, oh, it's every bit as deep as that sacrificial lamb story I was caught in before. Now I wasn't *allowed* to die. I was free."

"And that's when you quit the business," Ray said, rocking back on his heels.

Lena nodded.

"What about the vultures now? Aren't you afraid you'll be under that pressure again?"

She dropped the dandelion and found another one. "I felt it some today when I saw those fans running after the car. But basically, Ray, come on. I'm safe as houses. The story requires extreme youth. Nobody needs a middle-aged woman to die—it wouldn't signify at all. Now I'm just a rocker making a comeback. *That* story has its own perils, but they're more in the nature of the ridiculous. I've outlived tragic. But I just want to perform. On stage, in a studio, or, hell, on a street corner, so long as I've got a band behind me and a few people listening."

"Tell me something. Does that band have to have Gram in it?"

Lena shrugged. "Who better to back me up?"

"What about Jettie? Does she have to be there?"

Lena tilted her chin and gave him a long look. "She wants to be there. What are you trying to say, Ray?"

"Nothing." Wind slammed him with dirt, the grit abrasive against his skin. The flags whipped and the dog tags and dream catchers swung wildly against the juniper trees. "Is that a tornado behind you?" he asked.

She turned and looked. "You'll know one if you see it."

Ray stood up, ready to get out of the weather, but Lena made no move to leave. Instead she stretched her legs in front of her and crossed her legs at the ankles. "I think this is going great, don't you?"

Ray looked at the sky. "Definitely. But should we go?"

"Come on, switch the camera back on."

When the camera was on, she looked around and pulled a group of waxy berries from one of the junipers and began rattling off a history of the old Apache warrior, his sad end, his robbed grave, skull and bones, conspiracies. Dishonor. Honor. She sounded like a tour guide.

He interrupted. "Are you related to Geronimo? I mean, if you don't know who your ancestors were between him and you, how can you say you're related?"

She stared at him. "You don't believe me?"

"I don't disbelieve you."

"I suppose I don't really know," she admitted. Ray could tell the question hurt her. "But I believe it. Ruby, my mother, knew who she was and who her people were, and from what I hear, she used to tell people about Geronimo. I wish I knew what she knew, but things aren't cut and dry like that."

But they were. Genetics were pretty cut and dry. "It's just—you could have facts."

"Facts." She said the word as if it puzzled her, and he felt vaguely ashamed. He had assumed the Geronimo story was cynical self-mythologizing on her part. But no. Whether or not it was true, the idea that she was Geronimo's great-granddaughter was real to her. This grave was her place, and she was at pains to make it mean something to Ray, too. The way you do when you really love something.

Ray felt heavy raindrops hit him, even through the trees. He switched off the camera and crammed it back into its case just as the sky opened up.

Lena was already running for the car. He saw her swing open the driver's side door and dive into the car, reaching across the front seat to unlock the passenger door. When he got to the car, he flung himself in and sat panting, dripping water. Next to him, she was cranking the defogger, but in spite of her efforts, the inside windows steamed over in a few seconds. They were cut off from the outside world. A mile under the sea, or lost in space somewhere.

Ray looked at the seat. "Is this real suede?"

"It surely is."

"Then I'm ruining your upholstery."

"You surely are," Lena said, rubbing a hand across the wet spots. "Hell."

He pulled off his T-shirt and dropped it onto the rubber floor mat at his feet.

"Me, too," Lena said, peeling off her sodden blue tank top. Her hair was soaked and plastered around her shoulders, making her look even smaller than usual. She pulled herself up to look into the rear view mirror and run a finger under her streaking makeup. As the air conditioning hit Ray, he shivered, shocked to see Lena without her top. She looked pretty good in a plain, dark-colored bra. Then she turned to him and flattened her palm against his chest, running her fingers up along the base of his throat.

"I meant to ask you about your new music," he muttered.

"Ray." She smiled up at him and scooted close. He could feel her hard nipples against him as she looked up into his face. "We're stuck here for awhile. What do you want to do?"

Ray should have been prepared for what happened next, but he wasn't. Despite their flirtation on the drive home from the Signal Flare, the idea of having sex with Lena Wells was as remote and unimaginable as having sex with that poster on the wall.

Maybe he had imagined that. As they kissed and found each other with their hands, he remembered the poster his freshman roommate had hung above his bed in their dorm room, of Lena in a black velvet mini-dress and tall boots. Ray had often complained about the glossy, mass-market poster to his roommate, pointing for contrast to his own side of the room at the DIY handbills for shows by the likes of the Bad Brains and Lydia Lunch that he had personally stolen from streetlights and bulletin boards. He remembered that on nights when his roommate was out, he would finish his homework, then put on a mellow record, and let the music massage him while he, eyes fixed furtively on the Lena Wells poster, massaged himself. But now he came back to the current moment to find the real person moving under him, her pale throat catching the green tornadic light as she tilted backward.

8

JUSTINE

Sometimes I think Cy is my dad. But that would be fucked up because my mom and Cy are cousins, which is why I know it's not him. Even though he does seem like it. He's called me "son" since I can remember. Not in the real way, though, just like the way old dudes call young dudes "son." At least that's how I always took it.

While Martin clung to a hot coffee mug in the front passenger seat, Ray drove the Jeep and kept his eyes on the cloud of dust sent up by Cy's motorcycle, this one a dirt-caked silver Indian suitable for tearing around Indian Territory. Ray thought about the new note, which he had found under the door to his room when he returned from Lena's bedroom in the early morning hours. He had wondered before why Gram didn't land on Cy as the likeliest candidate for being his father, but now he understood. Cousins. Lena and Cy were cousins.

The day was bright and already hot, the grassy plains the same color as the sun. Ray rolled down his window as they headed south. The sweet smell of a hundred different grasses and wild flowers filled the air, and yellow was everywhere: a lemon-colored lichen flourished on the granite boulders of the mountains, prickly pear cactus flowers flowered between the rocks like caulking, yellow coreopsis bloomed in the shoulders of the road. Cy's house was down a gravel road off a dirt road marked by a wrought-iron sign, stretched over a cattle gate, that said DODGE CITY. Two dogs rose from somewhere in the yard and tore down to the drive, barking and snapping. They ignored Cy on his motorcycle and headed for the Jeep as it rolled to a stop in front of a blue door. The adobe house sprawled low to the ground, a warren of add-ons bracketing a courtyard in the middle.

"Go, damn dogs!" Cy ordered the dogs off and they obeyed, trotting down to the fence line by the road, where a pickup was passing.

Ray shouldered his camera case while he and Martin, who was carrying a duffle with lighting and sound equipment in it, followed Cy inside.

"Where are your girls?" Ray asked as they stepped into a bright, cool room and stared at photographs of two smiling young women in frames across the mantle of a white kiva fireplace.

"Bicycling in Alaska with their mother. Denali Wilderness. It's a two-week trek. Last year they did the Pacific Coast Highway."

Cy strode to the back of the house, and they followed him through a laundry room that smelled of detergent and past tall bags of dog food that stood by the back door. Cy grabbed three poles leaning in a corner and a small Igloo cooler sitting on top of the dryer before the three men set out across the close-clipped lawn, which turned into pasture. A big blue barn, tall enough to shade them from the morning sun, came into view. Ray felt good, riding a blithe sex buzz, cushioned between leaving Lena's bed that morning and expecting to return to it that night. The open air and sunshine were compensating for the lack of sleep.

"Your daughters, do you ever bike with them?" Ray asked.

Cy glanced back. "That's my ex's thing. I like my bikes with motors. Don't get no thrill out of wearing myself to a nub."

"I understand," Martin said. He drove a green Vespa around Austin. Then, in his deferential but insistent way, he began peppering Cy with questions about various recordings he'd made. Cy tended to answer in monosyllables, seemingly uninterested in reliving his recording past. He led them around the barn onto a path that wove through a group of dense scrub oaks to a small lake. Ray was in the middle, with Cy ahead of him as they marched single file down a path that wound along the edge of a scree leading them to a granite outcropping. There, Cy got busy preparing three fishing lines. He said, "We're multitasking today, boys."

Ray watched as Cy drew a live worm from a Tupperware container in the cooler. He pushed it through the tip of the hook and then looped it through a couple of more times and handed the pole to Ray. "I suppose you can do two things at once, Professor?"

"I can't hold this pole, crank the reel, and run camera, no."

"Turn the damned thing off, then," Cy said.

Frustrated, Ray said, "I'd rather put the fishing pole down and keep the camera."

"You can film later," Cy said. Martin was giving him a look that advised caution.

So Ray put away his camera and took the fishing pole. He cleared his throat. "Just promise me that if we have a good talk here you'll do it again for me later with the camera rolling."

"Maybe," Cy said, snapping shut his tackle box.

"Good enough," Ray responded, although it wasn't. Conscious of his probation, Ray felt like they were wasting time, and he could tell that Martin felt it, too. Cy was the last person he expected self-indulgence from, but he seemed preoccupied and was behaving as if Ray and Martin were there to hang out with him rather than to do their jobs. Ray added, "When I figured out who you are, I had it in my head that you and Lena were a couple, I guess because you seem so much like family. Now I know why—I never knew."

"Knew what?"

"Gram told me you and Lena are cousins."

"He told you that, did he?"

"It's not a secret, is it?"

"Guess not." Somewhere nearby a woodpecker started drilling, its insistent noise echoing off the water. Martin stepped a few feet down on a small ledge that brought him closer to the water. Cy sat on a broad, flat rock and cast his line. He wore sunglasses and a brown felt cowboy hat, so that it was impossible to make out his features. His voice, though, was suddenly thick with tension. "That's not."

Ray sat down next to him. "You lost me, Cy."

"Cousins—you were asking him about them being cousins," Martin called back.

"What if you didn't know?" Cy asked in a low, rough voice. "Do you think you could tell you were related to someone if you didn't know?"

"I never thought about it."

"She was an orphan. Lived with a foster family in high school."

"And you didn't know she was your cousin?"

"She didn't know. I knew. Knew about her all my life, but my parents always said they couldn't afford another mouth to feed. They felt too guilty to visit her, so she was kind of this dark secret in our house. Ruby's little girl. I knew exactly who she was, and I meant to tell her when we met, but the way I felt about her hit me so hard."

"The way you felt about her," Ray said.

"I know it was wrong. Don't you think I pay for it every day? But I couldn't help it. I just couldn't help it."

As if the woodpecker had been listening, the insistent hammering sound stopped. Cy didn't speak, but in the silence that spread around them, Ray scrambled to piece together what he was hearing.

On the other side of Cy, Martin leaned back and gave Ray a bewildered stare, silently mouthing "What the fuck?"

Ray looked at the spot where his fishing line vanished under the water. Cy and Martin both caught fish, and there was the business of reeling them in and reloading the hooks to further distance the three of them from Cy's statements.

Finally Ray ventured forth, trying to divert the conversation into less fraught territory: "Since you're cousins, I guess that means you're Geronimo's great-grandson?"

Cy pulled a face. "I don't put much stock in those stories myself."

"I knew about the orphanage," Ray said. "I assumed that meant she didn't have any family."

"My mom—Vivian was her name—used to say sometimes that Lena probably ate better than we did. My mom was never at peace about not taking her in, though, her sister's child."

"Did your folks finally go get her?"

"They never did. I met her one night in high school under this rusted old one-lane bridge on somebody's land south of town. She was sitting around a campfire with some other kids, just a-singing. I had my guitar, so I joined them. We hit it off right away. Head over heels. I knew I should tell her I was Vivian's boy, but I couldn't."

"Okay," Ray said, "I see."

Cy looked at Ray as if he wasn't sure Ray understood. "Our moms were sisters."

"First cousins."

"That's what I'm telling you, Professor."

"Are you saying you and Lena—what, you had sex?"

"That makes it sound like a one-time thing," Cy replied. "It wasn't."

Ray felt a pull on his line but ignored it. "Why are you telling me this? You can't want this in the film."

"You're not recording."

"Yeah, but—"

"Why should I pay for it the rest of my life? I've always helped her. Now she's changing her mind about everything I thought we understood between us. And"—he leaned forward, resting his elbows on his knees and staring out over the water—"I know what you and her got up to last night."

Martin stared at Ray.

Cy continued looking fixedly ahead, almost talking to himself. "She's been punishing me for tricking her all these years. Not that I don't deserve it, but goddamn."

"Did it stop once she found out you were cousins?"

"We tried. But no."

"So she kept on with you even after she knew?"

"We loved each other."

Ray felt like hot stones were sinking in his stomach, the sex buzz of the night before evaporating like steam. "So, I guess you know my next question."

"He's not ours."

Ray was surprised, maybe even disappointed. "That's a definite no?"

"Not a chance."

"Do you know who—"

"I'm only telling secrets that are mine to tell, Ray. Sorry."

"Fair enough. Are you and Lena still—"

"Relax, lover boy. We're not together. Not like that, not for years. But we're not *not* together. I see her almost every day." Cy's thick bicep stiffened and he began to pull in a fish. "So on second thought, maybe you shouldn't relax."

Ray's brain reeled. Who else knew about him and Lena? Did Gram know? Did Jettie? He fought to stay afloat in the conversation. "She's not going to like you telling me what you've told me."

As Cy's fish broke the water he stood and gave Ray a dark look, a wave of aggression coming off him like heat. "You need to know what you're stepping in. Have your fun, boy, just so long as you understand, when it comes down to it, all you can do is make her feel lonely. *I* know her, real as real."

Ray leaned away from the silvery fish that swung through the air and flopped on Cy's line, splashing him and Martin. He wiped drops of warm water from his face. From the beginning of his career he had been surprised by the way people will make a clean breast of things on camera that you wouldn't think they would want anyone to know. It always happened. Like the camera was a confession box, and it happened, like today, even when the camera wasn't on. The need to air secrets was strong. But that wasn't all that Cy was doing. Cy was warning him off. He told him what he told him as a way of staking his claim to Lena like some kind of alpha beast in a nature documentary. Screw him. He should have kept his dirty little secret to himself. Ray wished he hadn't heard it.

The prime directive came to mind like a bracing corrective. Captain Kirk would become entangled and then, always, disentangled in the nick of time. It would look like he was about to cave into the charms of some alien lady, green-skinned and stacked and beseeching, that feminized other, but he'd stand up suddenly and say he had to get back to his ship. Ray was always disappointed at those moments but also impressed by Kirk's surprising singleness of purpose. Ray set his fishing rod down and stood up, like Kirk rising from an alien chaise longue.

He cleared his throat and steered the conversation away from himself. "Cy, I want to tell you something. Gram wants me to find out who his father is. Badly."

Cy was closing up the bait box and didn't look up.

Ray continued, "And I can understand—I feel for the kid."

"Yeah?"

"I guess if you knew the answer to that question and felt free to tell Gram, you'd have done it by now. But if you can point me in the right direction—"

Cy's eyes moved to the blue barn. "Can't help," he said. He, too, seemed to have become embarrassed. The anger drained out of his features as he muttered, "Come on."

They lugged their gear back along the narrow, red dirt path to the barn. Cy led them through a side door and flipped a switch. Rows of fluorescent lights buzzed and sputtered to life, illuminating a number of vintage motorcycles and, at the back, several gleaming vintage cars. The inside of the barn smelled like engine oil, hay, and the pinewood boards of its walls, unpainted and rough on the inside.

"Is that a Packard?" Martin asked, eyeing a lemon-yellow touring car from the thirties facing them like a napping lion.

Cy was on his knees digging around in a row of cabinets below a long workbench of untreated wood that ran the eastern wall. Sitting back on his feet, he came up with a 2 × 2 metal box that he opened with a small key on his keychain. "Take this," Cy said, puffing to his feet and handing him the box.

Ray held the box, which felt full but not heavy.

"These are pictures you might want to use." He cleared a long space on the workbench, shoving wrenches and oily rags into drawers along its length and spreading a red-and-white checked plastic picnic tablecloth over the dirty surface. "You can go ahead and film this if you want."

Ray and Martin nodded at each other. Cy took the box from Ray and put it on the tablecloth while Ray and Martin set up lights.

When Ray was behind his camera, Cy opened the box. He took out one photograph at a time, glancing at some of the handwritten dates on the back and placing the prints on the tablecloth. "I'll try and keep them in order. These are probably a little more interesting to you than the professional photos. They're ours, our private pictures of the band. Like here—" He grinned self-consciously and pointed at a black-and-white shot of two teenagers, Lena and Cy, in bell-bottoms and sunglasses, the wind flattening their hair against their foreheads, as they stood on the side of a road in front of a highway sign that read LOS ANGELES, 1,216 MILES. "That's the day we left Oklahoma for California."

"Do you know the exact date?" From behind the camera, Ray's eyes took in the photograph. It had the artful-accidental charm of the sort of shot Walker Evans or Dorothea Lange took during the Dust Bowl.

"June '75. The 9th or 10th, I'd guess. We hadn't gone far yet—I believe that was taken outside Elk City. Lena wrote 'Black Ice' along the way, working it out while she drove."

The three men moved down the tablecloth as Cy narrated photo by photo. His whole demeanor had changed. He had become friendly and helpful again. "That's Lena in her waitress uniform. She waited tables when we got to L.A. That was not a line of work that suited her, I don't need to tell you."

"She's holding that coffeepot like she might swing it at somebody's head," Ray observed from behind the camera. "These are really good, Cy. Who took them?"

"Lady named Justine," Cy said.

"Is she around to talk to?"

"She passed."

"Who was she?"

"One of the gang. Lena's best friend. We went to high school together, and she stayed with us right along, not singing or playing music but doing damned near everything else."

From behind the boom pole, Martin said, "I never heard about her before."

"Is that her?" Ray spotted a series of posed group shots, in color, with Lena, Cy, and several other people perched on a paisley couch. Ray recognized their bassist, Desmond Jones, wearing a pukka-shell necklace, bare-chested, and with a white-man's afro, sitting next to a ferret-faced dude whom Cy identified as Chad Green, a piano player on the second album. In another photograph, clearly part of the same series, an additional person was there, a woman sitting knee-to-knee with Lena, their dark hair blending together as it fell to their laps. Justine. She smiled slightly, showing a gap between her front teeth and dimples in both cheeks. On her other side, Jones leaned his head on Justine's shoulder, his palms pressed together like a sleeping child's.

"There she is, yeah," Cy said. Ray zoomed in on the photograph then pulled back to catch Cy, pulling on his lip as he leaned over the image. The camera had a playback function, a new feature that Ray hoped would allow him to figure Cy out later. In the moment he couldn't read the signs, but Cy was showing them these pictures for a reason.

"She wasn't in too many of the pictures. That one, she fixed the camera on one of those three-legged deals and set a timer. We called it our Christmas card."

"Justine who?"

"Oxley. Justine Oxley."

"How did she die?"

Cy plunged his hand into the brushed steel box and came up with a manila folder that he quickly opened, pulling out another handful of glossy photographs. "Here's a bunch from backstage at the Grammys in '78," Cy said, his deep voice warbling. "You see who that is? That's Lena with Quincy Jones."

Ray considered restating his question, pushing Cy to see how he'd respond, but the sadness in Cy's face forbade normal behavior, like when you're zipping along in the fast lane and come upon a funeral procession. For a second Ray felt like doing the interview equivalent of honking and yelling, but his basic decency took over, and he decided that he would find another way to learn about the enigmatic Justine. "Quite a dress Lena's wearing. I see why Justine shot these in color."

Looking at this younger Lena in the slinky blue dress, her eyes shining, Ray felt the full force of what had happened between the two of them. Lena was no alien temptress on a sixties TV show, no green lady in Ray's own private drama; she was a real woman with a part in the nation's history, a person with deep roots and a trail of recognition that spread out behind her for decades.

"Can I take these photographs for a while, Cy? I'd like to get close-ups on all of them. They're great, they're going to give texture."

"I'll keep them on the premises if you don't mind. You're welcome to shoot them here, though. And we can get copies if you want."

"I want."

9

HIGHWAY GOTHIC

He had expected rock star sex. But Lena was not that kind of lover. She seemed bemused and moved tentatively, not inexperienced, but shy. A deep reserve never quite left her, even in the heat of the moment. That night, with her head on his chest, she had said, "It was easier when I was fucked up. You know? I could lose myself. Now I never lose myself. God, I would love to, even for a few seconds."

"We'll work on that," he said, suggesting some sort of promise in the plural pronoun.

Now he was lounging in her study, the room he had snuck into and where she had caught him sniffing her shirt. Things had sure changed fast. Then he had felt like a creepy freak; now, after their second love-making session, he felt like Anchises after he mated with Aphrodite. He felt like he should be glowing. Was he not changed? Should it not show?

As he waited for her to finish showering, everything looked warm and connected in the late night glow and postcoital haze, almost like he had eaten mushrooms. He even imagined giving her shirt back with a laugh, explaining how his attraction to her took him off guard, made him do weird things.

Martin had interrogated him about his "affair" with Lena on their way home from Cy's place that afternoon. His reaction teetered between admiration and alarm. "So are you seeing each other now, are you in a relationship?"

"It was one night. We're hanging out," Ray had answered.

"What does that mean?" Martin asked. "These things don't happen to me. While you were hanging out with Lena Wells, I was hanging out with the asshole youngest son of the Gack clan, who wants to be a director and had tons of ideas he wanted to share with me. Like have we ever considered using some kind of colored filter to make her drug years seem trippy? Do we know that if you smear Vaseline on the lens it makes everything look psychedelic?"

"Oh, boy." Ray laughed. "Sorry about that, Martin. I completely forgot about that meeting."

"Hanging out." Martin had flipped the air vent open and closed, considering the term. "You're going to keep on? After what Cy said?"

"Look. Lena started this. To me, that says she considers herself free and able to do what she wants with whomever she wants. Since when do jealous ex-lovers get to call the shots? They don't. What we witnessed back there was Cy having a tantrum. It changes nothing."

"What about that cousin business?"

Ray had already narrowed Cy's rambling story to the image of an innocent teenaged Lena being hit on by her cousin. He was trying not to think about the suggestion that the relationship had been long-lasting. "It is quite a story."

"Does it change the way you feel about her?"

"The way I feel? Martin, we spent one night together. We're just hanging out."

"Hanging out, right. With the subject of our film. You can call it what you want, but this still seems like a bad idea, man. A very bad idea. I mean, doesn't it?"

What if Captain Kirk had stayed with the green lady? Would that have been so bad? It might have been diplomatically advantageous, it might have given Kirk a better attitude on the bridge. "It's cool," Ray said. "Trust me."

Martin blew out a long breath. "Well, keep her happy, okay? Don't do anything to piss her off."

Ray leaned back on the couch and watched the rows of stained-glass balls dangling in Lena's window twist on their colored ribbons as the ceiling fan above stirred the air. He smiled to himself. Keeping her happy—he was pretty sure he had done that. While he waited for

Lena to emerge from the shower, he took out his cellphone and called his father. Lawrence Wheeler had been the star of Ray's first film, *Paper Trail*, which had been a modest success, winning notice on the festival circuit ten years earlier when Ray was thirty-four. Such a simple film, too. Ray had followed his dad into the odd, obsessive world of hardcore genealogists. According to an old family story, the Wheelers were descended from the first king of Scotland in the first century A.D. As Ray's dad followed the genealogical trails of the story, Ray tracked his efforts. Turns out the story was true. The audience had loved the thrill of the chase, the sense of history unfolding like a deck of cards with a lot of face cards you could shuffle to the top, allowing you to find the faces that look like your own. And they had loved Lawrence Wheeler, who was a genial goofball. He often told Ray that he was still a celebrity among genealogists, whatever that meant.

"Raymond! How goes it?" His father's merry voice came over the wire. Ray told him about Lena and her belief that she descended from Geronimo.

"Find out, would you?" Ray said. "If she really is his great-granddaughter, I'd like to let her know for sure."

He imagined Lena's face, her joy. He imagined filming her reaction, anchoring the film with a recurring Geronimo thread. His father told him he'd heard Native American genealogy was hard to take back too many generations; records were poor or nonexistent, but connecting the dots for the few generations between Lena and Geronimo should be easy.

"Through the mother. Ruby Wells, and her sister, Vivian," Ray told him. "Call me when you get something."

Then he walked over to the record crates in Lena's room and found her LPs there in alphabetical order between Wall of Voodoo and The Who. He extracted *Rank Outsider*, *Highway Gothic*, *Trip the Wind*, *Keep Your Powder Dry*, and the soundtrack to *The Ballad of Belle Starr*, and stretched out on the leather couch to read the liner notes.

He picked up *Highway Gothic*, an almost-forgotten album that had appeared a couple of months before *Ballad of Belle Starr* and was immediately eclipsed by it. Something about the album felt unfinished and incoherent; most of the songs, with the notable exceptions of

"Graveyard Jimmy" and "The Piano Bench Incident," were slight and whimsical. The album cover of *Highway Gothic* showed Lena leaning against the back of a blue pickup truck, arms crossed. On the back cover was a picture of the band he had seen earlier that day. It was one of the paisley couch series. He studied the acknowledgments and found the photograph credited to Justine Oxley.

"Learning anything?" Lena asked, standing in the doorway.

She was in a white silk robe, her wet hair combed out, holding a thin stick in her hand, a wisp of smoke trailing off its end. She strolled over to the mantle and slid the stick into an incense burner. Ecclesiastical smoke drifted over to Ray. "You look beautiful," he said.

She laughed and came across the glossy floor to join him on the couch. "What are you looking at?"

"Who was Justine Oxley?"

She glanced at the copy of *Highway Gothic* he was holding. "A photographer. She took some pictures for us."

Ray watched her expression. "A photographer?"

"She took pictures, yeah."

"You don't have a number for her do you?"

She studied the ends of her wet hair. "What do you need with her?"

"Just doing the due diligence."

"Oh," she said, pulling her feet under her and turning to him. "I couldn't tell you how to reach her."

Ray closed the album cover and stared at it for a few seconds. What had Cy said? Justine Oxley was Lena's best friend.

"How about Desmond Jones?" He pointed to the grinning, shirtless bass player in the photo.

She waved a hand. "Why would you want to talk to him?"

He had brought up Jones's name to steer away from the subject of Justine, since it was clear she wasn't going to be straight with him. He hadn't expected another roadblock. It was a tricky moment. "I'll be talking to all the band members, Lena. It's standard procedure."

"I see, I see. You know two concepts I'm not a fan of? Standard and procedure. You won't interview people I don't think are worth talking to," she said, and he could hear her straining to keep the steel out of her voice as she delivered her ultimatum, "if you want me in this film. But if you'd rather talk to Desmond Jones, go right ahead."

"Christ, Lena, he was your bass player for how many years?"

"I'm not kidding, Ray."

He stood up and began pacing in front of the fireplace, back and forth through the curling ribbon of incense smoke. She watched him from the couch. "I'm sorry," he said finally. He was getting tired of squabbling with her over content. "I know how private you are. It must mortify you to open up your life to us like this, and I get that you're scared. You don't like to lose control."

"I never lose control."

He stopped walking and gave her an imploring gaze. "I just wish you could trust me, Lena."

"Oh, I do, Ray. I do. I'm sorry to be so paranoid, I really am." She flexed her hands. "It just seems like I ought to have some say about who you interview."

"It's my job to shape this thing the way I think it needs to be shaped. It's *about* you, but it's not *by* you. Believe me, I am as interested as you are in making a good film."

"But you're not giving an inch."

"I—no—I'm not."

They stared at each other while the incense enveloped them in a sweet fog.

"You're on probation, remember."

He looked down, trying to hide his disappointment. He had hoped, even assumed, the last two nights together had superseded her unfriendly dictum.

She laughed and swatted him across the chest. "I'm just teasing, baby."

"Oh." Ray looked up and grinned. "So I'm not on probation?"

"You are, you definitely are, but I wouldn't fire you for trying to do what you think is best for the film."

"That's worth something," he said. "I am trying my best, you know. I need this to work. My soul can't take another catastrophe. Neither can my career."

"Mine, either." Her expression softened. "I guess this is as good a time as any to set some parameters."

"Guess so."

She pulled her legs around and sat cross-legged. "I don't want to talk about Van Elkins or any of his claims. I will not dignify him with a response."

Van Elkins was a drug dealer in L.A. who, from prison, had penned a tell-all book about dope peddling to musicians and actors of the seventies and eighties. Lena was one of his subjects. His references to her were a pastiche of crudely constructed sentences soaked in wishful thinking, crude assumptions, and a healthy dose of envy that Ray had read but hadn't countenanced. "I'm with you. That guy's a buffoon."

She let out a sigh. "Oh, good. Now, I also will not talk about Steve McQueen."

"Ah, come on!"

"No."

"You won't even say whether you—"

"No. Nor will I talk about the *Tonight Show* thing."

"Okay, but I will be using that footage." Ray was fine with the turn the conversation had taken. It was unambiguous. It was business. No small talk, no shadows.

"I'd rather you didn't."

"Lena, I won't ask you to talk about what happened that night if you don't want to, but that's as far as I'll go on that one. You've got to leave me some things."

"There are plenty of other things to discuss."

"Let's talk about that—what do you *want* me to cover?"

"Tell my story—it's zero-to-hero, you know. Real American stuff."

"Yeah," he said flatly.

What she wanted was everything he disliked about rock docs. He envisioned shots of a little cot in a long row of little cots at a dingy orphanage, her mother's humble grave, the footage of her playing the Hollywood Bowl, and her spread in *Rolling Stone*. Rags. Riches. He knew the story arc was compelling—half the people who watched rock documentaries were absorbing hope for their own would-be rags-to-riches journey—but he resisted the predictability of it.

He didn't know what kind of film it would be yet; it was still taking shape in his mind, but he remembered the phrase that had always prompted his earliest films. When he was fourteen, his mother would set him off on film projects by giving him prompts: "Tell me the truth about . . . why you hide those magazines under your bed? . . . Which of your parents do you think you're more like? . . . Why do our redneck neighbors hate us?" She had been diagnosed with cancer, and while she was fighting it, she lifted Ray's and his father's spirits by keeping them busy. For Ray it was the short films that he would make and show her, answering her questions. She sent her husband off on tantalizing genealogical treasure hunts. And when she recovered, they were both confirmed practitioners, Ray and his father, of their new coping mechanisms. At the moment his mother was on a Fulbright Scholar stint, teaching art history in Poland. Still, he could hear her voice: "Ray, honey, tell me the truth about . . ." He wanted to tell the truth about Lena Wells, but his understanding of her was more complicated than it had been twenty-four hours earlier, and he could foresee hard calls to be made about content coming up the road. Did her relationship with Cy go in the film? Gram's angst over his unidentified father? And what was the deal with Justine Oxley?

He said, "You're admirable, Lena. Relax. After this film, people will know how interesting you are."

"Admirable and interesting." She nodded. "Okay. But I swear to God, Ray, if you make me look bad—"

"How about the lawsuit?" She had battled Raven Records, her label, for years over missing profits. Finally, five or six years earlier, they had settled with her for a large, undisclosed sum.

"I wish," she answered, "but the settlement included a gag order."

"I was afraid you'd say that. It's okay. I think your years here in Medicine Park will be at the heart of the film."

"There's not much to tell."

"Twenty years?"

"I already showed you the buffalo. What else is there? Do you want to see the Toyota dealership?"

"You raised a child. There's your drug addiction. Recovery. There's the story of you buying the hotel you grew up in."

She interrupted. "I've got the title. *Live from Medicine Park.*"

"That's good," Ray said.

"So we agree on something?" Her eyes lit up and she slapped her palms against her thighs. "Let's stop there. I'm going to throw on some clothes. I want to go down to the theater."

"Right now? You know there are fans camping down there."

"Let's go say hi."

Ray jumped up from the couch and said, "Please let me film this."

She smiled. "Get your gear and I'll meet you downstairs in ten minutes."

The Quonset building where the concert would be held, its rounded roof curving to the ground, sat behind the revelers like a giant roly-poly. A campfire burned at the edge of Medicine Creek with several people sitting around it. More people were coming in and out of the water and moving among the tents. On the walkway across the waterfall two people bandied glow sticks in a mock sword fight. The air smelled like spicy food and pot. As Ray and Lena walked up the street from the Silver Sun, they could hear Cimarron barking in the backyard and voices singing down by the water.

As she walked beside him, Lena made an appreciative sound. "'Talkin' Dust Bowl Blues,'" she noted.

"That's not one of yours, is it?"

"Woody Guthrie." She had changed into a purple linen sundress that swung around her knees as she walked. Her hair was still damp on the ends and she wore no shoes.

"How many people does that place hold?" Ray asked.

"Five hundred," she said.

"You could have booked a bigger venue," he said.

"I like it there. It was a roller-skating rink when I was little. Besides, at least I don't have to worry about not filling the place. That would be embarrassing."

They strolled past three shirtless teenagers playing hacky sack under a streetlight.

"You think they're here for me?' she asked, her voice full of wonder.

"Everybody loves classic rock."

"There are people who just love to go to shows no matter who's playing," she said. "They probably never heard of me."

Steps led from the street down to the red stone promenade that followed the creek. Lena trotted down them and headed toward the campfire.

"Lena, wait," Ray called. "Give me time to set up my camera."

But she walked straight up to the circle of singing people sitting around the campfire and sat down. "Excuse me," she said, squeezing in between two men who looked like father and son, both with curly hair in ponytails. Four other people sat around the fire: a little blond girl, perched on a red igloo cooler holding a pair of plastic dinosaurs; a couple each wearing T-shirts that said "I Survived Y2K"; and a Hispanic-looking guy with silver rings on every finger who was playing the guitar. He was the first to notice Lena. His bejeweled fingers faltered and he stopped singing. "Hold up," he said. "You're Lena Wells."

Lena gave a little wave as she pulled her purple sundress over her knees.

The men on either side of Lena snapped their heads around to look at her. "My word," the father exclaimed. He put an arm around Lena and hugged her like they were long-lost friends. "So gorgeous to have you with us, love! Everyone, look!" The woman in the Y2K T-shirt put a hand over her mouth and squealed. They all grinned and nodded, extended their hands, and introduced themselves one by one, restraining their enthusiasm as if a deer had wandered into their camp and they were trying not to scare it off. The young guy with the ponytail got up and brought Lena a green bottle of mineral water from a nearby cooler. "I know you don't drink," he said as he leaned over Lena.

"Why, thank you." Lena smiled up at him.

Ray stood outside the group setting up his tripod and looking for a light setting that would capture the circle of glowing faces around the fire. He had the feeling he might have already missed the best part, the moment when they recognized her. For a few minutes they asked her questions: Was she really making a new album? How old was her son now? Was he a musician, too? How did she like small-town life?

Then Joaquin, the Hispanic guy, handed her the guitar and said, "Will you sing for us?"

"I don't want you to get sick of me before the show tomorrow night," she said, but she took the guitar.

"Right!" someone said. "Like that's going to happen!"

Lena grinned. "How about a new song?"

Ray knew that they would probably all rather hear her sing an old song, one that their own memories had laid down tracks with, but they acted as though they liked the idea, murmuring polite assent. But the little girl piped up and said, "I want to hear my favorite."

Lena smiled at her. "What's your favorite, sweetie?"

"'The Piano Bench Incident.'" Everyone laughed. It was a song that didn't yield its meaning easily, but it was sexy, a vibe the little girl wasn't privy to. "I'm taking piano lessons," she explained.

"'The Piano Bench Incident' it is," Lena said. "I don't usually play the guitar in front of people, I just compose with it, so bear with me." Several more people had gotten wind of Lena's presence and walked over. They ringed the people sitting around the campfire. She looked up to include them in the circle. "Now, this is the only song on my albums that I didn't write, I gotta tell you. Desmond Jones wrote this one."

"What's it about?" Joaquin asked.

"You'd have to ask him," she said.

"The Piano Bench Incident" was a slippery, atmospheric song, but Lena delivered a jaunty, almost comic version for the little girl, thumping the body of the guitar to keep the beat. When she sang "Major, minor, all at one go, my back can play a song you know," Lena leaned toward the little girl, widening her eyes as if she were reading her a bedtime story.

Behind the camera, Ray felt the documentary come alive. Lena had asked him the day before if he knew when he was getting good footage. He was getting it now. The amber glow from the fire lit the shot like a Rembrandt; Lena sat among her fans like Henry V minus the disguise, visiting his troops the night before the Battle of Agincourt; the crowd was avid; and the song was a good choice for a campfire song. He felt something like awe—for Lena, for the perfection of the scene he was filming—building like barometric pressure before a storm.

He had felt this way before, in Rome, when he saw Michelangelo's *Moses*. His mom had kept a paperweight replica of the statue on her desk, but the real thing was hidden beneath scaffolding and vast expanses of dirty plastic sheeting in the church of San Pietro in Vincoli, which was under renovation when Ray had visited. After finding his way to the alcove in the church, where his guidebook said the statue should be, he had lifted a plastic tarp, and there was the familiar figure looming large: Moses, with horns protruding from his forehead, the result of direct conversation with God. Those horns on his mother's miniature statue had puzzled Ray as a boy. They looked like the waggling fingers of a peace sign. His mother told him what the horns meant: they were rays of light or something, but he always thought it was a weird way to show that Moses had stood in God's presence. Horns. Standing in front of the statue, which was eight feet high and rippling with muscular tension, he had felt pierced by wonder, something bright and irrefutable only intensified by the contrasting heat and dust and indignity of the tarp.

As he watched Lena's effect on the circle of fans, her natural magnetism radiated outward and touched him with its electric fingers. He wanted to feel his head for horns, for some proof of contact with the divine.

When the song was over the group clapped and pleaded for more, but she stood up and said goodnight to them all. "Y'all don't stay up too late," she said, kneeling down to hug the little girl. "I'm going to wear you out tomorrow night!"

Ray packed up his camera, and he and Lena walked together down the promenade. A drunken redheaded girl stumbled by them. "Do you ever miss the drugs?" Ray asked.

"Oh, not at all. I go to my meetings, Cy and I do. It's a way of life."

"Sounds tough."

"Dying every day is tough. That's what getting high was like."

"I bet," Ray said, swinging an arm across her shoulders. He felt like an interloper, like a kid who has gotten backstage after a concert and is trying to avoid the roadies who will kick him out if they spot him. Martin's words flitted across his mind—"bad idea, man"—but for the moment he and Lena were together.

They climbed back up to the street level where they ran into the man in the silver lamé space suit, about to descend the stairs. His body odor was extraordinary—Ray hadn't smelled anything like it since the last time he had traveled in Europe. Under the streetlight Ray could see that he was a rawboned, sun-scorched man, just this side of elderly, with a blue chin and squinting eyes. When he relaxed his face, the skin inside his wrinkles was white. His expression was childlike and preoc-cupied, but the way he fidgeted, his gnarled hands twisting over one another, suggested energy ready to flood its container at the slightest provocation. He broke into a smile when he saw Lena and Ray, and bowed with his whole body. "Greetings, cats and kittens!"

"Hello!" Ray exclaimed. "That's some outfit, man. I love it."

The spaceman nodded, the silver planets in his headgear bobbing. "Life is an event worth dressing for. Don't you agree?"

"I do!" Ray said, suddenly self-conscious in his black T-shirt and jeans. "But not as much as you do, I bet. I saw you the other day. Are you here for the show?"

"I'm always here," he replied. "You can talk to me anytime."

"That would be great," Ray said. He realized the man knew who they were, but he introduced Lena and himself anyway. "And what's your name?"

But the spaceman's wild white eyebrows drew together, and a rigor overtook his face as his eyes darted to Lena. He backed away and then darted down the steps.

"Hey," Ray called, but the man didn't turn around.

"What was that?" Ray said, "I think he was afraid of you."

"Who knows?" Lena said.

"I really wanted to talk to that guy." Ray looked after the man as he hurried along the promenade, the moonlight limning his shiny shoul-ders.

"You don't need him," Lena said.

"How do you know?" he snapped, suddenly irritated. "He might have a lot to say."

"I doubt it."

"But it's my call," he reminded her. "Mine."

From somewhere above them, a familiar voice rang out. "You two look cozy!"

"What are you doing up there?" Lena asked, tilting her head up. "I need my bass player all in one piece, you know."

Ray looked up and saw Jettie on the roof of the Silver Sun. His stomach clutched at the height—she was fifty feet up in the same precarious spot where he had sat with her—was it only two nights ago? She was leaning forward, peering down at them.

"You be careful!" he yelled.

"Be careful yourself, Ray," she hollered back, and sat back against the chimney.

Lena grabbed his hand and pulled him toward the front door. "That one," she said. "Sometimes I can't make her out."

10

WHAT THE THUNDER SAID

There's this dude Eric who drops in sometimes. Creepy blond guy with a forehead that starts above his ears. He was one of Mom's session guys back in the day. He played pedal steel on a few songs—anyway, this Eric guy might be my dad. He and Mom go way back. He's skinny, like me, that's one thing. He has long fingers, like vampire fingers and so do I if you ever noticed. But I hope it's not him because he's a dick and only comes around when he's out of work. He mostly works in Nashville for shit country bands. "I bring the twang." That's how he describes himself. Cy does NOT like him, and Cy, man, Cy is cool with everybody. That should tell you something. Eric Barker. Sounds like a fucking dog. Woof woof. I do not want to find out I am Gram fucking Barker. Son of the twang. Pass on that.

Ray set aside the note. Why couldn't Lena just tell the poor kid? She of all people should have understood how it hurt not to know your parents. He had just returned to his room after spending another night with her and found the note under his door when he opened it. These notes—Gram had the communication skills of a twelve-year-old.

What was it like for Jettie to be married to someone like that? She had struggled on her own in Austin, waiting tables and writing music and trying one band after another looking for the fit she had found with the Black Sheep, while Gram had never lived on his own or held a real job, shifting from his mother to his wife like women from an earlier time were handed from father to husband, changing their names like cattle are branded. Maybe marrying Jettie was a way for him to get away from Lena, but it looked like he had married his mother, a younger version of her. Ray didn't know who he would bet on to win, Lena or Jettie, but it wasn't hard to see that Gram would be pulled apart if he couldn't decide who he stood with, what band he played for. Gram's sudden focus on the longstanding question of his paternity looked to Ray like a diversionary tactic. He was trying not to think about the decision he had to make.

When Ray saw him in the kitchen a little while later, the boy was in a mood. Ray took a muffin from a bowl on the counter and carried it to the kitchen table, where Gram sat scowling and twisting a cup of coffee in his hands.

"Where is everybody?" Ray asked.

"Martin's down at the theater already and Jettie's still sleeping. Mom left early this morning. She's got interviews on a couple of morning shows, one in Lawton, one in Oklahoma City. Cy went with her."

Ray had seen Lena slide out of bed when the alarm went off, but he hadn't realized she was leaving. He had told her he wanted to film those interviews. More lost footage. He slapped the tabletop so hard his palms burned. "When will she be back?" he asked.

"Afternoon."

"And Cy went with her?"

Gram flushed red and nodded. "You filming our rehearsal?"

"Finally. How are the new songs?"

"Fine, I guess." He leaned back in his chair, tilting onto its back legs. "I'm supposed to take you up Mount Scott today. Mom says you need *scenery footage, something of the real Comanche County.*" He raised his voice in a dead-on imitation of Lena's voice.

"That's pretty good," Ray said. "You sound just like her." He didn't need scenery footage, and he bristled at Lena's continual trumping of his plans, but he welcomed the chance to talk to Gram alone. He had only interviewed him once with Jettie, and briefly the day before while Gram tuned his guitar. Gram had told Ray the story of how he and Jettie had gotten drunk in a Lawton bar with a strange old bird who turned out to be some kind of itinerant preacher. He married them between tequila shots, and the next morning they hardly remembered him or the ceremony. "You never filed for the license?" Ray asked. They had not, and Gram was surprised to hear from Ray that this probably meant they weren't really married.

"We are," Gram insisted. "In our hearts."

They took Ray's Jeep, heading west on Highway 49 into the Wichita Mountains Wildlife Refuge. The Jeep passed over the tubular bars of the cattle grate, strung like giant guitar strings across the road at the entrance to the refuge to keep the buffalo contained. The grate thrummed as the Jeep passed over it. Next to the entrance, in the tall grasses lining the road, a sign with a color-coded pie chart declared the risk for wildfires HIGH today.

Gram directed Ray to a right turn, hidden by a dense tangle of blackjacks, which started them on a winding road up Mount Scott, the mountain that blocked the late afternoon sun from Medicine Park. "The WPA built this road in the thirties," Gram said, his voice tight.

"Have I done something to piss you off?"

"No."

Each ascending loop around the mountain showed more of the silver waters of Lake Lawtonka, and then, as the car rounded the mountain, the jagged spine of the Wichita Mountain range stretching west. The top of Mount Scott was covered by a blacktop that emanated heat like the mouth of a volcano. Ray pulled the Jeep into a spot facing east, away from the sun. There were no other cars in the lot, which canted at a slight angle high above the ground. Empty and floating, the vacant asphalt looked like a landing platform for some huge, unimaginable aircraft.

They got out of the Jeep and walked to the edge of the parking lot. Ray brought his camera and walked the perimeter, shooting the scenery that Lena thought he needed. The mountain, comprised of gigantic granite boulders, descended gently from the top in a series of prairie-grass plateaus and knotty spruces growing between the rocks, their sinewy roots like something liquid that had solidified. Ray and Gram walked against heat-heavy wind as they headed toward a concrete lookout that stood on the south side.

Below them a speedboat zipped across the surface of Lake Lawtonka. Hawks swooped and dived in broad circles. Gram bounded down the rocks surrounding the parking lot, scrambling across a wide boulder and landing on a narrow strip of prairie grasses littered with plastic soda bottles and beer cans. When Ray caught up, Gram said in a loud voice, "What I said about finding my dad? You don't need to worry about that."

"Why?"

"Just stop. Don't worry about it." He was yelling to be heard above the wind, which roared around them, seemingly coming from all directions at once.

Ray looked at the surface of the lake, furiously twisting one of the skulls in his earlobe.

"Why the change of heart?"

"Every song ever written about families is wrong," Gram said. "Nobody gets it right. You can't get it right."

"Does this include your mother's songs?"

"Especially her songs! They're all lies. Made up stories." He looped his fingers around his front belt loops and rocked forward. "Music is a lie."

"That's a hell of a thing for a rock-and-roll guitarist to say."

"It doesn't matter. It doesn't matter if it's a lie. I'm good at it. I've lived a lie all my life." He planted one hand against a boulder, startling a turquoise lizard with a yellow head. The lizard skittered away.

"You found out who your father is?"

"I was always kind of a fuck up. No good in school. That's what happens—incest makes for stupid kids."

"Incest. Listen—"

"I saw them this morning, Mom and Cy. In the kitchen. They were fighting. He grabbed her. I walked in and saw it. The look on his face."

"That's it? You saw a look on his face?"

"I'm telling you, it was a look I've never seen. Not the look of a cousin, Ray. Or of an old friend or of a band member. She was looking back at him the same way. My parents"—he bit the words off bitterly—"I walked in and they broke apart, played it off."

"What were they fighting about?"

"Fuck if I know," he shouted. "You, probably."

"Me?"

Gram narrowed his eyes at him.

"Look," Ray said. "I don't think Cy's your dad. After I got your note yesterday, I asked him point blank. He said no, straight up no."

"You're all up in our business aren't you?"

"Now just a minute"—Ray pointed a finger at Gram—"You're the one writing me notes."

Gram had swung himself up and stood astride two lichen-covered boulders, the wind whipping his dark hair around as he shaded his eyes to look at Ray. "I tell you what, my friend," he said, "any of this private business shows up in your stupid movie, I'll make sure you regret it. I'll help you to the bottom of that lake. You can show your movie to the catfish."

The threat had the odd effect of defusing the situation for Ray. It was so pathetic that Ray felt like he was having a run-in with a student who thought he could threaten his way to a better grade. Only in this circumstance, Ray felt sorry for the kid. In a conciliatory tone, he said, "Cy was in a truth-telling mood and I think he told me the truth about this. He says he's not your dad and I believe him."

"Well, I don't," Gram yelled. "They're fucking freaks, both of them. And I am the freakiest of all. A freak of nature."

The entire stretch of road between the Silver Sun and Medicine Hall was alive with people when they got back. Ray had underestimated the local hero effect. He doubted a Lena Wells concert without a new album release to back it up could have generated this much excitement anywhere else, but here in Oklahoma, they loved her and they were here to show it. Ray spotted DeAndre, Molly, and Dave, the extra hands Martin had hired from the local station, unloading their gear. Broadcast vans from Lawton, Oklahoma City, and even a Dallas TV station were parked in front of the Silver Sun.

Before they got out of the Jeep, Gram laid a hand on Ray's arm and asked stiffly, "Can you give me some advice?"

"Sure, man, sure." They had ridden in silence on the way back into town, so Ray was relieved they were talking again.

"I'm thinking I'm a Lighthorseman, not a Black Sheep."

Ray turned to look at him. So he had been thinking about his decision. "What about Los Lobos? Are you going to abandon your band? The band you started with your wife?"

"Well"—Gram sucked his teeth and stared through the windshield at the rusted Quonset wall of the theater—"Mom and I have been talking. Turns out she's known about our secret plan for a while."

"And she doesn't like it."

"She's pretty upset. I mean, she's on our side, but she doesn't think we're ready."

"That's horseshit."

"She thinks we'd get our asses handed to us if we went out on our own too early, and we might get permanently discouraged. You never get a second chance if you blow it. She wants what's best for us."

Ray felt blood rushing to his head. "Just a little while ago you were so mad at your mother you could hardly bear it. Now you're prepared to abandon all your plans at her say-so?"

Gram stared at his feet. "I am what she made me. She and Cy, they understand me because they're as fucked up as I am. But Jettie, she's not like us."

"You need to grow up, Gram. Cut the apron strings. Stick by your wife, for God's sake."

"Aren't you fucking my mom?"

Ray leaned back against the seat and rubbed his chin. "That's none of your business."

"But you're taking up for Jettie? That's not very loyal, dude."

"Loyal? Holy crap. You thought I'd side with your mom! You wanted me to sell Jettie out. That means *you* want to sell Jettie out. I've been feeling sorry for you, thinking you were ambivalent. You're not ambivalent, Gram. You're just too chicken shit to admit what you've chosen."

"You're the one who told me we're not really married."

"Gram"—Ray sat up and laid a hand on his shoulder and looked him in the eyes— "Your mother can hire other musicians. Jettie's alone in the world. She only has you."

"But my mom—"

Ray yanked his keys from the ignition and got out, slamming the door. He got his gear out of the back of the Jeep and walked into the theater, fast-moving from fury, with Gram scrambling out of the Jeep behind him, silent now.

Lena, Cy, Jettie, and Rinaldo, still dressed in their everyday clothes, were onstage rehearsing one of Lena's new songs when they walked in. Ray's eyes found Jettie first, her back turned to them, playing and grinning at Rinaldo, her green guitar slung low on her hips. She looked so invulnerable just then, but Ray felt like whisking her offstage and shooing her away from these people she thought she wanted, these people who were about to sell her down the river.

He and Gram passed rows and rows of folding chairs set up in three long columns. Gym-style fluorescent lights buzzed and flickered from the rounded ceiling. The soundboard was on a platform at the back of the room, where Ray would set up a wide shot from which all the moving camera footage would be synced. The stage stood four feet off the ground and was decorated for the show. The Persian carpets that usually covered the small stage in Lena's living room had been carried down here and unrolled, overlapping one another beneath the mic stands and amplifiers. Lavender tulle hung in long strips behind the stage, and artificial bare trees strung with white lights stood at both corners. A poster the width of the stage hung from the ceiling. It showed a stretch of empty highway, the yellow lines reaching into a dark horizon.

The music stopped. "There you are!" Lena called out, waving them forward. Martin stood next to the drum set, his camera on his shoulder. Gram bounded onstage like a rider swinging onto a horse, saying nothing to anyone. They gave him a minute to strap on his guitar and tune up, then they started into one of Lena's top-ten hits, "What the Thunder Said," a grinding, bluesy number off *Rank Outsider.*

Jettie had the opening, a thumping tumble cut off by Gram's lead. Ray turned on the camera and stepped back for a wide shot, hoping

Martin was getting decent sound. The song pushed Lena's voice into registers lower than any other song in her catalog. Jettie and Rinaldo brought the pulse, while the dynamic created by Cy and Gram on dual lead guitar wove a dizzying twist of melody lines that sounded, in the light of his recent conversation with Gram, like Gram chasing Cy around the room with a knife.

In front of her mic, Lena stood with her legs wide apart, braced for the force pouring from her throat. Halfway through the song, her black eyes flitted briefly toward Ray without a spark of recognition. She went back to staring straight ahead, crawled up inside the body of the song.

> *Let me tell you what the thunder said*
> *Said stay right there I'm coming to bed*
> *Said I got you where I've wanted you*
> *Now rise and sin no more*
> *Elemental referee, tell me the score*
> *The thunder said, da*
> *The thunder said, oh*
> *The thunder rolled in*
> *Where the lightning couldn't go.*

Ray watched Lena, Gram's bitter indictment of her on the mountain echoing in his mind. She was some kind of strange, that was for sure. Still, he waved at her. But as she stepped away from the mic and turned to watch Gram, she didn't see Ray. He felt foolish with his hand hanging in the air, the wave unreturned. Her inattention stung although he knew she hadn't seen him. Still, it was probably only a matter of days before their fling would stop. He didn't often get dumped—usually he was the one who got bored with having to pretend to care about things other than his work. But not this time. She *was* his work.

Patterns in his own behavior were usually pretty hard for him to detect unless he somehow got an aerial view, a moment of such remove that it was like sitting in the editing room of his own life picking up on recurring themes as they flamed out of the raw footage. Such a view was before him now, and it was hard to look at. When Chester Lord had been shot in Rio Marron, Ray had justified his non-interference by standing on his professional ethics. The prime directive. His job was behind the camera, period, no matter what.

But he *had* interfered, by letting Chester Lord bleed while he tried to think of a way to help Johnny Reyes, and now here he was, interfering maximally by screwing the subject of his current film.

So where were his ethics? Apparently they were there to justify inaction when he wanted them to, and when he wanted to climb out from behind the camera to get what he wanted, well, he did. He had lately found himself waking in Lena's bed with the streets of Rio Marron sinking away from sight, aware that he had spent his dreams there. The only thing that could justify his lapse with Lena would be True Love. But Lena wasn't even looking at him.

Ray moved the camera off Lena and got a shot of Gram and Cy facing each other, having a conversation with their guitars. Martin had turned off his camera and drew up next to him, whispering in his ear, "I have to go. I'm giving an interview at 4:00."

"An interview?" Ray whispered back. "You?"

"About the grant I got for the doc—the Gacks want it known what their money is going for. Apparently they're not just in oil, they own some newspapers."

"The Gacks?"

Martin gave him an impatient look. "The oil family."

"Right."

"Whoa!" Martin's voice lifted and he pointed at the stage. With an apologetic expression for the likelihood that his voice was now in the shot, he reduced his tone to a whisper. "Did you hear that? What Gram just did?" Martin was staring at Gram. "That kind of echoey screech? The casual fan doesn't notice. It's one of Cy's tricky sounds, you know. So far as I know, nobody else ever figured out that particular aural dog-leg before. Now here's Gram playing it like it's doe ray me."

Ray was in no mood to hear Gram praised, but he zoomed in on Gram's fingers anyway.

When the song was over, Martin went to the stage in front of Cy and reached up and tapped his shin. "My compliments, sir."

Cy looked down, his braids dangling like ropes sent down to pull Martin out of a hole. "Why?"

"Sharing that trick with Gram," Martin said, humming the sound. "My buddies and I used to listen to that over and over again."

Cy grabbed a beer from the top of an amp and told Martin and Ray he had never showed it to Gram. "I worked on that move for ages before I got it right," he said. "I came on the boy one day when he was noodling on his first six-string, and bingo—there's the move. He was sixteen years old. I never taught that to anyone, not even Keith, when he asked."

"Keith Richards?" Ray asked.

Cy nodded toward Gram. "He could do it in his sleep. He must have absorbed it when he was tiny."

"Excuse me," Martin said. He hailed Gram, who scowled but stood and waited while Martin climbed onto the stage.

"Sounds like a father's pride," Ray observed from behind the camera. He couldn't help himself. He was pissed off.

Cy jutted out his chin as he turned toward Ray, his face reddening. "Listen to me, you goddamned peckerwood, I told you no. That ain't the deal. And even if it was, it wouldn't be any of your goddamned business." He spun away and grabbed his guitar like he was throttling it.

But Ray doubted everything he'd heard from all of them. Was anybody shooting straight? Plus he hated the news that Cy had gone with Lena to her interviews that morning. They had driven up to Oklahoma City and back, talking, talking. What about? If he could feel the past-clogged, private space between those two, he would probably know everything there was worth knowing about these people.

As he watched Cy walk away, Jettie came up behind him and tapped him on the shoulder. "Lena's big night," she said.

He turned to look at her. She was flushed, the short hairs around her forehead curling with moisture. Sweat soaked through the underarms of her black T-shirt and left a wet line where it had run between her breasts and down her abdomen. She looked exhilarated and cheerful, as of course she would be—they were practicing. If she was aware of Gram's mood, she wasn't letting on. He told her, "You sounded great up there."

"We're going to blow this house down!" She raised her fists in the air. "Lena Wells is coming back!"

He grinned at her. "You really are a huge fan."

"You know it, old son. So are you!"

"Me? Sure, she's—"

"The woman, not the music," she said, rocking back on her hips.

"What do you mean?"

"I know what's going on. You're in love with Lena." She winced a little when she said it. "I understand perfectly."

"Love's a pretty heavy word, Jettie. I've only been here a few days."

"And I'm married anyway, so what's it to me? I'm fine. I'm happy for you!" She waved a dismissive hand and walked off. Ray stared after her. Jettie. Regret batted around in him like a startled bird as he realized he had crossed a line somewhere and left a choice behind. A choice he hadn't realized he had. Later, this moment would return to him often, Jettie searching his face and not finding what she needed there.

Lena came down from the stage and patted Ray on the back. "Hey, you." She looked a little the worse for wear, tension gathering around her mouth and flattening the look in her eyes, but she gave him a quick smile. "You get some good shots on Mount Scott?"

"Gram showed me around," he answered.

"Good, good. If you see Jettie, will you tell her I need to talk to her?" She patted him again distractedly as she walked past the rows of folding chairs to the front door. Apparently that was to be the extent of their conversation.

Ray looked after Lena, confused. He longed to catch up to her, yet he was thoroughly angry at her for jamming up the Black Sheep's plans with Los Lobos and was even angrier with himself for caring about any of it. But he cared about all of it, too much, too much. He wished the concert were not that night. He needed time to cull through the last few days' scenes to catch what he had missed. There had been something: a ghost floating in the air behind him, a quivering chandelier above his head about to drop, a rattling sidewinder poised to spring at his feet. Something.

He ran to catch up with her, grabbing the door as she pushed it open. "Hey, do you need a ride back to the Silver Sun?"

"It's just a few blocks," she said.

"I know, but it's a hot day and you've been up since dawn. You've got a big night tonight."

"I appreciate the offer, but I'd rather walk." Her voice was distant.

"Hey." He touched her shoulder. "Is everything okay?"

"I just feel like circling the wagons is all."

"What do you mean?"

She rubbed her forehead. "I've got a lot on my mind."

"Don't be nervous. I bet it's like riding a bike." His money was on Gram and Jettie's imminent departure as the source of her cross mood, but he wanted to talk her down, not rile her up. "Someone like you never forgets how to perform."

"I'm not nervous."

"What is it, then?" He started to put his arm around her.

She pushed him back, holding both hands in front of her. "Leave me alone, Ray! Shit! It was only three nights. I don't need you in my face right now! Couldn't you practice that goddamn prime directive of yours even once?"

11

CALAMITY

A little while later Ray was in his room, sitting at the table in front of a newly opened bottle of whiskey. He had already drunk all the liquor in the neck of the bottle. He wasn't sure how much that was. A couple of shots, maybe. He knew he needed to get down to the theater. The concert would begin in an hour. The musicians were all in their private quarters getting ready, but Martin and the rest of the crew were already at the theater, waiting for their director.

Martin's voice came over Ray's cell phone tinny and hard to make out. "Are you directing this thing or what?"

"I'll be there soon," Ray said.

"I knocked on your door a little while ago. When you didn't answer I thought you must be here already."

Ray had heard Martin knock. He hadn't been able to rouse himself to answer; the cloud of confusion that had settled over him acted like cotton wool, muting sounds from the outside world and their urgency.

"I'm here with Edmond Gack," Martin said.

"Who the hell is Edmond Gack?"

"The Gacks are the oil family—I'm not going over this again. He's the son, the one who wants to be a director. He wanted to see the show."

"See how the Gacks' money is being spent, you mean? My boss's boss. Damn, I've got a lot of bosses. And who does ol' Edmond answer to? Is there an *uber*-Gack?"

Martin ignored his question. "The show starts in two hours. Did Lena ever give you her set list?"

"Oh, hell no," Ray responded, with more heat than he intended.

"You're upset."

"I guess."

"That's no good."

"No, it's not."

"Uh-oh. What happened? Has she dumped you?"

"I'm not really sure. I think so."

"Shit." There was a long pause. At length Martin said, "All right, bro. Remember what you used to always say in class?"

"What?"

"'You gotta love your subject.' I never really understood how that squared with the prime directive and that whole cool objectivity thing, but I trusted that you knew. I'm not sure you do anymore, or if you ever did, but maybe you could look at it this way: you've blown the prime directive all to hell on this job, but at least you love your subject. And, according to you, that's when the magic happens. Right?"

Ray took a deep breath. "Right, Martin, right."

"So come show me what loving Lena Wells looks like through the lens."

"Martin," Ray said, "you're going to be a great producer." He hung up and rubbed his eyes.

There was a light knock, and Jettie stuck her head in and slipped through the door, leaving it open as she came toward Ray. She was dressed for the show in tight jeans, a black camisole, and green stilettos, wearing red lipstick with the brightness and shine of a candy-apple red Mustang. She looked like she had been crying.

"Come in, come in." Ray rose from his chair. "What's wrong?"

She streaked to the window and looked out on the street, which was by that time crowded with cars searching in vain for parking close to Medicine Hall, and throngs of people on foot weaving among the cars, walking with coolers and cameras from wherever they had parked. Even on the third floor, with the window closed, the sounds of cars honking and people shouting and laughing made their way into the room. It was still full light outside, and hot; the air conditioner trembled with effort.

Jettie faced away from Ray, her tan, muscled arms folded over her chest. She was in a state, shifting foot to foot, awkwardly balancing on the sharp, green heels of her shoes.

"You know that Los Lobos thing I told you about?" Jettie began, turning to face him. "Lena knows, too, turns out. She's acting like we were trying to trick her."

"You talked to her just now?"

"Can you give me a drink?"

Ray found a clean glass in the top drawer of the bureau and poured her a whiskey from his bottle. "Have a seat."

She dropped onto the edge of the bed and took the glass. "Don't let me get drunk. I can't play worth shit when I'm drunk."

She leaned back on her elbows, rubbing the bottom of her glass against the nubby ridges of the chenille bedspread. Evening sunlight from the window streaked across her abdomen. "Lena acted like we were using her. She's got this whole scenario in her head. She says we're just taking the money for playing with her, but really we're dying to shake loose of her."

"She gets scared. She's insecure," Ray assured her. "You wouldn't think it, but she is. I don't think she really thought ten people would show up for this concert tonight."

"But we're not using her! That's not it! We want to do right by her, we want her to do great. It's just that we have this chance with Los Lobos to go out *as the Black Sheep*. We'll almost certainly get signed if we do it. It's a time-sensitive opportunity, you know?"

"You don't have to explain it to me, Jettie. I get it. She doesn't think you're ready, or at least that's what she told Gram."

Jettie sprang to her feet. "Do you know I've been on my own since I was seventeen? Do you know how many songs I've written? More than she has. Maybe I wasn't struck famous when I was eighteen like she was, but I know my business. We've got enough material for three sets, never mind one. She doesn't know what she's talking about."

Ray put up his hands. "I'm on your side. I caught a little hell earlier, too." He felt unaccountably cheered by Jettie's news. It meant that Lena was in a generally bad mood, which could be taken to mean that she was not as specifically angry with him as she had seemed to be. "Tonight's got her scared. Let's just get through this show, and I bet you everything will be sunshine and birdsong in the morning."

"She just fired us. Me and Gram."

"Wait." Ray stood up. "What? Two hours before the concert starts?"

"No, *after* the concert. We're fired *after* the concert." Jettie stared, her eyes blazing. "Ha! How do you like that?"

"Fucking incredible. Why doesn't she think you'll walk away right now?"

"Gram won't. Cy won't."

"But what about you?" He rubbed his chin. "What if you don't play tonight?"

"I can't do that. All those people out there have come to see a show."

"Call her bluff is what I'm saying. Force her to rehire you. She'll have to, and the show can go on."

She looked at Ray as if he had just told her she could fly. "But she could get someone else. Desmond Jones might—"

"Desmond Jones? Her old bass player? You're not thinking straight, Jettie. How would she get him here from wherever he is and get him ready to play her new songs in"—he looked at his watch—"ninety-three minutes?"

"You're right!" she said. "I can say no. Fuck her!" She punched Ray in the arm and danced around, staggering on her heels and falling into him.

He grabbed her by the shoulders, a bond of solidarity sealing his hands to her body. Lena was The Man. They would stick it to The Man. Ray pulled Jettie to him and kissed her until all the whiskey in her mouth was gone and her underlying taste came through, full of sweetness and health.

They pulled apart and endured several seconds' thick silence. "Oops," she said finally, scratching her head and looking at the floor. "I'm sorry."

"My fault," he countered.

She cleared her throat. "So anyway, you're right. I will *not* play tonight under this threat. I'm going to tell Gram right now." She sounded like she was trying to talk herself into it. "Hey, you want to tell him for me? You explained it so great just now. Don't tell him we kissed, though—I feel so bad."

"I think it should come from you," he said.

"You're right, you're right." As she grabbed the door handle, her face broke into a broad smile, and she said, "I knew you'd be on my side."

12

REWIND, DELETE

Ray tucked several blank DV tapes in his bag and put a new one in his camera. He was about to leave for the theater when he heard angry voices outside his room. One was Gram's, louder than he had ever heard it before.

"You're quitting *now?*"

What was Gram doing on the third floor? Jettie must have decided she needed Ray's help explaining after all. Holding his camera, Ray opened the door and peered down the hallway. He heard the snap of Jettie's stilettos on the wood floor of the landing. She and Gram were twenty feet away, near the stairs, both of them yelling, both of them crying. Ray turned on his camera.

"But she fired us!" Jettie said.

"You can't quit before the show. This is a dirty trick, Jettie. She needs us tonight!"

"*This* is a dirty trick? But firing us, that's—what, exactly? You're crazy! Just like her." Jettie was pleading with her husband, holding onto his shirt while Gram was pulling away from her. "I swear to God," she cried, "you people don't make sense!"

Ray saw Gram's hand push out, push Jettie away, and Jettie grasping at him, working to reclaim her center of gravity at the tops of the stilettos.

Then she went over.

There was a moment when she hung in the air, all of her body straining for balance, reaching for a footing, her eyes casting about for something she could hold, and then she was down. In a haze of shock, Ray watched Gram's hand reaching out in space, empty air around it. Ray pushed a button, and Gram's hand drew close to him, and suddenly he realized that he was looking through the view screen of his camera. That he was recording, and had zoomed in on the hand that had pushed Jettie. A perfectly controlled zoom. He heard her ankle snap and then the sound of her body thudding down the hard wood stairs. Her body went limp as she tumbled down, coming to rest on the second-floor landing, the curve of her back caught in a bend in the staircase.

Gram sped down the stairs, calling her name. Ray dropped the camera and followed. He hit his knees in front of her, then felt her wrist for a pulse and found it. She was alive. He pulled out his cell phone. "We need an ambulance," he said into the phone. "At the Silver Sun Hotel in Medicine Park. I said the Silver Sun Hotel. The address—" He looked at Gram who was staring at Jettie and stroking her hair away from the side of her face that was smashed and bleeding. "Gram! I need the address!" Gram told him without looking up.

Ray's tears distorted the light in the room into bright, fracturing patterns like car headlights on a rain-spattered windowpane at night. He didn't remember hearing Lena coming out of her bedroom, but suddenly there she was, dressed for the concert, all mad, fluttering motion, emitting a keening, mechanical screech like the brakes of a freight train.

Gram stood up and caught her, whether to hold her up or fall into her arms, Ray couldn't tell. "The ambulance is coming," Ray said.

Lena got quiet and stared like she had that night on the *Tonight Show*. Yet she was present, too. She stood still, taking in the scene. Processing, processing—Ray could see her processing what she beheld, some part of her approaching and retreating from the reality of Jettie crumpled there on the floor, not yet accepting it, but some part of her mind combing every thread out to its ragged end.

"Mama"—Gram sobbed into Lena's hair—"she just fell. She was there and then—I tried to catch her."

She held him, rubbing her hands up and down his back. "Of course, honey, of course."

After a moment Lena moved him gently aside and went to Jettie. She got on her knees and put her hands all over her, rubbed her back, stroked her hair. "Come on Jettie, girl," she urged. "Come on, Jettie."

Just then they heard the front door open and Cyril's jolly voice boom from below, "Okla-Homa Rock-And-Rollas!" They heard him stomp across the Great Room and start up the stairs. "Any rock and rollers in this house? We got a crowd out there, folks. Let's get to it."

Everyone turned toward the sound of his voice. He came up the stairs and saw Ray and Gram. Then he saw Lena. Then he saw Jettie. "Oh my Lord!" He covered his mouth with his sleeve and dropped to one knee like a medieval knight. "Is she—"

"She's breathing," Ray said. It was hard to say how long they stood there, maybe a long time, watching Jettie breathe, not knowing if the next breath would come. Finally they heard the ambulance sirens come screaming into the parking lot. EMTs poured through the door, their entrance admitting the chaotic blatting of car horns, the talk and cries of the crowd as it pooled around the Silver Sun Hotel. Gram looked at Ray and asked, "Would you cancel the show?"

Ray was processing information like his blood was frozen. He stared and said, "I can't leave her."

"No, *I* can't leave her. We can't leave her," he said, nodding at Lena. "Please go cancel the show, Ray. Don't tell them anything. And wipe the lipstick off your face."

Ray went out the back, leaving the building through the gate behind the carriage house, at the edge of the property. The night was still hot, in the eighties at least, and the air smelled of blooming plants and creek water. He tried to rub the lipstick off his face with the back of his hand, but his hand was shaking. He walked around to the front and crossed the road, skirting the back of the crowd that had gathered around the ambulances. People were standing on the verandah, trying to peer into the windows as he had when he and Martin first arrived. When he got to the theater, it was half full with people who had come early to guarantee their seats. They were standing and talking, looking confused. Martin was at the back of the stage standing next to a bull-necked, tan young man in a golf shirt the color of raspberry sherbet.

"Finally," Martin said when Ray reached him. "Where's the band? The crowd's antsy all of a sudden. Do you know what's going on?" He eyed Ray, and the impatience evaporated from his expression as he picked up on Ray's distress. "What's going on?"

"I have to cancel the show."

"Ray! What's happening?"

"It's Jettie."

Ray walked robotically to the front of the stage and leaned into the center microphone. "I'm afraid I have some bad news. The show tonight is cancelled. I'm very sorry, the band is very sorry. Please leave the venue in an orderly fashion."

A roar went up from the crowd and he could hear their questions. *What's going on? What's happened? Where's Lena? Is Lena okay?* Ray looked down at a field of faces staring back, their heat and energy sliding across his shock like oil over water. He felt what Lena had described, their hunger for news, for a big event, for a death. At the back of the theater, standing in an aisle, stood the guy in the silver spacesuit, staring, arms straight down at his sides. He was still as a statue but for the bobbing of the Saturn rings around his head.

"Lena is fine," Ray said, hearing his own voice bounce off the walls of the room. "But there's been a terrible accident."

13

BLOODLINES

The bright lights of the Comanche County Memorial Hospital emergency room made Ray's eyes water. His cold blue shock was changing to a hot rage he could barely keep under control. He stood with Martin and Edmond Gack at the front desk, calling Lena on his cell. She wasn't answering, so he tried Cy with the same result.

"What about Gram?" Martin asked.

"I don't have his number," Ray said.

"I've got it," Martin said. He dialed and leaned over the counter with his hands over both ears. "Gram? This is Martin Parker. Ray and I are at the hospital. They won't let us in. But we just want to—no, of course, no cameras. I understand. Okay. Good, thanks." He looked at the nurse. "The family is calling you now."

The phone on the nurse's desk rang, and when she got off, she let Ray, Martin, and Edmond Gack sign in and directed them to the intensive care unit. Ray strode fast down the hospital corridors, with big, out-of-shape Martin and sporty Edmond Gack panting to keep up with him. The intensive care unit was a dimly lit, horseshoe-shaped room with a nursing station in the middle. Individually curtained areas went around the horseshoe, like pods in some sci-fi movie, with names written on small dry-erase boards pinned to their curtains. Ray saw "Waycross" at the top of the horseshoe and recognized Lena's purple velvet platform heels under the curtain. He stopped, suddenly terrified to go any further. Since the accident, he had stayed in the moment better than he ever had in his life, clawing minute-to-minute like a climber on a cliff-face, the roar of what-ifs and imagined scenarios drowned out by each minute's demands. But now as he stood in the dull green light, they flooded him. What was he about to learn? He wasn't sure he could take it. A smell of metal, of pennies, of blood filled his nostrils. The sound of heavy breathing emanated from behind the curtains, ventilators, multiple ventilators. Everything was animate, everything malevolent. The world had never shown him this face before. Edmond Gack tapped him on the arm and said, in a voice that could have been used for returning a borrowed pen, "I believe she's there." He pointed at Jettie's name.

Ray rounded on him, looking down at his waxy scalp that showed through the gelled clumps of short dark hair and the empty earring holes in both ears. "Who are you?" Ray asked. "What the hell are you doing following us here?"

Martin stepped up and smiled with all his teeth. "Ray, I told you this is Edmond Gack."

"I don't understand why you're traipsing around behind us, Edmond Gack." The supercilious kid, who reminded Ray of a certain type of privileged, dull-witted student he had never enjoyed, was bringing out the worst in Ray. People like Edmond Gack were hard enough to tolerate, but to have him here, at a time of utmost gravity, was too much. Ray felt himself sucked toward the possibility of violence. "We're not going to a keg party. Is that where you thought we were going? Why don't you run along?"

Gack smiled. "Nice to finally meet you, Mr. Wheeler. I've been reading about the lawsuit being brought against you. It's come up in our efforts to insure this project. You're hard to insure—did you know that?"

Ray shook his head. "Not surprised," he said.

"I certainly hope the lawsuit resolves itself soon, for your sake, or we may have to find someone else."

Ray rubbed the back of his neck and stared up at the long tubes of fluorescent lights. Then he pushed Edmond Gack hard in the center of the chest. Gack stumbled backward into a cart full of supplies, which went skidding out from behind him into the nurse's station. A nurse leapt to her feet. Gack landed on the floor, his eyes locked on Ray with wild incredulity.

"What the fuck—" Gack yelled.

"Gentlemen," the nurse said, "gentlemen, I insist that you leave. Leave now." Martin looked like he was about to cry.

In a low, reasonable voice, Ray said, "I'm sorry, but people are in crisis, Edmond Gack. Right now, in crisis. You have misread the situation. Now, I told you before—go on home."

The nurse stepped between them. While she was facing Gack, who was getting to his feet, Ray crossed to Jettie's curtain. He felt along it until he found the invisible seam. "Lena," he whispered, "it's Ray."

He stepped behind the curtain and was in a different world. He forgot about Edmond Gack as he saw Jettie in a bed, her wavy blond hair caked with blood, her eyes closed, and the right side of her face swollen and bruised. Her right leg was elevated. Lena and Gram were standing next to the bed, and Cy sat behind them on a black plastic chair beneath the heart rate monitor, his legs crossed at his ankles, his hands knitted together in his lap.

"Come in," Lena said, glancing at him.

Martin followed Ray in, and they stood at the end of the bed, the curtain brushing their backs. No one said anything for a few seconds until finally Ray said, "For God's sake, is she going to be okay?"

Without looking up, Gram said, "She's in a coma."

Ray felt his knees start to collapse under him and grabbed the bed rail.

"But she's breathing on her own," Lena said, giving Gram an encouraging nod. "And—and this is big—her brain activity is okay."

"Thank God, thank God." Ray rubbed his palms over his face.

"What are they saying?" Martin said. "Will she wake up?"

"Nobody knows," Cy said. He leaned forward. "Maybe tomorrow, maybe next week, maybe never."

"That's really the best they can tell you?" Ray said. He reached out and stroked the side of Jettie's elevated bare foot. Her toes were painted the same shade of car-paint red that she favored in lipstick when she was onstage. "Tomorrow or never?"

The next morning, Ray and Cimarron headed back to the Silver Sun Hotel from the Kwik Stop out on Highway 54 where Ray had gone to buy dog food. He couldn't get into Gram and Jettie's carriage house to feed the dog, and Gram hadn't returned home from the hospital. The dog had found him that morning, nudging his thigh with her huge head when he came down to the kitchen. Edith, who sat at the breakfast table staring vacantly out the window, said, "She's hungry. I'll go by the store later."

"I'll do it," Ray had said. "I need to feel useful." He had knelt down and massaged the skin under her collar and stroked the sides of her face back to her ears, running his fingers out to the thin, pink tips. Cimarron gave a low groan and pressed her face against Ray's palm. Jettie's dog. "What kind of dog is this?"

"Great Pyrenees," she said.

Ray drove with the windows down while Cimarron rode in front next to him, with her head high in the breeze, the wind flapping her gums and pulling back the skin of her head. It was a beautiful day, a day that didn't know who was lying in a coma. Cimarron barked all the way, and every so often she gave a high, hurting yelp, as if the piercing notes of the ambulance sirens had permanently challenged her range.

When he got back to the Silver Sun, the core group of would-be-concert-goers was still hanging around, some of the same ones who had come days early. There was the dude in the silver lamé suit. Not the same suit, surely. He wasn't sure what would be weirder, a guy who would wear the same silver lamé spaceman suit day after day or a guy who would own multiple silver lamé spaceman suits. Why were they still hanging around? The concert cancellation should have driven everyone home.

In the kitchen he found two stainless-steel mixing bowls in a cabinet and filled one with dog food, the other with water. He heard the stairs creaking and Martin's loping steps coming across the Great Room. Cimarron didn't look up from her food.

Martin appeared at the far end of the kitchen. "Poor Cimarron," he remarked.

"I'm babysitting."

Martin, who didn't drink coffee, reached into the refrigerator and pulled out a carton of milk. "Is this day real?"

"I can't say." Ray regarded him, wanting to reach out and say something that would share his hurt. He settled for "How you doing?"

Martin grabbed a peach from the bowl of fruit on the counter and stared at it as if he didn't know what it was. "Why were they on the third floor?" he asked.

Never interfere with the fate of a civilization. It had seemed cut and dry, the prime directive. But Jettie had come to him needing his advice, and he had given it. *Quit, Jettie. Call her bluff.* If he had stuck to his principles, Jettie wouldn't be in a coma. Why did he never see the line when he was stepping across? "I think they were coming to see me. Jettie wanted me to talk to Gram." Dread moved through him like floodwater as he watched his friend's bulky frame move toward him. "I have to tell you something, Martin. I filmed it."

Martin dropped into the chair next to Ray, his gut settling like a sandbag. "Say what?"

"I was on my way out the door to the theater, had my camera right there. When I heard them yelling, I turned it on. It was like a reflex."

"That's really—"

"Fucked up, I know."

"It's more than fucked up, partner. It's a pattern. Filming when you shouldn't have––it's exactly what you did in Rio Marron. First Chester, now Jettie."

"Hey, come on. I turned off the camera after we heard the gunshot." Ray covered his face with his hands. His objection sounded thin, even to him. He felt like a hole had opened up in his center that was quickly widening, chunks of himself falling through it as his ledge of self grew narrower. "I know, I know, I know. Martin, I know. But listen. Gram pushed her."

"What are you saying to me? Let's go back to the part about you."

"I don't think he meant to, exactly, but he pushed her. I got it on film."

"Are you serious?"

"I don't know what to do. I don't know if it's a police matter."

"I don't know, either," Martin said. "Is it, like, evidence? Where is it?"

"In my camera," Ray said. He looked around Lena's kitchen and wished for home, for his own, much smaller, much darker kitchen in his small house in Austin. He missed the peeling linoleum and the damp smell of mold from the leaking garbage disposal. He missed the incessant sound of I-35 traffic, his living room covered with vintage movie posters, and the ability to order out—pizza, Chinese, whatever, whenever he wanted. God, he was tired.

His cell phone rang. He stood up and fished it from his pocket, recognizing his father's number as he answered. "Dad." Calling from his office in the old, normal part of the world.

Martin left the kitchen and, after a few seconds, Ray heard his steps climbing the stairs.

"How's it going, Raymond?" The sound of his father's voice reached into him like an anchor.

"I'm still sucking air, Dad. That's about all I can claim today. What's up?"

"I tell you what, Native American genealogy is fascinating! Here's what I think, Ray, if we wanted to make a sequel to *Paper Trail*. I think we could tell some fascinating stories, untold American stories. The big chiefs—they were intriguing men. Most of them had lots of kids—we could find a few descendants and tell the story of what happened to the generations in between!"

"Did you find something, Dad?"

"Why, you bet! No challenge at all. It's not exactly like finding a link to the first king of Scotland. We're only talking a few generations, here. Your Lena Wells, she's got a great-granddad—her mother's father's father—who was probably some kind of distant cousin to Geronimo. He was Chiricahua Apache, like Geronimo. Came with him from Arizona, on the manifest for the same surrender. Tribe wasn't that big, so they probably are related somehow. There's no record of the generations before."

"She's not a great-granddaughter, then."

"Not as such. She and Geronimo probably do have a common ancestor, but so do we all if you go back far enough."

Ray tried to muster a grateful response for his father. The minor biographical note on Lena seemed like debris from an old, destroyed world.

His father continued, "It was easy—just a few generations to track down. It's kind of a shame her line dies with her."

"No," Ray said. "She's got a son."

"The adopted kid? Well, that doesn't count for bloodlines."

"Adopted?" Ray blinked. "What are you talking about?"

"Well, the birth certificate's sealed, even for a world-renowned researcher like yours truly. I was curious about his birth parents, but I couldn't find out a thing. Don't think I didn't try, though! Why, I flirted to beat the band with that little lady in the records office. Hard to flirt on the phone, I find, don't you, son?—"

Ray leaned his forehead against the sliding glass door and looked out at the gazebo, white in the sun. "Adoption papers. Gram Wells is adopted?"

"I figured you knew."

"I did not."

"Big news?"

"It is."

"Glad to help, Raymond."

Ray hung up the phone. "Son of a bitch," he said.

14

RANK OUTSIDER

As soon as he got off the phone, Ray heard the rumble of a motorcycle out front. Cy came into the kitchen a minute later carrying a small, white Styrofoam cooler.

Cimarron groaned like an old bear as she pulled herself up stiffly from the tile floor, revealing the air-conditioning vent she had been laying over, and lumbered over to Cy. He reached out his hand and scratched her long jaw.

"I can keep her outside if you think I should," Ray said.

"Too hot," Cy said. "You holding up?"

Ray crossed his arms. "I just—she was in my room, you know? Standing right there—"

Cy pointed at the Styrofoam cooler now sitting on the floor. "I brought y'all some fish."

"You've been fishing?"

"There was nothing I could do at the hospital."

Cy got to his feet, headed into the kitchen, and went straight for a cupboard where he pulled out a deep fryer and plugged it in.

"I'm not hungry," Ray said.

"Me either." Cy poured cooking oil into the fryer and switched it on. He whipped up a cornmeal batter and scraped it onto a plate. "Go fetch me the pepper," he said to Ray. Cimarron resumed her position on the cool tiles of the floor.

"I found something out today," Ray said. "Really surprising."

"What's that?" Cy was dropping pieces of fish into a bowl of Tabasco sauce and then rolling them in the dry, seasoned batter.

"Gram is adopted."

Cy's hand stopped in midair, a piece of fish suspended from his fingers. For long seconds, he stared at the yellow grease just beginning to bubble in the fryer. Ray saw that he knew all about it. What was it Cy had said about his relationship with Lena? He saw her every day. He knew her real as real.

Ray continued, "But she told me all about how being pregnant saved her. Did she invent the pregnancy? Adopt a baby and call it her own?"

Cy resumed his work, his hands moving in quick, efficient jerks. Without looking up, he said, "This is not the time for that, Ray. We're all pulling for Jettie right now."

"Of course," Ray said. "I'm sorry, but I just found out, and I'm trying to make sense of it."

"Stop trying. It's none of your business."

"Gram's been wondering who his dad is. I couldn't understand why she wouldn't tell him. I thought maybe she didn't know."

Cy leveled a gaze at him so dark that Ray took a step back from the sharp knife covered in fish gore and the boiling oil. He leaned against the refrigerator and crossed his arms. "But now I *get* it. It's not that she doesn't know the answer—it's because it's the wrong question!"

"Lena is his mother," Cy said. "She raised him, loved him. And she saved him, I tell you. From a bad life. Just because she didn't give birth to him—"

"Hey, I have no problem with adoption. You people are the ones who are lying about it."

Cy nodded, took the point. "I've always said she needs to tell him. She won't hear of it—" He stopped midsentence and busied himself with the fish as Martin lurched into the room.

"Something smells good," Martin said, then turned to Ray. "We need to talk."

"I'm in the middle of something."

"Soon, okay? I watched your tape." Martin gave Ray an uneasy look and then pulled a yellow sticky note from his hatband, handing it to him. "In the meantime, here's a message. Hope you don't mind I answered your cell. Desmond Jones." He wiped the back of his hand across his nose.

Lena's old bass player. Ray took the paper. "That's a local number."

"Cy? Do you know anything about this?" Martin said.

Cy reached into the cooler on the counter and pulled out another fish, rinsed it at the sink, and centered it on the cutting board. He sighted the knife along the body and took off the head with one fast cut.

Ray said, "Cyril, does Desmond Jones live around here?"

Cy rested his hands against the countertop, knife up, and made a show of thinking about it. "I believe so," he said finally. After a quick, evaluative glance at Ray and Martin, he added, "Saw him recently."

"How recently?"

"Let's see. A few minutes ago. I think it was him. Pretty sure," he said, and then walked out of the kitchen into the Great Room. They followed him, giving each other bewildered looks as Cy stepped out onto the front porch. He rocked back on his biker boots and nodded in the direction of the encampment of fans. "Down there."

Ray let himself be distracted. Down Medicine Park's heat-baked main drag toward the theater, he headed with Martin, knowing that Cy would be gone when they got back. The fans were playing the soundtrack to *Ballad of Belle Starr* on their boom box that afternoon. The final song on the album was starting, a mournful ballad called "The Bad Kind" that played over the scene in the film where Belle Starr is gunned down. Three tents were still arrayed in the dirty yard in front of the theater. Most of the remaining fans, nine or ten of them, were swimming around in Medicine Creek, a few feet below.

Ray nearly tripped over a kerosene lantern.

"Watch it," said a voice, and he looked around to see a round little woman in a sort of cheap, velveteen version of one of Lena's stage getups, flowy with feathers, and very, very insulated for such a hot day.

"My goodness," Ray said, turning to take her in. She had a pale, clear face with freckles and the barest trace of crow's feet. "Has anyone ever told you that you look like Lena Wells?"

"I don't look like her," she informed him, in the voice of someone who prided herself on straight talk. "I'm dressed like her."

"Maybe that's what it is," Ray agreed. He shifted into professional mode now, cheerful, forthright. Faking it.

She introduced herself as Penelope Scaggs, a CPA in the nearby town of Altus. "What can I do for you?"

"I'm making a documentary. Don't know if you heard about it."

"We heard," she said, not unfriendly.

"Why are you folks still here, if you don't mind my asking?"

She looked surprised at the question. "We're waiting for news of Jettie."

"Is Desmond Jones around?" Martin asked.

A long-haired man with round glasses stepped out of the water and joined them, running a towel across his bony shoulders. "He's not here." He introduced himself as Clark Pepper, owner of a chain of health food stores in Oklahoma City.

"Do you know when he'll be back?" Ray smiled at Clark, and the smile felt real. Sometimes the line between appearance and reality was that easy—step right over and make believe.

"Sure don't. He had to go feed his cats. He's got a lot of cats."

Martin walked toward the creek and scanned the group of people in the water, most of whom paid them no mind. "Say," he said. "He's not the spaceman is he? The dude in the silver getup? Because I don't see that guy anywhere."

Penelope laughed. "That's Desmond all right."

"I'll be damned." Ray raked a hand through his hair. "I'll just be damned. I thought I'd have to fly to L.A. to talk to that guy. Desmond Jones is the spaceman?"

Clark Pepper said, "Desmond's one of those who believes in opening the doors of perception, you know."

"Ah."

"The doors are pretty much hanging off their hinges now, if you know what I mean."

So Desmond Jones was fried. Ray had wondered why he hadn't been in the mix for Lena's concert.

"He lives somewhere up that mountain." Penelope pointed behind them at the mountain on the east end of town. A dirt road leading up it branched off Riverside Drive, the main road that passed in front of the Silver Sun. It was hard to see what was up there except a few rooftops and an adobe church near the top. "Is he friendly?" Ray asked, knowing he would have to go talk to him.

"Oh, he's a lovely man," Penelope said.

But Ray didn't have to trek up the mountain to talk to Desmond. As Ray climbed the stairs from the creek's promenade to the main street, with Martin following, he met Desmond at the top of the steps, where they had met before. Once again, the spaceman greeted him with a sweeping bow. "Did you get my message?"

"Yes, sir," Ray said. "I'm happy you called."

"How is Buzz?"

"Buzz?"

"Jettie. I always call her Buzz 'cause of how she's like a danged bee. Busy, busy."

"In a coma."

The white skin inside his crow's feet revealed itself as the bottoms of Desmond's mouth pulled down, stretching his features. He looked at the creek, seeming to lose himself in the water rushing over the waterfall. "She's still here," he said finally. "I can feel her. She'll be back. She's a fighter, is little Buzz."

"You know her, I take it."

"Of course I know her, know them all. I played with the Lighthorsemen right up to the end. I wasn't even consulted about this comeback—wasn't even invited! I know they've got Jettie on bass, but we could've both played. Am I right? You can't have too much rhythm section, am I right? Jettie's the only one that don't seem sick to death of me. Don't get a lot of respect, especially from Gram, but I guess that's to be expected."

"What's to be expected?" Martin asked.

Desmond turned his watery blue gaze on Martin. "I suppose he's mad. Gram's hurt. He doesn't know about me but he knows in his heart."

Ray folded his arms. "Doesn't know about you?" He was beginning to get it, but he needed to hear Desmond confirm the truth.

"Why I let Lena adopt him, yes. That's got to be hard for a boy to comprehend."

"Are you saying you're Gram's father?"

"She's going to tell him. I stay around for the day he wants to talk to me, but it hasn't happened yet. I'd be lying if I said I wasn't discouraged. He used to love the planets when he was little." He patted the springy planets of his headgear and began to walk off. "Buzz needs the waters," he added, nodding at Medicine Creek flashing in the sunlight. "I'll bring some to her. Tell Lena that. Tell Lena I'm coming."

Jettie had been moved to a private room. When Ray called the hospital, Lena picked up.

"How is she?" Ray asked.

"Same," Lena said. She didn't elaborate. After what seemed like a long time, Ray asked, "And how are you?"

"I'm fine. Ray, I need to get off the phone."

"I'm so sorry about all of this, Lena. You're not alone, are you? Is Gram still there?"

She let him know that Gram was on his way home to get some sleep.

"You should get some sleep, too," he urged.

"Later," she said.

Ray dropped his cell phone into his pants pocket. Her voice had been full of pain, but he didn't think the pain had anything to do with him. Him she was done with. What had happened between him and Lena had evaporated like a heat mirage on the highway. It was over like it had never happened, nothing more than a patch of dry asphalt no different from the rest of the highway once you got close and sped over it. He knew he should feel something about this parting, but he was too full to feel anything. The simple, shocking fact of Jettie teetering between life and death absorbed all the energy he had for anything else.

He did, however, register that Gram's departure from the hospital room meant it was a good moment for him to visit. He had so much on his mind regarding Gram that he wasn't sure he could talk to him at all. Ray had always hewed to F. Scott Fitzgerald's belief that the mark of a first-rate intelligence was the ability to hold opposing ideas in the mind and retain the ability to function, but his thoughts about Gram had taken him to the limits of his abilities. In the last day, he had gone from concern to near-hatred to mortification and back to near-hatred. As long as all those states coexisted in his mind, he doubted he could string two words together if he had to talk to him.

But as he was walking to his Jeep, Gram's white RAM truck pulled into the parking lot and drew up next to him. Gram got out. With a day's growth on his beard and blue circles under his eyes, he looked ten years older.

"I'm on my way to see Jettie right now," Ray told him, taking out his keys and rushing to open his door.

"I bet you are."

Ray ignored his hostility. "How is she?"

"How do you think?" Gram dug his hands deep in the front pockets of his jeans and ambled around the Jeep so that he was standing by Ray.

"I don't know, Gram, that's why I asked."

"I thought you were my friend, you know? I confided in you."

"I am—" Ray looked down.

"You're everybody's friend, I guess. What were you doing with Jettie? I can't believe it!"

"We were both upset—nothing was going on. Besides, you're in no position to get on your high horse with me, son."

"What are you talking about?"

"I saw what you did."

Gram shook his head. "*What* are you talking about?"

"When you were fighting? On the landing?"

"Dude, I have no idea what—"

"You pushed her."

Gram's expression stiffened. "Fuck you," he said. "Fuck you." He pointed at Ray as he pushed by him.

Some device near Jettie's bed was making a beeping sound that sounded like an elevator door opening and closing over and over again. Her hair had been cleaned and brushed and spread out on her pillow. One side of her face was still swollen and dark with bruising. Lena was still there, asleep in a soft chair next to the bed, her elbow on the armrest with her head propped up by the palm of her hand.

Ray wished he had his camera for a minute. Part of him was still making the documentary, and during the last few days, he had gotten into the habit of noticing moments that showed Lena in a flattering light. Here with her daughter-in-law—that was flattering. How Jettie got here, the stunt Lena had pulled when she fired her right before the Medicine Ball, was less so.

A man and a woman dressed nearly alike in khaki shorts and Dockers stood on the side of the bed gazing at Jettie. The small, sandy-haired man had his arm around the woman, whose face was in her hands. He had Jettie's eyes.

Ray cleared his throat. "Excuse me," he said. "I can come back another time."

Lena opened her eyes. "Beverly, Lou, this is Ray Wheeler. Ray, these are Lou and Beverly Waycross, Jettie's parents." As Ray shook hands with the Waycrosses, Lena said to all of them, "Excuse me, I'll be in the cafeteria."

"That Lena Wells," Beverly Waycross sighed, looking after Lena with red-rimmed eyes. "Jettie sure worshipped her. Since she was a little girl."

"Jettie's part of their family now. Lena loves her like her own daughter," Ray said. He wasn't sure it was true, but there was no decent impulse now but to comfort these people.

"Jettie's already got a mother," Mrs. Waycross rasped. "I'm her mother."

"I just meant that since she married Gram—"

"You're trying to take away the thing we could hate," Lou Waycross said.

"I beg you pardon?"

"Hating Lena Wells comes easy, Mr. Wheeler. I want to hate her. If it weren't for that woman, Jettie would be home with us. If we believe your pretty words about Lena Wells, then what? What do we do with all this feeling?" He was crying now, his face shining red.

Ray thought of Jettie's years in Austin, how long it had been since Jettie had lived at home, and he nearly corrected Mr. Waycross, but instead he said, "I'm sorry."

With ragged breaths, Mrs. Waycross said, "It's my fault, in a way. I used to like Lena Wells and the Lighthorsemen when Jettie was little." She looked to her husband who nodded confirmation. "If I'd known she'd take to that music like she did, I promise you, I'd never have played it. She ended up thinking she was a musician, too. Singer"—she drew the word out with bitter sarcasm—"guitar player. Of all the fool things. I don't suppose she really was, was she? A singer? A guitar player?"

Mrs. Waycross puckered her mouth with distaste, the skin above her lips wrinkled from frequent use of that expression. Watching her, Ray saw everything that Jettie had been running from, but then too, his pain made him sensitive to Mrs. Waycross's. She was scared and sad, and hurt, no doubt hurt. She felt rejected by Jettie. "Mrs. Waycross"—he reached for her hands, startling her—"of course she is a musician. Of course she is."

Mr. Waycross scratched his cheek and considered Ray. "She wasn't just lying to herself?"

"Oh, no. No, sir. She's good. She's on her way." Now it was their turn to watch Ray cry. He pulled his hands away from Mrs. Waycross and shielded his eyes while the full weight of Jettie's plight hit him. He could hear himself, but the sounds seemed remote, like they belonged to someone else. He saw the infinite silence that stretched around Jettie in all directions, the vast, terrifying silence she had tried to push back with her songs. With her music, she had cleared a space in the silence around her just a bit, like a lamplight in the desert, a small and finite soundscape in a surrounding silence that went on and on forever. Almost nobody had heard. Unless she woke up, nobody ever would.

"I never listened to her songs," Mrs. Waycross said. "She sent us a tape once, but I just couldn't make myself listen to it. I thought she would be terrible, you know. I put it in the junk drawer in the kitchen and every time I'd look in there, digging around for scissors or what have you, why, I'd see that little cassette and feel so embarrassed. Who does she think she is? That's what I couldn't understand." She reached into her purse and pulled out a black cassette tape, lifting her eyes to Ray. "Do you want it?"

"Are you sure?" He wiped the tears from his face.

"We were going to listen to it on the drive here. We couldn't do it."

"Won't you want it if she—"

"We've got a house full of pictures, Mr. Wheeler, from the day she was born. Recital video, graduation video, you name it. None of it will help if she doesn't wake up."

Ray took the tape. "If you don't want it—thank you." More was required, but he couldn't come up with it.

Mr. Waycross put both hands on his wife's shoulders. Responding to something he saw in Ray's face, he said, "You shouldn't judge us, Mr. Wheeler. Parenting is hard."

"I'll leave you," Ray said. He pulled out his wallet and handed Beverly Waycross his card. "If you ever change your mind and want this back, let me know."

15

DEAD GIVEAWAY

After leaving the hospital, Ray slid the cassette into the tape deck of his Jeep. He couldn't remember the last time he had listened to a cassette and was alarmed by its fragility, the thin brown ribbon that the music was written on crinkled and loose against the spools. The Waycrosses hadn't even carried it in its case, which Ray was sure Jettie would have sent, along with a track list. He heard the hiss of the tape slipping across the playback head, then he was nearly knocked into oncoming traffic by the sound of Jettie's voice. The tape started abruptly; all of a sudden her gentle laugh filled the space around him. It was a live recording. As Ray sped into the setting sun, he imagined her blinded by stage lights, looking out into the audience. "Well hey, everybody," she called out. She paused for a few seconds to let the applause die down, shading her eyes with her hand, just watching them. "This one's called 'Dead Giveaway.'"

The song was one of Lena's, the second track on *Keep Your Powder Dry*; it was never a hit in the United States—too grim—but it charted in England and Japan. In Lena's record collection he had seen a pristine 45 still in its dust jacket with Japanese writing and a humorously incongruous photograph of Lena in her Belle Starr costume.

The audio was sludgy, Jettie's voice carried off by the wind, but still, she was nailing it.

> *There's lots you can learn*
> *And plenty to say*
> *Once you can hear*
> *What the dead give away.*

When Lena sang the lyrics, there was solemn conviction—she knew whereof she spoke—but there was a winsome suggestiveness in Jettie's phrasing, like she was trying to lead you to some clarity even as the chorus ramped up.

> *Dead giveaway*
> *It's all very clear*
> *Dead giveaway*
> *I'm headlights*
> *You're deer.*

Jettie's delivery took some of the fear out of the lyrics, but Ray wasn't sure those lyrics didn't need their fear. As Gram's guitar lifted off, Ray noticed that the cold, reliable part of his mind got busy, analyzing and comparing, just as if the two versions of the song were mere data and not the work of these two women who had changed his life in less than a week. The realization scared him, not because it suggested he was heartless—he knew he wasn't—but because he was helpless against both parts of himself, the part that loved and the part that turned everything into material. Horrible, it was horrible.

He passed the Signal Flare and noticed the glowing marquee out front by the road, which said, in mismatched black-and-red plastic letters:

gET WelL s00n SWEEt JETtiE WAyCRoss
NO blACK SheeP SHOws tiL FUrTHer nOTIce
2 4 1 drAws All day

He switched off the CD player and drove in silence, passing two cars, a Camry and a 4-Runner, that bore Lena's dealer logo. Heading west toward Medicine Park, he sped by the turn to a dirt road that he recognized as the way to Cy's house. He turned around and doubled back, then he took the turn. In a few minutes he found himself creeping into the driveway marked DODGE CITY. The house was dark. A cattle gate was swung closed and locked across the drive. The sound of the Jeep's wheels crunching gravel brought Cy's two dogs flying up the yard. They got to the fence and ran along it, barking. He took out his cell phone and called Cy's number, letting it ring. Nobody home.

He was thinking of those pictures in the barn. He wanted to see them again. He thought he remembered Desmond Jones sitting next to Justine Oxley in one of them, but he wasn't sure. It would make sense if Justine Oxley were Gram's mother, but he would have to know the circumstances of her death to understand why Lena had adopted Gram and never told him. He would find out where Desmond lived, but in the meantime he wanted to see Justine Oxley's image again. In the light of the probable truth, he wanted to see the face of Gram's mother, this woman Lena had denied knowing except as a photographer she had used once. He got out of his car and tried the lock, feeling the dogs' hot breath on his hands as they pressed against the other side of the fence, yapping and snarling. Hopeless.

He climbed back into the Jeep and drove back to the Silver Sun. Within minutes he was parking in its gravel lot. Light poured through the purple and orange stained glass of the front door. He slammed his car door and trotted the length of the verandah, his footsteps loud across the boards. Before he walked in, his phone rang. Lauren.

"Ray, I realized I didn't explain your settlement options to you well enough. This offer to pay for Lord's kid's college—this is a good offer. I worked hard on getting you a structured settlement like this. The other option is you get hit with a big bill up front, and I mean big. And here's another thing—you wouldn't have to pay the full sticker price. Rice would assess what you can pay and make up the difference. They're good that way."

Ray leaned against a red stone pillar. "You think I'm going to lose!"

"They got a statement from Johnny Reyes saying you put him up to it."

"That's not true—" he began. But he stopped. The truth was, he wasn't sure.

"Ray, I think there are certain kinds of responsibility you've never taken. You're naive—you think you can just wander this earth and film what you want with no obligations. It's not true. It's the same way you treated our relationship. You thought you got to hang out in my life, enjoy everything in it, and accept no responsibility for my happiness. I don't know where you got this idea, darling, but it's long past time to grow up."

"I didn't need this lecture today, Lauren, I really didn't." He told her what had happened with Jettie.

"Oh, God, I'm sorry. So sorry. But Ray," she persisted, "this is exactly what I mean. You want to stand behind that camera and leave no trace of yourself, but you leave more than a trace, you leave flaming wreckage behind you. You need to think about this settlement offer a little harder."

"I can't," Ray said. "I promise to think about it tomorrow, Lauren. I'll put on my thinking cap."

He was exhausted, and more darkness crowded his mind than he had the energy to keep at bay. He walked into the Silver Sun intending to go directly to bed, but Martin called out to him. He was sitting in the living room watching *Hail! Hail! Rock 'n' Roll*, the Taylor Hackford documentary on Chuck Berry that was his bible for this project. Ray's camera was sitting next to Martin on the leather couch. No one else seemed to be around.

"Where is everybody?" Ray asked.

"Lena came in a few minutes ago and went straight upstairs. She couldn't figure out how she beat you home."

"I took the scenic route."

"There's catfish under the paper towels on the counter," Martin said. "And Edith made coleslaw. It's in the fridge."

Ray dropped into a recliner and wished again for his own dark, smelly little house in Austin. If he were in his own recliner he'd be staring at a poster for *Ride the High Country* instead of Martin's dour face. "I think we should clear out. I feel like we're intruding." He couldn't imagine that Lena or Gram, or Cy for that matter, wanted him around now or ever. It dawned on him that the weeklong probation Lena had put him on wasn't even up yet. He laughed.

"What's so funny?"

"I don't think I'm going to survive my probation."

"They want us to stay, Lena told me. A few more days, just to wait and see. I got the feeling that if we left it would feel like losing hope for Jettie. I told them we'd stay a while longer."

"Well, I need to do some things in Texas. We won't be doing any work for the next couple of days, and I'll leave in the morning and be back the day after. I've got my phone." Ray hadn't known what he was planning until he said it, but there it was. He was feeling superstitious, like if he fixed the mess from his last film, the mess of this one would right itself too. He needed to see Johnny Reyes, get him to retract the statement he'd made to Chester Lord's lawyer. He had to talk sense into Lord in person, minus the lawyers. He had accepted Martin's statement earlier that day that Chester's and Jettie's injuries amounted to a pattern. His pattern, his fault.

"Bring some real beer when you come back," Martin said. "Did you know all the beer in this state is 3.2 percent? It didn't bother me in high school, but I'm not used to it anymore."

"I didn't know you cared that much about beer."

"Neither did I. A twelve-pack of Lone Star. No, make it a case."

"You got it, boss. Do you think anybody would mind if I took Cimarron with me?"

"In the current state of things I don't think anyone would notice. Are you ready to talk about that tape you made last night?"

"I'm going to get me a 3.2 beer. Want one?"

When Ray came back from the kitchen with a beer in each hand, Martin had paused *Hail! Hail! Rock 'n' Roll* on an image of Keith Richards waving a cigarette, sitting eye-level with a bathroom sink. Martin had turned on Ray's camera. He patted the space next to him.

"Should we turn it over to the police?" Ray asked. For almost the first time in his life, he was happy to have someone else's judgment to defer to. He set the beers on the coffee table in front of them. "I can't process it. When I think of Jettie, I want justice but when I think about Gram, I get confused."

"Sit down, Ray." Martin leaned forward with his elbows on his knees and gave Ray a look that made him feel like the younger man. "You've been in a tailspin since the night Chester Lord got shot. I've been watching you, hoping you'd right yourself. The work you're doing on this project has been great—but I think you're still spinning."

Ray looked at his watch. 6:30. "Twenty-four hours ago Jettie was in my bedroom telling me her troubles. Now she's in a coma. I am most definitely spinning, my friend."

Martin gave Ray a careful, sympathetic look. "Eyewitness testimony is so unreliable, you know. And people don't mean to lie. It happens all the time, Ray, we talked about it in your class. People see things according to their feelings. They're trying to make sense of chaos as it happens, and their minds put it into patterns that make sense to them. They don't see anything else. It's as honest a mistake as there is, but Ray, I got to tell you, it's still a mistake."

An eerie sustain trailed off the end of each passing second. "I don't understand what you're saying to me, Martin. Did you see that tape?"

Martin took a long drink of beer. "The tape is what I'm talking about."

The two men stared at each other. "I didn't want to have to watch it," Ray said finally. "But I'm afraid I'm going to have to."

"I think that's a good idea." Martin picked up Ray's camera and hit play. Ray leaned forward to watch the footage play in the small screen below the viewfinder. When it began, Ray had a strong impulse to flee. His breath was coming fast and shallow, and he had to grip his knees to keep still.

The tape began with lurching shadows and then shifted to a shot of Ray's shoes. Then he had raised the camera. Light. The hallway and sounds. Then Jettie and Gram, in full view, perfectly framed, in the hallway walking with their backs to the camera, yelling at each other, hurt in both their voices. It was exactly as Ray remembered it. The last thing Jettie said was "I swear to God, you people don't make sense!"

Ray thought Gram had pushed her in the chest, but that wasn't quite right. Jettie spun to face him and took the last few steps to the stairs sideways until her right ankle boomeranged under her and her whole body jerked, reaching to reclaim her center of gravity at the tops of the stilettos. Ray's shot was wide enough to catch all that—her ankles, even. It was after that when the lens zoomed in on Gram's hands. He was reaching out all right, but he was reaching out, Ray could see clear as day, to grab hold of her. To save her. Then she went over.

Ray jammed the heels of his hands into his eyes. "Okay, stop," he said.

Martin stopped the tape. He was watching Ray, waiting for his reaction.

"I can't believe it."

"I think you panicked, Ray, when she started to fall. The camera jerks when it goes close on Gram's hands—maybe you closed your eyes?"

"I don't know." Ray sat and stared at his own hands. He had been dead wrong about Gram. What scared him most was his own certainty. All day his vision of those events had remained bright and definite in his head. Even now, in his mind's eye, he could see Gram pushing her. But that was—what?—a lie? Yes. A visually complete, perfect lie that only he could see.

Martin handed him his beer. "Look, it's good news. There's no need to turn this over to the police. It was an accident."

"It's just shocking that I could be so wrong," Ray said. "I've always thought the camera doesn't lie. When I'm behind the camera I feel *right*, like I can't possibly be wrong. But I sure can. The camera didn't lie, but I did."

"You didn't lie. This whole deal is a mind fuck," Martin said. "But I have to tell you something." He twisted to face Ray. "I wish I'd never met Lena Wells."

"Are you saying you don't want to finish the film?" Ray asked.

"We have to finish. Tonight I'm just sick at heart."

"You've wanted to meet Lena all your life."

"I know, but I should have left it alone. Her music, the fantasy— that's what I loved. The reality is just"—he shrugged—"like anybody else's reality. And she barely noticed me. Same with Jettie."

"They thought you were okay, Martin."

"Yeah, okay. They thought *you* were more than okay—they both did. I'd rather live in my fantasy world where I'm more than okay. We shouldn't have come." He looked at the frozen screenshot of Keith Richards holding forth about Chuck Berry. Martin didn't say what Ray knew he was thinking: if they had never come to the Silver Sun, Jettie would probably be safe tonight.

And if Ray had not encouraged Jettie to confront Gram. . . . At least Martin didn't know about that. But Martin's ignorance hardly mattered. Ray knew. His guilt was no less true for being private. To Martin he gave the advice he himself needed. "You can't start second-guessing the chain of events." He reached out tentatively and patted Martin on the shoulder. "That'll drive you crazy."

"Right, that's right. We meant no harm. We were just doing our jobs."

But Ray had been trying to keep the same doubts at bay and now they came tumbling forward. "Our jobs. But somehow we did more than our jobs. At least I did."

"You sure did. Jesus, that was a bad idea."

"That's not what I mean. What I mean is, nobody's asking whether we set out to hurt anybody. What we thought we were doing doesn't matter. Do I give students grades for the paper they meant to write, or for what they actually got on the page?"

"Oh—"

"Right! So, what I'm saying is, who the fuck cares what our intentions were? What happened is what happened, a human being is damaged, is broken." He heard Lauren's reproach in his head: *There are certain kinds of responsibility you've never taken.* "Now I just don't know, am I responsible? Are we responsible, Martin?"

"I thought you said no second-guessing?"

"I know." Ray crushed his empty beer can in his fist. The two men sat and stared at the screen for a long moment before Ray said, "Remember when Johnny shot Chester? I'm starting to think we should have stopped Johnny when he broke the pharmacy window."

"Stopped filming?"

Ray nodded. "Stopped filming and stopped Johnny. There was almost a minute from when he broke the window to when he fired the shot."

"What about the prime directive? You think we should've interfered?"

"I interfere all the time. Why not then?"

"You're not saying you think this Chester Lord guy is right to sue you?"

"I don't know if I'd go that far," Ray said. "I just know I don't feel good."

16

UNDERWATER

When Ray left the Silver Sun, it was barely dawn. Closing the big front door as quietly as he could, he stood with Cimarron on the verandah, drinking coffee and watching clouds oxidize the apricot-colored sunrise. Then he drove, making Dallas before ten o'clock, missing both morning rush hour and the lunch rush. He had promised Martin that he would be back the following night, so he had to make good time. From Dallas, El Paso was almost ten hours away. He couldn't bear to listen to Jettie's tape anymore, nor could he bear to choose other music over hers, so he drove in silence, which wasn't silent at all. It was full of the hiss of brakes, the thump-thump of his tires rolling over expansion joints on bridges, the pounding of wind battering billboards, punctuated occasionally by the long bray of an eighteen-wheeler's horn. Sometimes he heard birds overhead, or the sounds of babies or music from other people's cars. Sometimes Cimarron stuck her head between the seats in front of her and rested her head on his shoulder, wet nose against his neck and her breath in his ear, steady and regular. He called the hospital in Lawton to check on Jettie. No change.

The last time he had taken I-20 from Dallas to El Paso was just after the trip he had made to Rome, and he hadn't been able to get over the contrast. The layers and layers of civilization in Rome, centuries below your feet, made his own part of the world look brand-new. The slanting raw-wood homesteads and disintegrating barns, the new, prefab strip malls and gas stations all looked so temporary, and this, the topmost layer, was the only human layer. Millennia of Plains tribes had tread lightly on the earth, leaving few physical traces, and the first white settlers were barely dead. It would take hundreds of years to stack history in this dirt. Ray had always felt himself, as a citizen of the present, to be riding the ever-moving tip of the timeline into the future, but after Rome he felt like he was at the beginning of history, practically a caveman. In four thousand years some archaeologist would find one of his films and think, What is this primitive form of communication? The leveling effect of time was oddly comforting. He shook with the road and passed from hot to cold sweats, from blasting the air conditioning to cranking up the heater.

Late that afternoon, he got out of the Jeep at Odessa and realized the shaking he felt wasn't just from the motion of the road. He was sick. He pulled into a motor lodge intending to rest for a couple of hours, but he spent the next two nights and days there, sweating with fever.

Jettie came to him in a dream both nights. In the dream, the sun lit up Jettie's fair eyelashes and brows. It was a dry, bright day and she was sitting on top of the waterfall in Medicine Creek, strumming her green guitar as Ray approached her through the shallow creek. Suddenly there was a boom. "I can see it all, old son," she said, like she did that night on the roof. Then terror seized her face, and Ray swung around to see a wall of water rushing at him. The water surged and rose until they were both submerged, the water as high as the roof of the Silver Sun, which Ray could see underwater. Jettie stayed seated, in that strange nature-defying way of dreams, and gripped her guitar as her hair floated around her. She was saying something, and he floated closer. "I'm herding," she said.

He questioned her. "Herding?"

"Hurting," she said. "I'm hurting." Then she let go of her guitar and the green Höfner floated to the surface. He couldn't tell if Jettie had drowned, or if he had, if they were both dead or transformed into sea creatures that lived and breathed in the healing waters of Medicine Creek.

He awoke disoriented and wet with sweat every few hours, and took the ice bucket down the sidewalk in front of his room to the ice machine. Cimarron shuffled along beside him and peed in a patch of grass behind the building. Sometimes he heard her barking in his sleep, shoving her face into the front window of the motel room, bending the plastic horizontal blinds as people walked by. Messages piled up on his phone from Martin and Lena, who were wondering where he was. But they had no news about Jettie, so he ignored them. Every time he slept, he felt the flood of water in Medicine Creek with Jettie. Every time he woke up he couldn't distinguish grief from guilt. Exhaustion, dehydration, these things had made him sick, but late the second morning he opened his eyes to the sea foam–colored wallpaper and knew he had been making some kind of crossing there in that room and that this had been the main source of his illness.

Now he had crossed. What he knew now that he hadn't known before was that no amount of public humiliation—from lovers, lawyers, or employers—could be worse than not being able to live in his own head. He felt invigorated by a plan. "I was wrong!" he announced into the fetid room. Cimarron, asleep next to him, raised her head and gave him a baleful look. "Look at me any way you want," he said, patting her side, "but I'm going to say it." He had driven to Texas to tidy things up in his life, to fade heat, to persuade Johnny and Chester to go easy on him, but now he would continue his journey for a different reason entirely. He would come clean.

He sat up and he wanted a biscuit.

After showering and packing up, he left the hotel room, blinking in the bright sun, and drove down the highway access road to a diner, where he picked at a plate of biscuits, eggs, and coffee. He couldn't handle meat yet, but he ordered two sides of bacon to take to Cimarron, waiting in the Jeep. The waitress, a flat-faced girl with curly blond hair, told him he looked like hell.

"Why, thank you," he said, and nodded as she raised the coffee pot. "Half a cup."

She refilled it all the way. "No offense. I don't mean you're ugly— you're not. You just look bad. Are you a tweaker?"

A blind man. A liar. But a meth addict? "No."

"You don't look like one, but you never can tell. Drugs are equal-opportunity destroyers, and besides, it's bad to stereotype. I got stereotyped once, and I tell you what, it hurt my feelings."

"I'm just a poor wayfaring stranger heading home."

"Where's home?"

"El Paso. But I live in Austin. "

"You can be to El Paso by lunch."

Ray filled the Jeep up with gas and jumped back on I-20, heading southwest through the Chihuahuan Desert to El Paso. He called Martin and told him he had been sick.

"I thought you'd quit," Martin said. "Lena is asking about you. She's a bit put out. She thought you'd hang around like they requested."

"How's Jettie?" Ray asked, although he knew Martin would have said so in his messages if she were awake.

"Desmond said she squeezed his hand," Martin said.

"Really?"

"He was dead sure. He'd brought her a jar of Medicine Creek water, so of course that's what he credits."

"You're the one who told me about the good medicine."

"Yeah, but I didn't mean—"

"Whatever works," Ray said. "Whatever works. She squeezed his hand? Man, that's good to hear."

"Now the bad news."

Ray grimaced. "Hit me."

"The Gacks say I have to fire you."

"Give me a break. I don't usually go around shoving people, did you tell them that? Edmond Gack probably gets shoved all the time."

"Because of the insurance. The lawsuit makes you too expensive to insure. I don't know what to do, Ray. They kind of own me."

"Don't worry," Ray said.

"Are you kidding?"

"If it's about me being insurable, I'll see if I can't change the equation."

"Try to change it for the better, Ray, please. I'm going to feel like shit if I have to fire you."

When he hit town—the waitress was right, he reached El Paso around noon—he stopped for beer and a pack of Marlboro cigarettes on Montana Street, then drove straight to the Concordia Cemetery and walked the rows with Cimarron until he found the grave of John Wesley Hardin. He sat down in the dust in front of the wrought-iron cage surrounding the grave, popped open a beer, and drank it. His hands still shook from sickness and silence, and he was still dehydrated. He drank another. Never had alcohol hit his system so fast. He sang:

> Oooohhh, out in the West Texas town of El Paso
> I fell in love with a Mexican girl
> Nighttime would find me in Rosa's cantina
> Music would play and Felina would whirl.

Cimarron sat back on her haunches and watched him. Ray sang every verse of the song: falling in love with Felina, shooting the handsome stranger, fleeing to the badlands of New Mexico, returning, his love for Felina stronger than his fear of death, sitting atop his horse in the mountains overlooking El Paso, getting shot, dying, oh, dying, and singing while he died. Cimarron felt the music, began to make wounded little howls, her chin up like one of those coyote silhouettes that appears on truck stop lighters across the west. Ray leaned back and held his beer aloft as he warbled the majestic finale. *One little kiss and Felina, good-bye.* He wiped away tears.

He had no bullet to leave for John Wesley Hardin, but he took out the pack of Marlboros and tore them open. He ripped the filter from one, as he had seen Lena do at Geronimo's grave, and scattered the tobacco through the bars across the top of the grave. He left the pack. It probably didn't signify: American Indian ritual and John Wesley Hardin. Hardin had been a sonofabitch, truth be told. Ray wasn't sure what it was about these Old West characters that made everybody forget their basic sonofabitch natures, but there it was. Maybe Hardin had been a smoker, anyway.

He ate a plate of enchiladas at a Leo's on the north side of town, which sobered him up, then headed up I-10 a dozen miles to the federal prison. La Tuna. When he was a kid growing up in this city, he and his friends made jokes about the name and told scary stories about the place. He remembered the general location and trusted signs to point him the rest of the way, which they did.

From the road La Tuna seemed bucolic, like a church camp or a private school. The white adobe Spanish-style administration building at the front of the prison looked like a church from a distance, but as he drew closer, he saw that what looked like a bell tower was a watchtower, and then he saw the tall barbed-wire fences. In the parking lot at the front of the building he left the Jeep running and the AC on for Cimarron, and yanked the emergency brake as tightly as it would go. Surely nobody would steal a car in front of a prison, especially not a car with a 130-pound dog inside. He had never visited a prison before and didn't know how they felt about unannounced visitors, but maybe because La Tuna was a minimum-security unit, Ray managed to talk the guard at the front into letting him in.

The guard took Ray's ID, made him sign in, and made a couple of calls. Ray sat and waited for about thirty minutes. Then the guard received a call, said "okay" into the phone, and motioned to Ray. He patted him down, ran a wand over him, and led him through a couple of sets of coordinated electronic doors, like canal locks, that emptied finally into an empty cafeteria that stank of sour processed food and pine-scented cleaner.

Johnny Reyes was sitting at the end of a long table.

A guard stood behind him staring out the window at a basketball game happening on the yard. He didn't look at all interested in Ray or Johnny. Maybe it was the inadequate air conditioning, or maybe it was an illusion of the moment, but La Tuna felt indolent, a place that used extreme boredom for punishment.

"What the fuck, man?" Johnny looked baffled. "Could it be my old buddy Ray? You come to take pictures of my pretty new house?"

Ray sat down across the table from him. It had been almost a year since the night he robbed the pharmacy in Rio Marron, and Johnny looked different. That boy-to-man transition had happened. His trendy asymmetrical haircut had been replaced by a buzz cut that sharpened his handsome face. The piercings in his lips, nose, and ears were closed. Although he was sitting in prison, he seemed less a victim of circumstance than he had when he was jonesing in Rio Marron.

"Johnny, how's it going?"

He laughed and stretched his arms to encompass the room. "Magnificent! How are you?"

"I was in El Paso and thought I'd come by. I think a lot about you being stuck down here."

Johnny made a face. "Why?"

"Well, you know. I feel bad."

"You are very sensitive, Ray, huh? Very sensitive. I didn't know that about you. People do stupid shit all the time, man. You get tore up about all of it? My aunt was like that. She couldn't watch the news at all. I didn't know you were like that."

"Other people's stupid shit isn't my fault."

Johnny tipped his chair back onto one leg. "But *my* stupid shit is?" He considered Ray and let the chair drop back to all four legs. "Ray, this is very serious. A very big moment for me. Are you trying to tell me that you're my papa?"

"What? I just—I should have stopped you. Instead of filming you. I'm sorry."

Johnny pinched a cuticle between his teeth. "So you're not my papa?" He laughed. "Just fucking with you, man. My mama likes tough guys."

"I wanted to say I'm sorry. That sounds insincere, but I mean it. If there's anything I can do—"

"I see. It's your fault I'm in here." He shook his head. "You make me sick, Ray. Really. You must think I'm a monkey. And you're the man, huh? I'm not in charge of my life—you are! See, I didn't know that!"

"You don't think I should have stopped you?"

"Shouldn't have, couldn't have. I guess you never known a drug addict before. If you ever did, you'd know—there ain't no talking somebody out of that need. I was going into that pharmacy to get me some medicine, and that was that. And you know what else I learned? This place, this prison, it's part of my spiritual journey."

"Your spiritual journey?"

"I fucking hate it, but it's my journey. I don't know about your journey, but I don't see how you can even turn that movie camera of yours on if you go around thinking every goddamned thing that goes down is on you. You're just a witness, man. Get over yourself."

"But you told Chester Lord's attorney that I am responsible. You said I put you up to it. Did I or didn't I?" Ray rubbed his hands together and admitted what he had never until that moment admitted, even to himself. "I kept saying stuff to you about how I wished something would happen, somebody would do something while I was filming. Dropping hints. I didn't know what you might pull, but I knew I might get something—"

"You wanted a big bang for your movie. I saw that. You think I didn't? If you were fooling anybody, you were fooling yourself."

"But if you knew I was handing you a line, why did you go along with it?"

Johnny reached over the table and popped him on the shoulder. "Because I wanted to, man! I wanted the big bang. I wanted to *be* the big bang. And I *was* the big bang, man. I was it. You saw me."

Ray pulled an earlobe and looked at the ceiling. He had really thought he was in charge on that film. He really had. "You knew what I was doing better than I did."

"You were lying to yourself. I could see that. We all do it, you know?" Johnny thought about it. "I tell you what. You want me to take back what I said to that attorney? You want forgiveness? Then do something for me. Will you?"

Ray looked at the guard, who looked back at him, alert now. "Yes," he said under his breath, convinced he had just agreed to smuggle drugs.

"My girlfriend needs money. She's four hundred bucks shy on her rent, keeps writing me about it like they got money trees in prison. Go to Rio Marron and give her the four hundred, and you can call yourself forgiven. No, I tell you what—give her eight hundred. For next month, too. That's not a lot of money."

"I was going to Rio Marron anyway. Where does she live?"

"221 Pecos Drive. Not Pecos Avenue, Pecos Drive."

"Pecos Drive."

17

CONTRA ENVIDIA
Y PELIGROS

The two hundred block of Pecos Drive in Rio Marron dead-ended at the train tracks and consisted of four clapboard houses shadowed by old cottonwoods. Jim-Anne Towson, Johnny's girlfriend, lived in the second house on the right. Her place was the nicest on the street, which wasn't saying much, but some landlord had cared enough to put siding on the house, and oleander bushes in hot pink bloom grew under the front windows, lending the place an accidental grace.

Accidental grace described much of Rio Marron. Driving back into town, Ray passed the Holiday Inn Express, where he and Martin had stayed during their filming of *What's in the Water?*, and the string of fast food chains that led to the old downtown, a square of mostly deserted storefronts. The businesses still operating on the square were antique stores, as if the town had given up all new enterprise and was now trying to eat itself, selling off old bits of its previous prosperity. There was a Mexican restaurant, Los Loros, in an old Arby's building, its windows hand-painted with purple parrots and tropical trees, and Cut Upz, a beauty salon in the spot where an old barbershop had been, the striped barber pole still turned by the front door. The middle of the square was a small park, a miracle of heirloom roses and azaleas, cracked sidewalks and benches dedicated to local casualties of the world wars.

Everything was different. Rio Marron was exactly the same, but what he had been through in Medicine Park, was still going through, had changed how Ray saw what he saw, like a grainy blue filter on a camera lens. A year ago he had felt brisk and preoccupied, bored with

Rio Marron. But those were his salad days. He had been 100 percent his own boss, making a documentary with no shame on his head, with no doubts about his own abilities, with no sense that he could or would hurt anyone. There had been nothing to do but tell a story, find and focus on a spot of truth, and blow up the image until everyone saw something they hadn't seen before. And truth had been easy; you could see it right there like a flame-colored rose blooming out of a field of green leaves.

In Jim-Anne's driveway, Ray pulled up behind the rusty bumper of a red Ford Taurus and got out. Cimarron wanted to come, and Ray was feeling guilty about keeping her pent up in the La Tuna parking lot, so he opened the back and let her come with him. He had stopped at an ATM and withdrawn almost all he had. The money was now folded in his pocket, ready to hand to the lovely Jim-Anne. Salvation for eight hundred bucks.

She came to the door, a heavy-set young woman with long, dark hair that was permed. She wore jeans and a black tank top that revealed profound cleavage. She opened the door and then closed it halfway when she saw Cimarron. "What?" she said.

"Hi there. Johnny sent me."

She narrowed her eyes. "He's at La Tuna."

"I visited him this morning," Ray said. "He wanted me to—"

"Who the hell?" The door swung open all the way, letting out a big gust of pot smoke and a big guy, at least six foot two, who stood glaring down at Ray. He had a face like John Lennon's, but huge—John Lennon pumped full of devil juice. Without the glasses.

The guy was dangerous, but also, somehow, hilarious. John Lennon with most of the intelligence drained from his features, a face diluted. Ray stared and tried not to laugh. Maybe he'd gotten a contact high from the gust of pot smoke, but he couldn't make up his mind to take the money out of his pocket. From his side, Ray heard a low growl coming from Cimarron.

Big John Lennon looked at Cimarron, who growled louder with the eye contact. "What do you want?"

Ray had met Jim-Anne once before when he was in Rio Marron.

He'd been talking to Johnny, taping him, at a café in the town square when she'd come in. Ray didn't think she'd remember him, but she said, "You're that movie guy."

"That's right! That day in the café—"

Blue fingernails flitted over her cleavage. "We don't get too many cute guys come through, you know?"

Ray smiled. Her cleavage was simply astonishing: a place to hide things. A place to hide. Big John Lennon read his mind. Just like that, he came around Jim-Anne, pushed back the screen door with his wide shoulder, and punched Ray in the face. Acute pain shocked Ray into a new state of consciousness. Colors streaked, sounds strobed. He held his nose and Cimarron started barking, deep and loud and fast. She knocked Ray out of the way and jumped on Big John Lennon, her massive front paws planted squarely on his chest. He twisted his face away from her snarling jaws, pushing her away and kneeing her body until he got her off. The screen door slammed between them and Big John's finger, pressed against the mesh screen. "Tell Johnny—Jim-Anne's with me now!" The front door slammed. Cimarron kept barking, bounding up and down on her front legs.

Ray reached for her. "Cimarron, Cimarron. Hey. Calm down, girl. It's okay, it's okay."

She gave one last warning bark to the door, took a step back, and became quiet. In a few seconds, Jim-Anne's blue fingernails opened a space in the blinds, so Ray took the money from his pocket and held it up for her to see. He mouthed Johnny's name and looked around until his eyes lit on a terra cotta pot containing a dead cactus that sat on one of the front steps. Dripping blood all over the steps, he lifted the pot, slid the money underneath, and looked up again to make sure Jim-Anne saw him. He blew her a kiss. The blinds snapped shut.

"Cimarron, we're outta here." Ray opened the back door of the Jeep so she could jump in. Then he looked down at her and saw blood, a lot of blood, gushing from her right front paw. She limped toward him and left bloody paw prints on the driveway. "Shit!" He pushed down on her hindquarters until she sat and gave him her paw. While he peered at the wound, Cimarron growled, but he got a good look. The pink middle pad of her paw was sliced open, a piece of green glass sticking out, blood pulsing out around it. "Shit," he said, "shit, shit, shit."

He reached into the backseat and pulled his duffel bag onto the pavement. Unzipping it, he reached in and felt around for a piece of fabric. He pulled out Lena's plaid shirt. Bringing it around the back of Cimarron's paw as gently as he could, he slid the green glass from her paw and pulled the shirt tight around the gushing wound, cinching it tight. He had to straddle Cimarron, and it took all his weight to keep her still as she howled and struggled. The blood soaked through Lena's shirt while he put pressure on the wound, talking to Cimarron the whole time. "You'll be okay," he told her. "Be still, be still." Blood appeared on the white fur of Cimarron's head, and for a minute he panicked, convinced some other wound had opened up. Confused, he thought she had been shot, wondered how that could have happened, but then realized he was the source of the blood. His nose. He tried to tip his head back while holding onto Cimarron.

Behind them, Ray heard the screen door open and turned to see Jim-Anne scampering down the front steps to the pot where he had put the money. She took it and tossed a glance over her shoulder at Ray and Cimarron before she hurried back into the house. Under Ray's weight, Cimarron let out a frustrated sob, as human a sound as imaginable. They held steady like that for a few minutes until Ray was satisfied that the bleeding had stopped, then he lifted her into the backseat and they got out of there, leaving Jim-Anne's driveway looking like a crime scene.

Ray and Cimarron shared a bottle of tequila and a few Tylenols, and then he drove with one hand pinching the bridge of his nose. Cimarron fell asleep in the backseat, her white fur blowing in the air conditioning, with Lena's shirt a bloody ball cinched around her front leg. Poor dog. Ray drove around Rio Marron until he found a veterinary clinic, where the vet, an efficient woman in magenta medical scrubs, got Cimarron's paw all bandaged up and assured him he had done a great job with the makeshift tourniquet. The vet handed him a bottle of pills and Lena's bloody shirt when they were finished. "Here's something for her pain. No more alcohol," she said, "at least for the dog. And you should get that nose of yours looked at." Ray thanked her and left the clinic, holding the door open for Cimarron, who limped into the glaring day and stood patiently by the Jeep while Ray opened the rear door.

There was still one stop to make in Rio Marron. Chester Lord and his family lived a few miles outside town in a weathered pink trailer. A large, fenced garden extended from the east side of the property, and a green Subaru Forester and an old black pickup sat in the driveway. When Ray's Jeep rolled onto the property, four big dogs appeared from under the trailer, running headlong at the moving vehicle and baying. Cimarron woke up and began to bark, trying to stand on the backseat but held back by her wound. Ray pulled in behind the pickup truck and let the Jeep idle. He held up his hands on the steering wheel, surrendering to the dogs while he waited for someone to come out and call them off. Caught out by the dogs, a jackrabbit squeezed its enormous body under an invisible gap in the mesh around the Lords' garden. Its ears lay back and its body compressed like it was boneless, then its giant heels worked like hinges and he was gone, vanished into the desert.

In a minute a teenage girl with Buddy Holly glasses and black dreadlocks stuck her head out of the front door. She yelled something in Spanish and the dogs backed off, trotting away to the far end of the fence line.

Ray rolled down his window. "I'm looking for Chester Lord."

She stepped out of the trailer and clomped down the cement steps in crimson Doc Martens. "What for?"

"My name is Ray Wheeler." Ray left the air conditioning running for Cimarron and got out of the Jeep. "I've got some business with him."

"Why do I know that name? Ray Wheeler?" Then, at the top of her lungs, she shouted, "Dad! Ray Wheeler's here to see you."

There was silence from the trailer. She squinted and looked him up and down. "Why do I know your name?"

"Your dad is suing me."

A wide grin broke across her face. "Oh my god! You! Are you crazy? He's probably in there getting his gun. Good news is, his arm is so fucking weak, thanks to you, he probably can't fire it. That's why he lost his job."

She invited Ray inside and he followed her through the small, dark doorway into a tiny living room. A television laugh track sounded from a back room. Window seats were built into the walls and decorated with yellow-and-turquoise Santa Fe–style cushions. A small kitchen table extended from the wall, crowded with loose change, keys, a row of prescription bottles, and three voodooish religious candles—the kind they sell in the Hispanic section of grocery stores. He had a girlfriend once who had loved these candles and used to put them all over the house: Contra Envidia y Peligros, Chango Macho, Immaculada Concepcion, and his favorite, Alleged Controlling Candle. "Alleged by whom?" he would tease.

"Hang on." Four steps took her from the living room, through the kitchen, and into the back room. In a minute the girl returned with Chester, slight and redheaded, about Ray's age, who held one thin arm at the elbow as he walked.

Ray stood up. What was he going to say? He hadn't thought it through. But he was going to get clean somehow. Purpose burned in him. "Chester Lord? I'm Ray Wheeler."

Chester cracked a crooked smile and sat down on one of the window seats across the table from Ray. "Soledad told me." He glanced at the girl, who stood in the kitchen like a sentinel. "I don't know what you want, but my understanding is that our lawyers do all the dealing. Us, we're not even supposed to meet."

"I don't have any money, Mr. Lord. That's the thing. Pay in my business is pretty unreliable. I had one reliable source of income—I was teaching some college classes in Austin—and now that's gone. The university dropped me like a hot potato when your lawsuit showed up."

"I don't give a good goddamn about your problems, Wheeler. What are you thinking, coming here?"

Ray held up a hand. "I want to do right by you. I do. Not so much for you as for me, if you want the truth. I can't go around feeling this shitty for the rest of my life."

"So what's the plan?" Chester asked. "You want to be my butler?" He laughed and laughed.

Ray looked down. There was no plan. He had just wanted to say the words "do right by you." He had no idea what they might really mean, and now that he saw Lord's shriveled arm for himself, he felt ill. He could make gestures and say nice words all day long, but there was no fixing that injury.

Chester glanced at his daughter. "Can you give us some Jarritos?"

Soledad opened the fridge and pulled out three glass bottles of brightly colored Mexican soda pop. She handed them to her father. "Mama just put these in this morning. They're not real cold."

Chester grabbed a bottle opener from the table and popped off the tops, handing Ray a bottle.

"Guava," Ray said. "My favorite."

"You see my daughter, Wheeler?"

Ray nodded.

"She's pretty ashamed of me. Thinks I'm a loser, don't you, hon?"

Soledad shrugged elaborately.

"She does, Wheeler, she does. See, I used to be a cop in Lubbock. It was a good gig, but I got hooked on meth and fucked that up. We came home to Rio Marron, and Maria, that's my wife, she transferred with Chili's. That new one off the highway, she's the assistant manager. I got a second chance with that security job for the pharmacy. Nobody would hire me, but that old geezer who owned the pharmacy, he was so tired of getting ripped off by tweakers, he took me on. Paid almost nothing, but he hired me. He didn't know I was a tweaker myself, and I figured that was my business. I was going to work my way back up to a real job from there, but now, see"—he lifted his injured arm like a wing—"I'm screwed."

Ray took a long draw of the warm, sweet soda. Lauren would kill him if she knew he was here. "You should go easy on your dad," he said, looking cautiously at Soledad. "Most people can't kick meth. It shows real fortitude that he's clean. He must love you a lot. I bet you're pretty sharp, aren't you?"

"You just think I'm smart because of the glasses. They're fake."

"She's got an offer from Rice," Chester said. "As you know."

Ray looked at Soledad. "I know a woman who you kind of remind me of. She's smart and tough like you even though she's not doing so great right now. She writes songs, she's a singer. Have you ever heard of Lena Wells? Lena Wells loves this woman's songs. Maybe there's something up the road like that for you."

"Lena Wells, the singer? How do you know what Lena Wells likes? I happen to know she hasn't put out new music since longer than I've been alive," Soledad said.

Chester spun his soda bottle on the table. "Shit. Lena Wells."

"Do you know 'The Bad Kind'?" Soledad asked her father.

"You don't hear that one much."

"That's a really good song."

"I just saw Lena a couple of days ago," Ray said. He suddenly wanted very much to impress this little girl. "I'm making a documentary about her. She'd like you."

"Bullshit. You don't know any rock star."

"Just a minute." Ray ran out to the Jeep, where Cimarron was asleep in the gelid air, and grabbed the press kit. He held it up to Soledad when he got back inside and let her look it over.

She flipped through the laminated pages and said, "This is just stuff. It doesn't prove anything."

"My name is on the cover sheet. It says 'Prepared for Raymond Wheeler.'" Ray found himself bragging about the rockumentary. "Lena's about to do a new album and go out on tour. I got lucky. I needed a job." He nodded at Chester. "After what happened to your dad."

"Call her." Even through her grimy nonprescription glasses, Soledad's eyes were black and fierce, not her father's eyes. "Call her or I don't believe you."

He looked at Chester and took out his phone. He had six missed calls, three from Martin, and three from Lena.

"Where are you?" Lena asked when she picked up.

"I saw these missed calls—"

"She's awake, Ray!" Light flowed around her words like sun through an opening door.

Ray closed his eyes. "Oh, thank God. Is she okay? Is she the same?"

"Same old Jettie. Groggy, and in pain, but she's all there."

"When?"

"A couple hours ago. We've been calling you."

"Forgot to turn it back on." He collected himself and looked up at Chester and Soledad, who were watching him closely.

"Are her parents still there?"

"Jettie's? Yeah, they think she'll go home with them."

"And she's talking and everything?"

"And everything—maybe she'll give you another kiss when you get back."

"Oh, Lena."

"Never mind. Where are you?"

"Rio Marron."

"I'm not even going to ask."

"Could you speak to someone for me? This is Soledad Lord. Her dad is that security guard who got shot. Remember?"

There was a long pause. Finally, she said, "You want a *favor* from me?"

"I'm trying to set things right, Lena."

"Not with me, evidently. And did you really accuse Gram of pushing Jettie down the stairs?"

"We have a lot to talk about, I know," he said. "But could you please just say hello."

"What does she want?"

"To hear your voice."

There was another long pause. At length, she said, "I guess I'm too happy about Jettie to worry about you today. Put her on."

Ray handed Soledad the phone and could hear Lena's voice, *Hello, Soledad? Hey this is Lena.* The girl leaned forward with her elbows on the table, playing with the bottle opener, intensely absorbed. "I thought this guy was full of it," she said, then Lena said something that made her laugh and look at Ray.

His stomach felt like he had swallowed a bunch of vibrating phones. The idea that he would be able to look Jettie in the eyes and speak to her made him giddy. She was alive and Chester Lord was alive. Not all together well, not undamaged, but at least Ray's casualties would walk away from the damage he had done. He was dying to get in the Jeep and head back to Oklahoma, but he sat and drank his soda. He watched Soledad talk to Lena. They were agreeing that high school sucked.

He began thinking. He scooted around the table closer to Chester. "She'll need a security guard on her tour."

Chester had been thinking, too. He brought his good hand to his chin. "Would she do that?"

"Probably not." Ray didn't even know if there would be a tour. "But maybe."

"My arm—"

"You'd have a staff. Your people could handle any guns."

"My people." Chester looked afraid, but then a tremulous grin sneaked onto his face.

Ray nodded. "Soledad could come."

Chester watched his daughter as she chipped black nail polish from her thumbnail, nodding and laughing with Lena, and Ray saw him reach a decision. "You can't buy me off that easily. I want Soledad to go to college."

"Right. I was going to agree to that anyway."

Chester fixed his gaze on Ray. "Say that again."

"I'll take the settlement. I'll pay for her to go to Rice." He hadn't known what he was saying until he said it, or that it was what he had come here to say. And now it was done. He felt like a rock had rolled off him, like he was flattened grass grown pale and sickly under the rock that could now begin to unbend and to reach for the sun. "And in return you'll drop your lawsuit."

Chester set down his soda and offered Ray his good hand.

"All four years," Ray said. He had no idea how he would make good on what he had just promised, but he meant to find a way. "Whatever the scholarship doesn't pay for."

Chester nodded and they turned to watch Soledad as she giggled into the phone, wrapping up her conversation with Lena. "Okay. Okay, you, too. Yeah, I will. Thank you, Lena!"

18

THE LAST DAY
OF PROBATION

Jettie was inconsolable about Los Lobos. "Gram said they were real nice on the phone. They sent those flowers"—she nodded in the direction of a large bouquet of yellow roses by the hospital room window—"but they can't wait on me." Her right eye was still swollen shut—that whole side of her face was purplish and difficult to look at—but the left side was attempting to smile. No one else besides Ray was in the room. It was almost two o'clock in the morning, and now that she had regained consciousness, the twenty-four hour vigils had stopped. "I may never get another chance like that."

"You will." Ray was still jangling from the long car ride, his fingers cramped from gripping the steering wheel. He pulled up a chair facing the undamaged side of her face and took her hand. "I'm so glad you're okay," he said. "I shouldn't have talked you into fighting. You were going to do the show. You were thinking about other people, about the fans, and you were right."

She turned her head stiffly on the pillow to look at him. "It was the damned heels," she said. "I don't know what I was thinking. I can walk in wedgies or platforms, but spikey heels, for-get-it! I'm throwing those damn things in the trash!"

"Why'd you wear them?"

"I told you I was a little bit of a perfectionist."

"They did look pretty good," Ray conceded.

"See, I know. They matched my shirt perfectly."

Ray rested his forehead against the edge of the bed. He felt her reach out and pat him on the head. He said, "Cimarron's out in the car."

"They told me you had her. I sure do miss that old thing. Why don't you sneak her in?"

He lifted his head. "I'm too tired to get into any trouble tonight."

"Then hug her for me. Tell her I'll be out of here real soon." She smiled with half her face. "You do look tired."

"I thought Gram pushed you. Did you know that?"

"That's what he said. He's still pretty pissed about it. So is Lena."

"I guess I deserve it."

"They're not so bad, you know. They're a little weird, but they're not killers."

"I feel like they take advantage of you, Jettie."

She tried to smile. "That's real sweet of you, Ray, but I feel like that street runs both ways. After all, I'm the one who came up here to get what I could get out of Lena. And I got a lot."

"Her son."

"Sure enough! Not bad for a bisexual barfly with more unrecorded songs than dollars to her name. Are you really fired?"

Ray looked up. "Is that what you heard?" He looked forward to telling Martin that the lawsuit was settled, or soon would be. Now the Gacks could insure him to their hearts' content.

"Thought I did. I probably don't know what I'm talking about. I'm pretty doped up." She laughed.

"Don't worry about it. And don't worry about Los Lobos," he said. "You'll get your shot. You're alive, old girl. Everything is possible."

Ray didn't feel quite right about returning to the Silver Sun, but he did it anyway, waking up the next morning under the familiar peach chenille bedspread with Geronimo's grim countenance staring fiercely from the wall. He sent down for a cup of coffee and received one in the dumbwaiter, same as before. There was no sound coming from Martin's room, but it was still early. From his window he could see the sun just beginning to sparkle off Medicine Creek and stretch down the asphalt of the road between waving shadows of tree branches.

Cimarron must have still been asleep in the backyard.

He pulled Lena's black-and-blue plaid shirt from his duffel bag and rinsed it in the bathroom sink. Cimarron's blood ran and ran. He squeezed it and opened it again and again until the water finally ran clear. Then he found a hair dryer under the sink and dried it, waving the hot air across the fabric. The shirt was still stained, but its dark colors hid the worst of it. When all the moisture was gone, he tucked it under his arm and took the stairs to the second floor. As he crept down the hall past Lena's bedroom, he realized that the door to the study was open. He stopped.

"Who is it?" Lena's voice rang out.

Ray took a deep breath and stepped into the study. "Just me," he said. "Wanted to let you know I'm back."

Curled barefoot in the corner of the couch in a frayed yellow robe, Lena looked like someone recovering from a long illness. She had showered and the ends of her hair made wet spots on the robe. She wore no makeup. Without her characteristic black eyeliner she looked wan and tired. Her lips had the shiny dryness of fever. Her eyes fell on the shirt. "I wondered if you'd return it."

The morning sun slanted through the windows of her study, passing through the blown glass orbs and casting colors across the surfaces of the room. Ray caught the residual scent of incense and coffee. He stood just inside the door.

"Come in," she said. He took a seat at the other end of the couch and tucked the shirt into the crease where he had originally found it. That night seemed like lifetimes ago. It was hard to believe it had been only—how long? A week.

"You know what today is?" she asked.

"May 25th?"

"The last day of your probation."

Ray leaned back and pushed his hands across his scalp. "I know you're pissed off—"

"Pissed off?" She rested an elbow across the back of the couch and stroked her chin. "Pissed off. You've been going around saying my son tried to kill his wife?"

"I believed what I was saying, Lena. I didn't want it to be true."

"You had lipstick all over your face when Jettie fell. Jettie's lipstick. God, you make me feel like a fool. Yeah, Ray, I'm a little pissed off."

"Look, we kissed. You had just blown me off. 'It was only three nights'—remember saying that? She was pissed at you, so was I. It just happened. Can't you understand how we might have been pissed off?"

She picked up one end of the sash to her robe and twisted it around her finger. "You must think I do what I did with you all the time. But I don't, Ray. Not easily, and not often. I don't make the decision to let someone that far into my world lightly. What I said to Jettie and to you, that was uncool, I know—"

"Uncool? You're pretty easy on yourself, Lena. Firing Jettie and Gram? That was very, very uncool."

"Okay, I hear you, but I was under a lot of stress, I was having a bad day, and you betrayed me at the first opportunity. The moment I wasn't perfect, you let me have it."

He wasn't prepared for the idea that he had hurt her. Not her. He had hurt nearly everyone else in his life, but he didn't think he had the power to hurt Lena. "I didn't mean it," he said plaintively. "I really liked you. A lot. I did. I do."

She wiped a tear from her cheek. "It's all right. You've helped me see things more clearly."

He had no idea what he felt or what he wanted in that moment. A passionate reconciliation might have been within his reach, if he would reach out for it, but he continued to sit and stare at a stone coaster on the coffee table. He wanted a drink of water. He didn't know what to say, so he reached for something small to console her with. "I've been meaning to tell you. I had my dad—he's a genealogist—research your family tree."

Her eyes flew to his face. "You did what?"

"I checked into the Geronimo connection."

"Oh for God's sake." She stared at him. "Are you going to humiliate me further, Ray? Is that what you're about to do?"

"The story's not quite what you said."

"Oh no?"

"You're not his great-granddaughter." He paused. Her eyes were chaos, and the idea that he had humiliated her made him feel like the very walls of the Silver Sun were squeezing him, trying to push him out like a splinter. "You're his great-*great* granddaughter. Geronimo's great-great granddaughter. How cool is that?"

She flexed her toes, winced like he had fired a bullet right past her head. "Great-great granddaughter. So it's true?"

Ray nodded. He liked it as a question. *It's true?*

"I am?" She stared at him. "I am. I—I knew I was, I told you that." She shrugged. "You must not have believed me, Ray."

"Oh, I understood. I'm a storyteller, too, you know."

For a second her eyes roved over his face. Then she looked down. Her fingers moved busily along the sash of her robe. "So I'm not a mother—according to you—but I am a granddaughter. That's something, at least."

"According to me?"

"Cy told me, Ray. You found out Gram's adopted. I guess your father dug that up, too. So, okay. Now you think you know something."

"Why did you keep it from Gram?"

"You're Gram's advocate now, are you? Done accusing him?"

"I just want to understand." He reached over and took her wrist, her thin skin sliding over the balls of the joints as she tried to twist away. He let go. "I talked to Desmond."

"What did he tell you?"

"Not who the mother is. Not why they gave the baby to you. It's Justine, right? Justine Oxley. She's his mother."

She blinked hard. "You're so determined to think the worst of me."

"I'm not, Lena, I—"

"I was fostered out to this couple in Lawton, the Browns, when I was in eighth grade. Justine lived down the street. We became best friends, together all the time. Then in tenth grade she was gang-raped." She pulled her legs beneath her and clutched a red pillow to her chest. "January of tenth grade."

"Like in 'January Ground.'"

"What I put in the song is just what happened. I never saw anything lower than the way her parents dealt with the rape. The day after it happened, all the grown-ups met at my foster parents' house. I was in the room when the Oxleys apologized to the rapists' parents." She half stood, holding the pillow close, and then sat back down.

"Wait? What?"

"They blamed Justine. Her parents. They blamed her. This 95-pound, 15-year-old girl. Had it coming, asked for it—they said those things about little pubescent Justine, who was still such a child she was afraid to even use a tampon. And the boys, well, apparently no one can expect a boy to control himself. I mean, the way they saw the boys was vile, too, although it served them well. Like a teenage boy isn't a real human, doesn't have a mind or a moral capacity." Her bare feet dug into the seam between the back and the bottom cushions. "I tell you what, I think the boys' parents were all shocked as shit. They came ready to bargain, ready to apologize and make deals. I do believe they would have paid Justine's parents off. I believe they came with their checkbooks handy."

"So Justine's parents sold her out."

"It was like they wanted the boys' parents to like them, like they thought if they didn't make trouble the boys' parents might invite them over to swim or something. There was no thought to defending their daughter."

"Were the boys' parents rich?"

"What passed for rich in that town. Middle class, really, not even upper-middle class."

"Where was the law? The lawyers?" Ray rested his forearms on his thighs and studied the weave of the rug, listening.

"We were all under sixteen except for the kid who got his license, so the parents decided to deal with it privately, no lawyers. Justine's parents—they didn't seem to understand they were the injured party. They treated the rapists' parents like *they* were the ones wronged, falling over themselves to assure them they didn't have anything to worry about from the Oxley family. I'll never understand it. I just—can you imagine?"

"No. God."

"When we left Lawton a couple years later, Justine never called them, not even once. We were all together, a family, me and Cy and

Desmond and Justine. I believe she and Desmond loved each other. When she died—I just had to keep Gram. You see? I couldn't turn him over to her parents. Those people were horrible."

"What about Desmond?"

"Desmond was devastated. He could barely take care of himself on his best days, and after Justine died, there was no question of letting him take care of an infant. He begged me to take Gram." Her gaze flickered over him. "Ray would you take a seat?"

Ray had stood up without realizing it. He glanced around, then sat back down, closer to her, and they faced each other across a short expanse of shiny leather.

"I get it. So that's what Cy meant when he said you saved Gram from a bad life."

"He said that?"

"Remember how you told me being pregnant saved you. Did you make that up? Were you ever pregnant?"

"I was pregnant."

"Well, then—"

Lena grimaced. "I miscarried."

He could have filmed her face in black and white, and it would not have looked much different than it did at that moment. Black eyes, white face. Black hair, shades of gray under her eyes. "I'm sorry," he said.

"When Gram was about two months old, this was December 16th of '79, we were sitting around my place in West Hollywood, the four of us—Justine and Desmond and Cy and me. I was fucked up, Ray. Real fucked up. I had lost my baby a few weeks after Gram was born and took it hard, feeling so sorry for myself. I'd told the world I was having a baby, too, blabbed it to every reporter I could find the minute I missed my first period. Justine and I were just silly, pregnant together, shopping, painting, knitting—knitting, man! We were so happy. I told the world I was clean, but I wasn't, not totally, and the dope is probably why I miscarried. I was terrified for anybody to find out I lost the baby. I didn't want to hear all the bullshit speculations, the cruelty."

"Who was the father?"

"Fuck you."

"Cy?"

She looked off. "What does it matter? I miscarried. There were a lot of other factors besides us being cousins. The dope. I don't know. Meanwhile, here's Justine, clean and beatific with this precious baby. Lord, that baby—Gram was like a ball of light in our hands. Changed everything. Justine was happy for the first time since the rape." She paused, then continued. "So this night, December 16th, I had just bought *In Through the Out Door*."

"Zeppelin," Ray said.

Lena nodded. "Cy and Desmond and I were all shitfaced. Everybody except Justine. Cy and I, we were wading through deep waters together. We were trying to break up for good."

"By spending all your time together?"

She ignored him. "We ran out of beer. Gram was in his crib asleep in his room, and Justine didn't want us driving, so she slipped out for a beer run." Lena grimaced and ran a finger across the top of the couch, becoming absorbed for a long moment in rubbing the leather. "Car wreck," she said, finally. "Just like that."

"So you took over raising Gram—"

"What else would I do? Desmond had a complete breakdown after Justine died, and the child was living in my house."

"So look, your decisions are perfectly understandable. It sounds to me like you were trying to do right by everybody. But I don't understand why you never told Gram about Justine and Desmond. Why lie and say you were his birth mother?"

She pursed her lips, and something of the camaraderie they had shared showed in her expression as she sought his eyes. "See, I was in charge of this baby all of a sudden. Justine was gone, my best friend. Gram looks like her." She paused. "I saw how if Gram was my baby it would help me out of the mess I had created for myself telling the world I was pregnant."

"Oh."

"Yeah."

"Wow, Lena."

"Cy and I were out of our heads with grief. At the time we thought it was short-term, we'd tell Gram when Desmond got better, but Desmond's been in and out of institutions since that time, and up until recently he's begged me not to say anything to Gram. Plus, we didn't know what it would really be like raising a child. How a child's identity is formed and how fragile it is. Being my son is who Gram is. I've been scared to tell him."

Her voice lowered as she talked. She seemed to forget about Ray, but now her eyes snapped up to his. "So I haven't."

He reached for her.

"No, fuck you," she said.

"Lena—"

She pushed him away. "I don't trust you anymore. You betrayed us."

Suddenly he was sick with anger. You never trusted me, he wanted to say. You put me on probation. You second-guessed my every impulse and made it hard for me to do my job. These things were true. But then he remembered Jettie in his room, remembered kissing her and sending her out to confront Gram because Lena had wounded him. To get back at her. To take her down a few notches. That was also true. At a loss, he said, "I think you're an amazing woman."

"I'd like to believe you." She reached over and patted Ray's thigh like a cowboy telling his horse to move. "I just don't."

He tried to catch his breath. He had expected her to relent. "What makes you think you're right all the time?" As if from a great distance, he heard himself lashing out. "You think your judgment about the Black Sheep is sound? You only heard them play once, but you tell them they're not ready for Los Lobos like everybody can't see what self-serving bullshit that is? You kept Gram and Desmond apart—you, a drug addict who just lost a baby. You thought you deserved another one? What made you so sure you'd be the better parent?"

Her face fell open and she bolted to her feet. "Out! Get out, you motherfucker, get out!" She pointed a finger at him. "But I tell you what. Before you go, get out your camera. I have a favor to ask of you. And I think we can agree you owe it to me."

19

EAT CROW SPECIAL

Ray turned left out of the Silver Sun parking lot. As he rounded a corner that would take him out of Medicine Park, he saw a flash of silver on one of the dirt roads that led up the mountain from the main thoroughfare. He spun his steering wheel, making a hard right and catching up with Desmond in a few seconds. Desmond was leaning into his walk, head down, headgear hanging like a wilted plant from his head. Ray rolled down his window. "Get in," he said.

Appearing reluctant to stop thinking about whatever preoccupied him, Desmond stepped back from the road and rocked back and forth on his legs for a minute like he was limbering up for a run. Finally he answered, "My cats need their lunch."

"This won't take long," Ray promised.

After Desmond had walked around the front of the Jeep and climbed into the passenger seat and Ray had unrolled the windows to release the nearly unbearable body odor emanating from Gram's silver father, Ray told him where they were going. "Lena couldn't tell him herself, she's afraid of his reaction, so she had me record her spelling it out about you and Justine and the whole deal. I'm charged with finding Gram and playing the video for him."

"Dangit," he said, looking straight ahead out the front windshield. "Big day. It's a big day. Did she ask you to bring me along?"

"That part's my decision."

Desmond's red-rimmed eyes filled with tears. He grabbed Ray's shoulder with both hands. "You are one righteous cat, Ray-man. You shook this place up, didn't you? By God, you did!" He roared with a kind of ho-ho-ho laughter that blasted rotten breath all over Ray. Rocking back and forth in the passenger seat, he plucked the silver planetary system from his own head and placed it on Ray, gently pressing it down over his forehead. "There," he said. "For you." He sat back and beamed at Ray.

"Thank you." Ray patted the bobbing planets. They were lighter than they looked. With more emotion than he meant to show, he said, "I've admired this headgear since the moment I saw it."

Desmond nodded in a courtly manner and crossed his hands in his lap, looking around and beaming at the day, his knees jittering like a kid's.

"I'm not sure I'm doing you any favors," Ray said. "Gram is attached to the idea that his dad is Steve McQueen."

"A compelling man," Desmond said, "but dead. And I don't believe he could play guitar. I am, you know, one hell of a guitar player. As is"— he paused like a gymnast preparing for a challenging series of flips, approaching the rest of his sentence with his whole body—"my son."

"Good point," Ray said.

"I need to go home for a minute. Do you mind?"

Desmond gave him directions to a small house at the top of the road, where it dead-ended in front of an impassable arroyo. The place was an alpine affair adorned on the outside with dark cross beams and Bavarian folk art carved into wood that lined the A-framed roof like old lace. Three llamas stood behind a fenced enclosure, slowly chewing as the men approached. Cats were everywhere. Ray wondered how they kept from being eaten by coyotes. The Bavarian-style house looked out of place, surrounded as it was by scrub oaks with Indian Blanket grow-ing in wild orange and yellow profusion across the yard.

Ray threw the Jeep into park. "I heard Lena say you wrote 'The Piano Bench Incident.' What's it about?"

Desmond was already out of the car. About to slam the door, he paused. "Justine," he said.

The acrid cat reek inside the house was mostly suppressed by the smoky odor of some pungent herb. Ray stood in a narrow, paneled kitchen while Desmond disappeared into a back room concealed by a wool blanket nailed above the doorframe. Cats climbed across the kitchen counters to rub against Ray. In a minute, soap-smelling steam reached him. Desmond was getting clean. Ray walked into the living room and found it filled with tall piles of *Guitar World Magazine*, *Rolling Stone*, and *Sports Illustrated*. Big bags of cat food stood next to a stained, corduroy La-Z-Boy in the center of the room behind which three cats raised their heads to look at him. There was an old television set inside a wooden console, the kind Ray remembered from the seventies. The wall behind the TV bespoke Desmond's devotion to his son. It was covered with photographs of Gram at all ages, school pictures from kindergarten through twelfth grade, and lots of informal shots. Lena had kept him well supplied.

On the adjacent wall there was a density of University of Oklahoma football plaques and Woody Guthrie sketches, posters, and pictures. Guthrie had played a guitar with THIS MACHINE KILLS FASCISTS scrawled around the body, and there were at least two black-and-white photographs of him performing with that famous instrument. His likeness was interspersed by an equally insistent sprinkling of OU plaques, signed posters of players, wooden cows with hinged limbs wearing crimson OU jerseys, pink-cheeked cherubs in OU jerseys, muscle cars in OU jerseys, cartoon pigs and chickens wearing OU jerseys. The piece de resistance, where the two themes came together, was a caricature drawing of Woody Guthrie wearing a crimson OU jersey.

Behind him, Ray heard Desmond walk into the room.

"You're a football fan," Ray said, reaching down to pet a cat that was pressing itself insistently against his leg.

"Oh, it's okay," Desmond said.

Ray laughed. "Okay? Your walls are covered—" He had turned around and now stood looking at Desmond, whom he hardly recognized. The smell of Old Spice emanated from him, and he wore a green-and-yellow plaid, button-down shirt and a pair of old Levi's. His face was closely shaved, and his still-wet, blondish-silver hair was combed back from his forehead. "You look great," Ray said, only then noticing that Desmond still wore the silver tennis shoes that were part of his spaceman ensemble.

"Shoelaces broke on my boots," Desmond said, following Ray's gaze.

"You look great," Ray repeated.

"I prefer the silver," Desmond said. "But I don't think Gram cares for it."

"Are you ready?" Ray asked.

Desmond's hands twisted over each other like kittens. "Let's rock and roll."

They hit Lawton, and after a few minutes, Ray turned right onto Fort Sill Boulevard and headed north toward the stretch of seedy dives that serviced the base. Gram's white pickup sat in the gravel parking lot of the Signal Flare, where Jettie had said it would be. She had sounded upset when he talked to her; she said Gram had just visited her and "stormed off to go get fucked up like the immature SOB that he is." The OPEN sign flashed on a window otherwise blacked out with paint.

Ray left the silver headgear sitting on the dash of the Jeep. Inside the club, the jukebox played Pink Floyd. For some reason British existential angst was the soundtrack of Oklahoma; every time Ray turned on the radio he heard something from *Dark Side of the Moon* or *The Wall*. That or Led Zeppelin. His eyes took a moment to adjust to the darkness as he breathed in the sickly sweet smell of alcohol and cigarettes. The bottoms of his shoes stuck to the floor as he crossed to the bar. There was a lone guy sitting at a bar stool, a heavy man with a long tail of hair hanging down behind his short-cropped sides. He glanced over his shoulder at Ray and Desmond. Torres appeared from behind swinging doors that led to the kitchen, wiping his hands on a towel that hung from his belt.

He looked them up and down. He had been friendly during Ray's last visit, but he wasn't anymore.

"We're looking for Gram," Ray said, setting his camera on an empty stool and sitting in another. Desmond remained standing, rocking back and forth in Ray's peripheral vision.

Torres gripped a cardboard coaster and flicked it back and forth like it was a ninja star he was about to send spinning into Ray's chest.

He leaned over the bar, bringing his acne scars up close where Ray could see them. "Why? You ain't hurt him enough? I heard what you said about him. I can't believe you're here, man, really."

"I came to apologize."

"Apologize? Well, well."

"Could we have a couple of beers?

Torres reached into the cooler and set two cold bottles on the bar. He grinned. "You're gonna eat crow, huh? Boy, oh boy. Dean, did you hear that?" He gestured at the big man down the bar, who was laughing like he was personally sick of Ray's shit and glad he was going to get what he had coming to him. Then Torres pointed to the red vinyl booths that lined the back wall in front of the stage. "He's back there."

Ray grabbed his camera and his beer and slid off the stool. "What do I owe you?"

Torres waved a hand. "Eat crow special, one day only."

He couldn't see inside the booths until they were nearly on them. Then Gram came into view, in the first booth, the one where Ray and Lena had sat to watch the Black Sheep. His feet were stretched out along the booth, his back against the back wall. He had a drink in front of him, eyes on Ray and Desmond.

On the other side of the booth sat Cy, who greeted them. "Hey, you two." Swiftly, he took in Ray, and Desmond trailing behind him, clean and normal-looking. He ran a finger over his eyebrows. "Fuck," he said.

Ray slid in next to Cy. Desmond, looking terrified, gave Gram a sheepish grin before scooting across the slick red expanse of his seat. Gram sniffed the air near Desmond with surprise and pushed himself to the booth's far corner. Ray set his camera case on the table and started talking. "Gram." He flattened his hands against the table and apologized.

Gram stared, saying nothing.

Ray continued, "If it helps at all, I believed what I was saying. Not that I wanted to believe it—I didn't—but I've always thought of myself as real objective, like, I don't get in the way of what I'm filming and I don't have personal opinions about it. So I guess—"

Next to him, Cy chuckled.

"I know, laughable. Believe me, I'll never laugh at that joke again. But that's how I've always operated, or always tried to, so I wasn't in the habit of, you know, doubting my own eyes. I didn't think I could distort what I was seeing that badly. But I did. I damn sure did."

Gram jabbed a straw into the ice of his drink. "You had her lipstick on your face."

"Well, now—"

"Did you really think you could have my mother and my wife?"

"I said I was wrong." Ray reached for the camera. "And I'm sorry."

"That's all? You're wrong and you're sorry?"

"What else do you need, Gram? Would you like to go to college? Just send me the bill. Now, I've just come from talking to your mom. She has something to tell you. She asked me to show you this." He looked at Cy and gave him what he hoped was a significant wide-eyed look. "It answers a question you've been wanting answered for a long time."

Under the booth, Ray could feel Gram's knees going like pistons. He looked like he had been doused with ice water. "Don't fuck with me, Ray."

Desmond turned sideways, facing out of the booth like he might take off.

"I fuck with you not. This is what you think it is. And more."

Panic flitted across Cy's grave features, but he nodded at Ray and ran a hand over his mouth. "Geronimooooo," he intoned in a low voice.

"What?" Ray asked.

"I said go for it." Cy picked up his drink and took a long swallow.

Ray pushed the camera toward Gram. "See this little screen? Watch that. Playback button is right here. I'll be back in a little while—want to give you all some privacy." He slid out of the booth. They barely glanced at him.

20

KING OF STRANGE

Martin was sitting on the verandah alone when Ray finally pulled in to the Silver Sun. He had left Gram and Desmond and Cy getting drunk together at the Signal Flare. He couldn't tell how Gram was taking the news—the boy may have been in shock. He seemed to be okay with Desmond, staring at him with a remote but gentle seriousness, but the story of Justine Oxley had opened up a hole inside him that was visible to Ray when he returned to pick up his camera. His mother was not who he thought. "Do you want me to tell Lena anything?" Ray had asked.

Gram had knocked back a shot. "No."

As Ray had promised Lena, he ejected the tape and gave it to Gram. "That's yours," he said.

Now Ray stomped slowly up the stairs of the old hotel to the verandah and paused in front of Martin's chair. "You look like you just lost your best friend."

"I like your hat," Martin said.

"Thank you." He patted the silver headgear. "I'm the new King of Strange."

"That's not new," he said. "I've always thought of you that way. Remember that first semester I took your class, that Intro to Film class, and you played the rape scene in *A Clockwork Orange* in fast motion?"

"Oh, well, I played it fast to get it over with—there were a lot of young women in that class. I find the scene hard to watch."

"But it made the scene look so ridiculous—the whole class was laughing."

"I don't remember that," Ray said.

"I'd never met anyone like you. I've wondered why you make films the way you do."

"With no money?"

"Exactly. That DIY aesthetic of yours seemed to really hold you back. But I understand it now. Boy, do I. You work the way you want to work, beholden to no one."

Ray was about to object, to explain what Lena had figured out about him from the get-go. He had sold out when he agreed to make *Live from Medicine Park*. But he could see Martin wasn't finished, so he was quiet.

Martin raised despairing eyes to Ray. "The Gacks really do want me to fire you."

Ray grinned and took the chair next to him. "Don't worry about it."

"You keep saying that, but I'm serious. They want me to fire you."

"It's all okay now—I cleared up my lawsuit."

"Hey," Martin said, attempting enthusiasm. "That's big news! Congratulations, Ray!"

Ray was dismayed at how little the news lifted Martin's spirits. "So I'm insurable again."

Martin slumped his shoulders. "Edmond Gack wants to be a director. He wants your job. I think the insurance was just an excuse. Then when you punched him—"

"That was a bad move. I admit that."

"Well, he wants you gone."

Ray let the news settle on him. The sun was beginning to set, and the sky over Medicine Creek was pink and orange, framed by the porch pillars, stacks of those strange red balls rising to a point. He could hear the wind chimes from the house across the creek and Cimarron barking in the backyard. He liked this place. Medicine Park, Oklahoma. There was something about it. He remembered his dream, where he found himself underneath the rising waters of Medicine Creek with Jettie. "You still think there's good medicine here?"

Martin shook his head. "I don't know."

"I do," Ray said.

Martin looked puzzled. "You do?"

Ray stood up and slung his camera case over his shoulder. The news wasn't what he wanted, but there was an air of inevitability about it. "I never wanted to make a rockumentary anyway, Martin. Now that my lawsuit's over, I want to finish up with *What's in the Water?* To tell you the truth, I'm glad to be free of this gig." He wasn't telling the truth, but what would be the point of admitting how attached he had become to this place and its people? It had been a week—what was a week out of his life? He would go home and forget all about Lena and Cy and Jettie and Gram.

Martin stood up. "Seriously? You're okay with this? No hard feelings?"

"Call me if I can answer questions. Does Edmond Gack have any experience at all?"

Martin shook his head. "I'll pay you for the work you've done," he said.

"I'll let you," Ray said. The money he had given to Jim-Anne Towson in Rio Marron had been almost all he had. He wasn't sure what he would do now, except find a new film project and beg for his old job back at the university now that the lawsuit was settled. When he had told Lauren that he had settled the lawsuit himself, she had been too aggravated to offer much advice about handling his former employer.

"Does Lena know what the Gacks are doing?" Ray asked. "What does she say?"

"She said she wouldn't fight for you. You failed your probation. She told me to make it work with Gack; she didn't care how."

"She doesn't mess around, does she?"

"Guess not," Martin replied. "She just hangs out."

"I was hanging out," Ray said. "She was—well, I can't say what it was for her. Is she around?"

"She and Jettie just got back from the hospital."

"Jettie's here?" He would drop by to say goodbye on his way out of town.

"They let her out today. She's on crutches and she's still"—he shook his head—"pretty beat up, but she insisted on coming home."

Ray didn't want to see Lena, but he felt duty-bound to tell her he had completed his mission. He climbed the stairs slowly, feeling odd and empty, clean of the old baggage and the new. But no elation rushed in. Instead he felt tense and scared as the understanding settled over him that he had been doing the best he could when he made the messes he had made at Rio Marron and here, at Medicine Park. He had been trying to live by a code, to do what was right, and instead he had backed into mistake after mistake, like Oedipus setting out to avoid the prophecy that he'd kill his father and marry his mother and doing those very things along what he thought was the road away from them. How to proceed? He would cut loose of the prime directive, that was for sure. It was a great code for somebody else, but he wasn't that guy, wasn't the cool observer. Love your subject still seemed a tenable code. Looking back, that seemed the only one he was capable of, and he wasn't sure why he had ever decided he needed to be more like James T. Kirk than like himself.

When he reached the second-floor landing and was about to turn down the hall to Lena's room, he saw Cy standing in front of Lena's door. Evidently Cy had parked by Gram and Jettie's carriage house and come in through the back door. He heard Ray and turned. "Thanks for lying to Lena about Geronimo."

"You knew all along?"

Cy shrugged. "She needs that particular fantasy and I need her."

"I came to tell her about Gram," Ray said.

"I'm going to do it myself," Cy said, his expression friendly but firm. Without knocking, he opened the door to Lena's bedroom and stepped inside. Ray imagined Lena and Cy in her room together, a room where he had spent a few nights but where Cy could enter without knocking, and the image comforted him, replacing the ragged realization that he had hurt Lena with the truth of her deeper story. Cy was with her, had always been with her, and would always be. Cousins, lovers, an old unmarried couple, a dirty secret, whatever they were to each other was the heart of the family story Ray had stumbled through like a drunk on a rampage. They would set right the furniture now that he was leaving. They would clean up what had been knocked over and maybe even do some rearranging.

It only took Ray a few minutes to pack. He lugged his suitcase down the stairs and out the door. When he got to the Jeep, Jettie was standing next to it on crutches with Cimarron, on a leash, and two suitcases. She looked like she should still have been in a hospital gown, but she wore shorts and a green shirt, and carried a backpack.

"Hey, there," he said. "I was about to go looking for you to say good-bye."

"Martin told me you're leaving. Can you give me a ride?"

"Where to?"

"I'm going to stay with my parents for a while. Waco."

"You're a Waco girl? I didn't know that. It's right on the way. Going for a visit?"

"I don't know."

"Gram coming with you?"

"Not at the moment."

"Don't want to talk about it?"

"Let's talk about your problems instead," she said, grinning painfully.

"Is this a good idea, getting a ride with me? How's Gram going to take it?"

She shrugged. "I'm not worried about it."

He helped Jettie into the passenger seat, letting the seat back as far as it would go to accommodate her ankle cast. He helped her slide the backpack off her shoulders and offered to put it away, but she said she wanted it on her lap. He loaded his luggage and hers into the back of the Jeep and laid Jettie's crutches over the top. Then he opened the rear door so that Cimarron could climb to her now-familiar spot on the back seat, where she stood with her head between the front headrests. Ray ran his hand down the dog's flank and pushed his face into hers. "Looks like another road trip for us," he said to her.

From the front seat, Jettie remarked, "You and my dog sure do get along."

Ray agreed. "Maybe I need a dog." They pulled out of the parking lot of the Silver Sun, the gravel churning under the wheels until they got on Riverside Drive, which took them out of Medicine Park, on to Highway 49, which emptied them on to I-44, which would take them into Texas and hook them up with I-35, which would carry them south like a mighty river. Ray envisioned the drive gladly. Out of the Wichita Mountains, into the plains, and across the Red River, they would follow the branching, arterial highways with the pleasure of yielding to somebody else's dull but effective argument.

He felt shy with Jettie in the car. Small talk was never easy, but it seemed that everything he and Jettie might say would be big small talk, the impossible kind, the kind he invariably screwed up. She was pitiful to look at, like a broken bird, and he wanted to protect her at the same time he wanted to give her lots of space. Neither of them spoke for quite a while. As they drew close to the Texas border, Jettie finally said, "What have you got to listen to in this car?" She started punching buttons on the dash, shuffling the CDs in the changer, and ejecting the cassette tape in the cassette player.

"Hey, a tape," she said, more brightly. "I didn't figure you for old school." She pulled out the black cassette and read her own handwriting across the front of it. "This is—me? How did you get this?" She frowned.

Ray didn't know what to say. He thought he had received and delivered all the bad tidings one person could be expected to in one day, but apparently he was wrong. He cleared his throat, staring ahead at the yellow centerlines flashing by on the road. "Your parents gave me that. I met them when you were in the hospital."

"They said they met you. But why—they didn't want it?"

"They mentioned it to me, and I was really interested in it, so they gave it to me. They said they had a copy. Told me how great it was—they're so proud of you, you know."

"Ray, my parents wouldn't know how to duplicate a cassette if their lives depended on it. This is the only copy." She held it up at him. "My whole life, right here." They were coming up on the bridge across the Red River, the border between Oklahoma and Texas. She unzipped her backpack and took out a jar of water. "This is Medicine Creek water.

Desmond got it for me."

"He says it healed you."

"And who's to say it didn't?"

"Shit. Not me." They began crossing the bridge, planks thumping below the wheels of the Jeep. "You're not thinking of dumping it in the Red River, are you?"

"I just wanted to hold it," she said.

They rode in silence again, all the way through Wichita Falls. Finally, Jettie spoke up. "So listen, I don't think I want to stay with my parents after all. Why don't you take me to Austin? My ex will let me stay with her for a little bit."

"Are you sure? You can crash at my place."

"Not a good idea, old son, but thanks. I want you to come by and visit Cimarron, though, whenever you want."

Ray reached up and ran his hand along the dog's long muzzle. "I'll do it," Ray said. "Are you going to play that tape, or what?"

"Oh yeah."

Her own laughter at the beginning of the tape startled her, but after that they became quiet and listened to the music while the road unrolled beneath them, taking them farther away from Medicine Park. The waters were with them, though, sloshing in the jar that Jettie held in her lap. Ray told her about his dream, the one where the two of them were submerged in the flooding creek, and they agreed that, while it was impossible to say what dreams meant, it was probably a good sign.

21

LIVE FROM MEDICINE PARK

"A Bittersweet Spoonful of Lena Wells," *Rock Steady,* July 2002

Casualties, burnouts, and hermits—rock and roll is full of them. The documentaries that inevitably come along to solve the mystery of these vanished figures are usually depressing, revealing squalor, mental illness, or, what's almost worse, utter mediocrity, making you wish the filmmaker hadn't turned over that rock. A rash of soft-focus hagiography documenting the life and times of the saints of classic rock have marked—or perhaps marred—the millennium. Add to the pile *Live from Medicine Park* about Lena Wells, the Oklahoma rock and roller who gave us "Black Ice," "Graveyard Jimmy," "Rank Outsider," and other perennial rock favorites. Wells has also released a new album, *Silver Son,* and is touring in support of it. The album is fresh, and Wells seems to have gotten better with time, as has her band, the Lighthorsemen, featuring Cyril Dodge, Desmond Jones, Rinaldo West, and her son, Gram Wells, who is the Silver Son of the album's title. What works about the documentary are the scenes when the camera simply shows these artists at work. There is also a memorable interview of Wells at the grave of her great-great-grandfather, Geronimo, where the artist shows a private side of herself that is surprising to watch. Too often, though, the film, directed by first-time director Edmond Gack, is full of obtrusive editing and cheesy techniques. Structurally, it is a paint-by-numbers documentary, strictly serviceable. A must-watch for any diehard Lena Wells fans out there, but not for the rest of us.

"Ray Wheeler Dives In to Discover 'What's in the Water?'"
Cinephilia Files, July 2002

Ray Wheeler is a documentary filmmaker who has been slowly estab-
lishing a reputation for tight little projects that run truth to ground
like blue heelers on the scent. In his first film, *Paper Trail,* made on a
shoestring budget in 1992, Wheeler's camera follows with detached
amusement his own father, semi-pro genealogist Lawrence Wheeler,
on the trail of an old family legend, allowing viewers to form their
own opinions of the senior Wheeler and the surprisingly zany world
of hardcore genealogists. This loose, cool approach tightens and heats
up in his second film, *Barking Mad.* A series of interviews of illegal
immigrants speaking on dark sets that hide their identity, it is as visually unappealing a film as I have seen, but one which, piece by riveting
piece, assembles a horrifying picture of a serial rapist who, for years,
found mute prey by acting as a "coyote," running illegal immigrants
across the border for a price. From this confident exercise, in which
the filmmaker's presence is nearly invisible despite the thesis-driven
editing, Wheeler, a Texan, turned to another strange tale from his
native state. Released six months ago after a yearlong legal battle,
What's in the Water? unspools the wacky story of a small West Texas
town where low doses of lithium had appeared in the water since the
early sixties thanks to a couple of forward-thinking city councilmen
concerned about keeping crime rates low despite the high percentage
of ex-cons in the local population. Lithium made for a tractable population, ex-cons included. When the lithium came out of the water, the
entire town went a little bit crazy, and Wheeler was soon on hand to
tell the tale, going a little bit crazy himself if rumors surrounding the
filming are true. The result is a compulsively watchable documentary,
not to be missed. Wheeler shows in this latest film an understanding
of human frailty that serves his desperate and ailing subjects well and
should come in handy on his next project, *Calamity,* reportedly a portrait of one of Austin's up-and-coming female musicians.

ACKNOWLEDGMENTS

I am grateful to my intrepid editor, Kathleen Kelly, at the University of Oklahoma Press, for her interest in and advocacy for this book, and to Rilla Askew for first bringing us together. For their generosity and energy I am obliged to those who read this novel in its various iterations: Rilla Askew, Angela Morris, Amy Little, and especially Steve Garrison, to whom I also owe a big thanks for penning the film review "The Decline of the West-ern," found in the press kit section of this novel. I needed help with details on the arts of music and filmmaking and gratefully acknowledge the assistance of Brian Johnston for the musical inspiration and love, as well as Ace Allgood, Bradley Beesley, and Sterlin Harjo for patiently answering my questions about documentary filmmaking.

Many people contributed their experience, strength, and hope to the composition of this novel and the way of life it depicts—my love and thanks to them all. Always and above all, I thank my daughter, Nora, for her gentle, loving spirit and the inspiration of her presence in my life. Finally, I must thank all the great rock musicians whose music has played through the scenes of my life since earliest memory. This book is nothing if not a big thank you for a lifetime of felicitous audio.